D1476546

TAR BEACH

New American Fiction Series: 23

TAR BEACH
Richard Elman

[signature] Elman
Knoxville
April, '95

Sun & Moon Press

LOS ANGELES

Sun & Moon Press
A Program of
The Contemporary Arts Educational Project, Inc.
a non-profit corporation
6148 Wilshire Boulevard, Los Angeles, California 90048

First published in paperback in 1991 by Sun & Moon Press

10 9 8 7 6 5 4 3 2
FIRST EDITION

This book was made possible, in part, through a grant from
the California Arts Council and through contributions to
The Contemporary Arts Educational Project, Inc.,
a non-profit corporation.

Cover:
Felice Casorati, Midday (*Meriggio*)   1922

LIBRARY OF CONGRESS CATALOGING IN PUBLICATION DATA
Elman, Richard
Tar Beach
p. cm — (New American Fiction Series: 23)
ISBN: 1-55713-117-1
I. Title. II. Series.
811'.54—
CIP

Printed in the United States of America

Author's Note

Children are told many strange things, and then try to understand what they are told as best they can. In Hebrew School, long ago in the Forties, some kids learned the British Government once offered the Zionists Uganda as a Jewish National Homeland.

Der Yidisher Sprach has variants of dialect, according to the geographical locations of the speakers. I've been guided by memory, with the assistance of a neighbor, Rochelle Steinfeld, to whom many thanks are due; and aided by the late Uriel Weinreich's *Modern English-Yiddish, Yiddish-English Dictionary* (Schocken Books).

An earlier version of "Tar Beach," comprising a draft of the fist two chapters and called "Uganda," appeared in the *Bennington Review* in the summer of 1981.

THIS BOOK IS DEDICATED TO CHILDREN I HAVE LOVED (and other such misfits voila!) — to Herb, for Hannah, and Lem, and to my long-lost friend, Yvette Fronval, of the Rue Henri Barbusse, Paris.

"...Of the Past, familiarly risen...appealing in its whole aspect a little too positively to the mind, over-exciting it a little, as should not be surprising...there, in our midst, approached, pressed against, touched, motionless, in the sun."
Marcel Proust, "On Reading"

Kafka in a lecture to some members of the Jewish community of Prague: "...You know more Yiddish than you think you know...."

ONE

UGANDA

Some lions roaring in the park: Maw Maw Maw! Giggi-hama beaks clicking at the tar sands.

Mostly lions we hear as they glide across the high grass of the wadi Prospect Park. Big slow trolleys down Flatbush Avenue.

Bwana Izzy Berliner is on his gin rummy schneider again. He has to knock with the king and has only one small black three left over.

Holding a fan of cards up to his face, Umpapa glares behind thin silver wire-rimmed glasses. "For nothing like that you get nothing."

"Sez you Sam."

"Name of the game Iz."

Gin! Twenty points and a box for Umpapa.

A hot sky over Tar Beach mirrored in watchbands, sunglasses, goldteeth. Glint of rings and Ronson cigarette lighters, thick humid reek of roofing tar.

Sitting under the dangling bare feet of Umpapa, Little Sam, and his friend, Izzy, the child Peter Pintobasco says, "*Jambo* Uncle Izzy. O *Jambo*."

Izzy aside, he thinks, who is presently losing his jock to Umpapa in gin rummy, there is also *gornisht* to be said for this place in the sun, up here on the roof in Uganda, especially when it's so hot.

A *gribben* feels no worse....

Scawa Scawa. He's been abandoned, thrown into a pit surrounded by Umpapa's beastly chums. Without his brother Benjamin and his friend, Billy Ruben, for most of the whole long summer, the sun against his bare shoulders oppresses Peter.

Being here like this, with nothing but these grown-ups, blinded by my own *shvitz*. Who really cares how I feel when these games start? Out loud Peter says, "How about we play Go Fish? No cheating...."

"Who ya talking to boychick?"

Next to Izzy and Sam, like a big knot of burl in a log, sits Dr. Piggy Baer, retired obstetrician. Bulging brown kneecaps like candy apples swell against his chest, hiding *dushik* and bloated old sack of wrinkleballs.

Piggy's eyes are clots of solid clotted cream. His skin has a high color, a sheen just like rayon. Fine tiny wrinkles galore. A pongee belly. He looks like that big insect preserved for thousands of years in one of Memsahib's amber beads.

Umpapa says now Piggy has been declared legally blind for his "disability" he no longer even pretends he can see.

"Never even says boo to a patient," says Sam. "Just stares and turns brown all over like a cheese dream. Pretends he can't even hear a word's being said...."

Izzy asks, "How does old Piggy get by?"

"He's got coupons he can clip every single month. Municipals," Sam, in a low whisper, "and I bet he still collects on his disability, maybe a little Social Security...."

"...From my tenants I get a little something extra, too," the blind man confesses, eyes runny now like pizza pie cheese. "And I even win at Goshen at the trotters, pinochle and pisha-paishe...."

"Good for you, Dr. Baer," Izzy shouts, showing a little respect. "*Inshallah!*"

"I hear plenty good. Nice of you to keep track of all my resources Pintobasco," Piggy says. "Just don't count me out yet fellas. I don't need from any charity. Thank God ...from being thrifty at Brooklyn Jewish, when I was a younger man...."

His hand gropes with a palsied tremble toward Peter's boiling forehead. He pats the little boy who flinches, as he usually does, even before contact is made.

"Thrift," says Piggy. "Hard work...I delivered you sonny...from der momma's womb...."

"Why don't you listen to Dr. Baer?" Umpapa commands.

"But I was just a baby."

"Lucky for you," says Piggy. "We were so poor I almost never grew up...."

"But you did," Peter reminds him. "You got old...."

"O *Jambo!*" Izzy responds, with a wink and a shrug at Peter.

"You tell him. Tell the boy Piggy," Sam says, hardly hearing his own son, or Izzy, if he can help it. "Kids have it so good nowadays it's a different world, I tell ya...."

"That suits me just fine," Piggy says. "The dollar's maybe no longer a dollar but I got a lot more than I had in the old days...believe you me...a *shisl*...."

"That's just what I like to hear," says Izzy. "An optimist...."

"Cigar and all," Piggy adds. "Go fish!"

"You don't know the half of it," Sam says. "Why the

other day Dr. Piggy Baer here challenges me to a game of handball. Said he'd play me by sound...."

"Against you I said I could." Piggy laughs.

"If worse comes to worst fellas I'd probably even deliver babies at Brooklyn Jewish again. The women used to swear by me. You think I don't know my way around a belly by now...."

"By sound. Imagine," Sam repeats. "Pinochle I can figure...."

"Don't forget touch," Piggy blurts out. "A vagina is a vagina, after all...."

"The things you find with your eyes closed," Izzy says. "Capital!"

"If you ask me," says Sam.

And Piggy says, "Who asked?"

All the men laughing, with Sam and Izzy and Piggy, like thick heavy colds, snigger laughs.

Cards shuffled again. Noon precisely, the hottest slice off the day; this sun could boil water. Peter sees good enough when he wipes the sweat from his eyes. Gonna be such a long hot one. A little sleep, a closing of the eyes, might help to get him through till lunchtime, in an hour or so.

He shuts them and sees the sun make garish wallpaper on his vision.

When he came back from the war overseas Mickey Rivlin told everybody he could clean his rifle in the shower bath with both eyes closed. Crazy Mickey. Eyes like the iodine bottle. A quart low from the war...lots of static on the brain...all he talked about for a week and then he turned quiet again, unplugged.

Peter's rapt small brown face recalls him to Tar Beach, and Mickey's suicide attempt 3 weeks ago. He had one leg practically over the roof when they ran and pulled him back....

Peter sees Mickey mounting his death like Tom Mix and shudders *Gotenyu*....

Maroon zipper marks along Mickey's hairline led to a bog of maroon skin covered by hair above Mickey's right ear, as though some lady had just bashed him one with her steam iron....

It was the Japs did it, of course, shrapnel, Izzy says. Does it still hurt? Peter wonders, and touches the hot intact skull above his right ear, near the temple, and the tiny stitches from when Umpapa got mad at his report card with the "D in deportment" and shoved him back against the radiator from pillar to post.

That felt cold at first and then it hurt real bad, with lotsa blood, and he had to wear a white bandage around his head a whole week like a mummy.

Mickey can't always look people in the eye because his face is a little lopsided from what happened to him.

What about my face? He touches himself there again...

His cheeks feel streaked with tar. And when Peter wipes the sweat he puts tar streaks on his nose, and chin, drying in the sun, red Indian markings. Pugnacious, frail, a little naked boy, "tall for his age," according to Umpapa, "not normal." In a sunny patch of large red tiles, embedded among grouty creeks of shiny black tar, he squats alone, cooking beneath the gin game.

"A least can I make the shuffle?"

"The last time I let you cards flew everywhere," Sam

says. "Off the roof."

"Regular shuffle off to Buffalo," Izzy adds. "Just like Mickey. Two sheets to the wind. That's show bizz Sam. The kid's gotta learn somehow...."

"Later," Sam says. "Between you and me this is serious."

Peter thinks, everything is serious when it comes to Sam, and I'm just a spit in the ocean. I will count to ten and they will all go away, men, sun, heat, whole damn gin game, even Izzy, Sam, Solly, Piggy, whole shebang.

Moja mbili tata, alle alle infree.

Such a day. The cloudless sky so very blue. Hot hot: In the zoo he hears seals bark.

Only here in this veldt, where Bomba still lives, we can all be ourselves as Jews, even kids like me, if I had my own friend, here in *Eretz Uganda*. "Miracles do happen," Izzy says. "Like scrambling eggs. Look at me kiddo. I was born in Terespol near Minskgobernya in Byello Russia on Leap Year, so I'm really not much older than you...."

"You don't look it."

"Use your imagination, boy of my heart. Uganda is the Turner Towers compared to that little sandbar along the Mediterranean they want to call a homeland...It's the Roney Plaza of Colonialism," Izzy adds. "Lots of cattle and coffee. Little forest folk. Water up the wazoo...why in Toroland are great kings seven feet tall...."

"And are there trolley cars and movie theatres like the Rodgers Izzy?"

"Not too many in the bush, I'm afraid. This is Africa, after all...a Dark Continent...."

"A Pearl of Africa!" he adds.

Boring, if you're naked and broke, sent home from camp a month early, without a friend in the world this summer, and nearly 8 years old. The things he's seen this summer....

"Mpapa?"

"Boychick...."

Piggy's voice a boom: "Little boy...little Pintobasco who I delivered...."

"O *Jambo*!"

Looking up into that runny wrinkle of a face blocks the sun.

"Why don't you play with yourself somewhere?"

"Why don't you?"

"At my age, I dare say," Piggy roars, "if I could find...."

The wind picks up his toothless gusts. The boy, meanwhile, is stuck to his spot, chewing gum.

With nubby hanging breasts, almost like a woman, Piggy gropes to his feet, and totters toward the fire door leading down the dark stairwell.

Peter's shoulders are on fire. At least camp had pine trees. Needle beds of shade. Lily pads in a lake. Ten floors up like this, on Tar Beach, no building tops poke above his naked collarbones. The sun really bakes, a *soyne*, enemy. Some grimy yellow bricks form a parapet, maybe a foot and half above his dark curly crown.

Umfasu, he thinks. *Gevald*. Regular steam bath...worse than any jungle. El Alamein....

From the rusty showerhead with the pull chain, water bubbles and drips soddenly down against the darkly spotted radius of the drain, ricochets beneath a long grey slatted wooden bench, set at a 45 degree angle to the parapet beyond.

Twenty naked men, including the *Umfundisi*, Rabbi Elias Zuckerman, are lying out, or sitting upright, on this bench: A griddle full of BLTs, he thinks: puffy and brown, grilled almost black, big water blisters, pancake batter dropped from a *lefle* to bluster at each other with their lingonberries on display. Spooned out like that they lie there, endlessly playing gin or Michigan rummy, talking business, tribal stuff.

"If they read from those cards tomorrow night, I'm personally going to take myself a long walk...."

Mushy Cohen is just being a cheapskate again. Just no *frum*.

A former set-shot artist at LIU, Mushy was once almost as famous, Izzy says, as Mangiapanl, or Jacky Goldsmith, though now he wears a *shuba* greatcoat of his own flab. With his hands from the foul line, or the left corner, he's still got the eye, the hands, quick. A pretty chubby *shickseh* for a wife. Little armored pillbox on the handball court as well.

"Honest to Christ," he adds. "Every *shabbes* and *yontiff*, they put on the bite. It's embarrassing...."

"Never mind talk like that," Umpapa says, "the roll call can't be avoided...."

"Hooray for Mushy," Izzy adds. "Bucking *harabee* by standing up for his bucks. No more give until it hurts. Give until Palestine is the Kingdom of Heaven. A waste anyway. Better a glass of Seagram's Seven...."

When Izzy talks no one really listens either. Like he's deaf and dumb. "Money talks," says Solly Cohen, "shit walks."

Besides, as Peter knows, grown-ups give big to feel big. A check, bills rolled inside a rubber band, even under the table money, makes a good impression. The more you reach into your pocket the more esteem....

This weekend all the men have a lot on their minds. The old *yekke* Abraham Abraham died only yesterday, the most important man on Tar Beach, in *shul*, everywhere: so many years President of Temple, the Men's Club, and Sefer Torah Society....

In days gone by he was like Stalin himself up here on Tar Beach. Never naked himself, but bossing all the naked men *azoy vee ferds*. *Dein nomen* acclaimed, as Izzy says.

It does not matter, Peter thinks, that he was called the *Emesireytse* more recently, when in his 80's, a little stuffed bear on the *bima*, during High Holidays, prayed for a homeland in benighted Palestine, a subway series, that good old Pete Reiser should get well enough to play centerfield again.

Caught being unruly in glaucoma thickets of that old man's glare, Peter always felt his teeth begin to chatter. Abraham Abraham was a colossus among olives. The shad roe and bacon, Izzy says.

Tomorrow, being Sunday, comes the funeral, ten floors down below in the Sanctuary, high, with white tiers of lily flowers, and later tonight, in the evening, as had been previously scheduled and now cannot be unscheduled, the annual congregational dinner, to raise a lot of money for the DPs, and select a new Prez. Umpapa Little Sam, his dad, is in the running for Scribe, and maybe even Presidenke. They'll read telegrams from President Truman, and Chaim Weitzman: Condolences! Congratulations.

UmPeter thinks, thanks be I will not have to go to that, too, and be bored. Boring....Maybe they'll even get me a baby-sitter tomorrow. Not just grandma again. *Hamduillah*....

He hears Mushy: "Catered affair or not. I mean it fellas...."

"They'll read anyway," Umpapa says. "You gave $150 for the Journal last year so give $200, so we can burn the first mortgage, finally, and get it over with, and then a small contribution for the stained glass window memorial...."

"I'm no millionaire! I work hard for my living...."

"*Ohmain*" Solly Cohen says. "So don't be such a piker. Abraham Abraham always said, if you give you get. The law of business...."

"It's a hard dollar. Besides," Mushy says, "my wife isn't even Jewish and it's her money, too."

"Is that our fault? Give anyway," Sam says.

Mushy: "You know what Brooklyn is like nowadays. Slow...."

"Slow?" Umpapa's wink is sly for the others. "You're slow Mushy...."

Seems Sam wants to get people to vote for him by insulting them. Polishing his glasses with the liner of his athletic trunks, Sam says, "New York slow? Where did anybody ever get that idea?"

Abruptly, the *kaffir*, dog-faced Harry Halpern, who jobs hearing aids, erupts: "There ain't no better real estate in the whole world...."

Shifting the dangle of his ruby-tipped cock from one upthrust thigh to the other, Harry adds, "Who can compare? They haven't given me the *maftir* on the five boroughs, but I got a few bucks, and whenever I got a few extra I buy class A locations through syndication...second mortgages too...Right now I'm all over Astoria near the Pearlwick sign, right opposite Sutton Place. That's gotta get better I say...."

"It's been two years since the Duration," Mushy warns.

"That's nothing. You wait. Gonna get better and better. Wait and see if you don't see. Manhattan Island was a treasure even after the Crash. It always will be. The Bronx had pearls to offer. So did Kew Gardens around the Van Wyck and even some parcels in Brooklyn are like 18 karat solid silver...."

"And Staten Island?"

Solly's mouth is open; he looks like a thirsty dog.

"*Gehenem*," says Harry. "I wouldn't even dump my garbage there. It's all cemetery and woods. No improvements, setbacks, variances. Abraham Abraham he knew all that like the hair on his knuckles...."

Grunts of approval mingle with the cement-mixer crowd noise of a Dodger baseball game on Harry's yellow Emerson portable, as Umpapa, Sam Pintobasco, takes up where Harry has just left off.

"Abraham Abraham was a German. Cheap was his middle name. Bought his last suit when Hoover was President. He used to make me drive him to the Bowery just for haircuts. Up here on Tar Beach we're all on the make for lost time. So when we give people notice. Look at Big Sam over there. He knows...."

Umpapa points at his biggest enemy, and former client. Big Sam Rostok. Such a primadonna. Glasses catching sun. His whole life a fire between the eyes. The chaff of his hand on one naked hip. The press calls him Buster.

Staring down Rostok, Sam Pintobasco tells his friends: "Giving restores confidence so then you get it back with investors. Syndications...Only kindly do me a favor Harry. Don't ever sell me Brooklyn again because that was a total loss...."

"I'm not selling I'm telling."

Harry shrugs and dangles, dangles and shrugs, an animal without hooves. "You think 150 Montague Street was *bobkes*? If Joe Trunk was still alive...."

"NOW 120 Church Street, THAT WAS A PARCEL, as I live and die."

Bwana Izzy Berliner's nasal tenor has broken through sharply above the roar. His brother lives in a palace in Sands Point. The man who "practically invented" instant coffee, Izzy says, though he never drinks the stuff himself. Izzy drinks "Savarin dark and thick as mud...from the railway buffet is best" he always adds.

Now he says, "As I live and die we could all have retired to Palm Beach on 120 Church Street. And you could have gotten financing, you know that, Sam. It was your own damn fault. We had war bonds, you, me, Etta, Lillian...."

Behind a pair of large black and silver bat wing reflectors, Bwana Izzy cooks his face medium well done for his *memsa*, Etta Berliner.

He isn't usually interested in real estate, or making money. A *fiener shtimme* for singing. Just no *kop* for business.

"Izzy's vain and he likes the girls," his father always says. "He'll never get out of the poorhouse, but such a voice he has, Lillian. He's my friend. I admire him...."

"The feelings must be mutual," she observes. "We've got a friend in Izzy all the way...."

In the annex to the sanctuary, when he's needed and there's overflow, on the High Holidays, Izzy sings *Kol Nidre*. He's actually a Communist, I think, "but not dangerous," Sam always says; and he has the finest smoothest skin in all black Africa.

"A skin like that should get baby oil," Peter's mother always adds, with a little high-pitched nervous giggle. "Tincture of violets...smooth...."

Izzy once told Peter Uganda was a land of milk and honey, and then some. He spoke of the soul revisiting the body, the weighing of the heart in *National Geographic*, in color photographs, and the German and the British "colonialist despoilers." When has Little Sam ever said anything to him worth remembering? When kept a promise? Sam even gave away my dog and behind Izzy's back he makes fun of *Bwana*. "That Bolshevik palooka," he says. "Where does he get off?"

Now Peter hears his father again: "War bonds? It was the Goddamnt war itself. I tell you. A patriot didn't cash in. Taxes could have killed you on a parcel that size. You'd have to refinance and that would be the end of it. Taxes taxes, then receivership. And when I asked you, against my better judgement, if you thought your brother Mel might be interested, you threw gabardine all over that...."

"I didn't want Mel mixing in my business. You could have always gotten a mortgage back from the Dime, or maybe Trunk himself. How should I figure? I'm ignorant when it comes to practical details...."

Izzy shrugs like an accordion.

"A lot you know Izzy, Trunk was up to his ears in Seagate. Trunk never owned the property...."

"A lot I know...." Izzy indulges in a deep gulp of spicy summer air. "I never said I had facts at my fingertips. It's true I don't know a lot about real estate Sam. I know about people. I'm talking courage, not dollars and cents. I figured if you wanted Mel you could please forget Izzy Berliner...."

"Dollars and cents are courage." Sam is grimmer than usual: "Bite your tongue."

By mid-summer Izzy's face looks like the end cut on an eye-round: so much sun makes him just a little crusty, with frontlets of oil or cream, an eye full of juice whenever he looks at Peter.

The way his hair, after shampoo in the shower, fluffs out like a big fur *streimel*.

Now he says, "The richest man in Mount Ararat I'll never be...." And to Peter adds, "Money is to spend. Silks and satins, a good time...."

His very thought, so Peter says: "Spend money Umpapa. I want we should have a new Pontiac and a 12 inch Dumont television."

"Shut up sonny. Please mind your own business. This is grown-up talk."

The boy's eyes film over. If he leaves now he'll miss lunch. And Izzy has promised to play Uganda with him later.

Suddenly Harry Halpern says, "Just look at Sam Rostok. He never was timid, took chances, and now he's living on easy street. That's not so hard to take...."

Umpapa: "I think you got it all ass backwards Harry, Izz. Rostok's father was the big success before him...."

"They came here with diamonds sewn in their *gotkes*," Sam adds, arguing with himself, as usual. "Big Sam was just parlaying what there was to begin with from his father's live chicken stores. The father had three cash and carry stores in Yorkville alone as soon as they got off the boat...."

"Come on," Izzy chimes in. "Even you got to admit," as he shifts his weight from one adhering buttock to the other on this hot deck, like he's sitting on top of a big muskmelon, "there's a heck of a difference between live chickens in Yorkville, and building the Whitestone Bridge, and the Lincoln Tunnel. Rostok was an operator from the day he landed here...."

"I thought we were just now talking real estate. Construction is different," Sam says, "nobody denies. A talent. A man has it or he doesn't. Uris, Zeckendorf, Tishman, Trunk, are master builders, brickmen par excellence. Some of us are just not so ambitious...."

"Shit through the mouth Sam...."

"Don't insult. I'm trying to explain not justify. First came his hospital operation and then the live chickens... like *aleph, bes*...."

Now it's Izzy's and Harry's turn to grunt assent, and then, *genug*, close their heavy, sleepy lids, bake a little more in all that hot sun.

The world's unjust, and everybody knows it always has been. Even Izzy, Peter notes, is slumbering, his oily bald spot, in the center of his hair, tips toward his right shoulder, a *ziden kepeleh*.

A commission man. Never going to make his bundle, but never harsh with Peter. Mammileh says, "Izzy has different values. He just doesn't think like other people."

"On which side of my balance sheets should I put Izzy's values?" Sam asks.

Sweat from Peter's armpits cools in trickles along his rib cage.

When Rex Barney threw the wild pitch all the men got *fertig*, so angry, somebody even silenced Harry's radio.

Then all the rest of the men looked as though they were
slumping into little catnaps, a nasal zissing....

Cut out of living flab, like stone, to echo off the golden
scales and sun/eye figures of an ancient world on the brand
new library facade down below, across the Parkway, they just
lay there, solid and stolid, in an aching yawn of sunlight.

Three summers before last was just a big hole in the
ground, it seemed, with a high grey fence around it, a
public works sign, a sump filling with muddy water. While
the men dozed, brick and building blocks piled up, and
gold figures shone in the sun: Gods of the sun and of the
Dead. Izzy told him, the old Gods.

"See how our taxes go?" Big Sam Rostok said then, "It's
much too fancy for the likes of some...."

That was just after Roosevelt *plotzed*, I think. Then came
atomic bombs and the Duration, the men returning to Tar
Beach from the War. Izzy and Sam with their cards, Mammileh unwell, and Izzy telling me Uganda stories when he
babysat sometimes....

Now it seems like I'll never be getting off this roof the
whole summer long. We'll all melt together up here. You
can't tell some of these men apart anymore from the sun.
They all seem so grizzled, and old, so heavy against the
grey bench, as though their flesh seeped out from under
their shadows in large soppy bundles.

Some lie spoon fashion. Others sit up, propped against
the slats, or bent over, like they have cramps....

Peter notices how many of them seem cockless because
they've folded so much midriff behind heavy, hairy thighs.
They're almost like girls, he thinks, except for that
hairiness, a thickness of muscle. On others, dark red tips

are showing like tulips before they open up, maybe little pieces of ripe plum, cast to one side against those hot wooden slats so that they hardly seem to touch on them.

They're all so shiny brown, and black, and red, too, glistening with different oils and smells. Iodine and mineral oil, olive oil with Mercurochrome, gentian with Crisco...Harry Halpern wears *gornisht* except for his big, grey Zenith hearing aid, like he's sending and receiving from the planet ZUG; and the self-same Buster Rostok, sitting almost out of earshot, richest man in *shul* and between here and maybe Africa, looks just as naked as all the rest, except for his bifocals and his *Wall Street Journal* with the *New York Times* crossword cut out.

Rostok says, "Out on Long Island Bill Leavitt's practically broke already...."

"So he'll refinance," says Umpapa.

"And you and I and the banks will pay for that one just as sure as I'm sitting here baking."

Rostok's bee stung lips are as white as Red Sea salt, as lime. He practically lives off Gelusil, Izzy says, big stacks of them like poker chips always by his side. "Acid stomach," Izzy maintains. "Bleached mud walls like Timbucktoo inside Rostok's tummy tum tum...."

Izzy personally swears by one Alka Seltzer daily. Greets everyone with a *greps* sounds like Mombasa, and he sometimes smokes an old yellow pipe like a big horn. "Nothing like a good shag," Izzy says. "Prince Albert in a can. Believe me!"

Now the radio has switched back on again. Dodgers are licking St. Louis 5 to 4, top of the eighth. Red Barber says,

"This one is a tempest in a pea pot, and, folks it looks as
though it is going right down to the wire."

"Mombasa," Izzy says, "take me out to the Dodgers
Rogers...."

"Pardon his French," says Rostok. "He means Goody
Rosen."

"Sometimes the hardest work of all for some of these
men is vacationing," Umpapa says. "Even for a big man like
Mr. Rostok over there. He cries all the way to the bank...."

"All the way to his broker," Halpern corrects.

"I personally cried all the way to New York on the
Seabright Express the day of the Big Crash," Rostok once declared. "That's when I vowed the market was not my cup of
tea. Real estate.... that's another matter. The war made some
of us greedy. No denying. That's why so many *mavinim* are
going south of the Border. Lots of work for the asking and not
much law to worry about. A man can get rich between mid-
night and morning. I'm building railroads and garages...."

They've heard it all before. Too often. "I'll take Manhattan," Sam says. And Peter's eyes are closed to the juicy
sunlight when he hears his Uncle Izzy start to sing, sweet
as seedless:

"South of the border
down Mexico way
that's where I fell in love
when stars above
came out to play...."

"Turn that off," shouts Harry.

"Never you mind," Umpapa says. "Sing Izzy! Sing!"

"Sounds to me like he got his needle stuck in a groove,"
Rostok says. "Gene Autry got no worries from this here
crooner...."

DORTEN!

In the tranquil air of this high mountain valley, suddenly, sleek Heshy Anuskiewicz lifts his shiny bald head like a seal through ice: "We got a theatre party tomorrow night. Anybody else going? A musical....Gracie Fields...."

"I wouldn't waste my money," Solly Cohen contributes with another shrug. "Now a movie, I could take in a movie, and maybe some Chinks later...Hey kiddo," he's talking to Peter, "you like Chinks?"

Making little beady slant eyes at Peter: "Porky flied lice?"

Peter nods. All of his fingertips ache, where he has bitten back the skin a ways to rawness, and that means he has to pick more tar, with the other finger of his almost-crippled-feeling for a hand.

Kuk im on, but Peter loves Chinks, especially greasy spare ribs with tart duck sauce...and he has been promised all this and "My Favorite Brunette," with Bob Hope and Dorothy Lamour, either tonight or tomorrow night, if he stays good all day long on Tar Beach both days, and doesn't bother anybody because his mother is not having any amour right now. She is on the other side of that partition marked "WOMEN," having her curse again *chavar*.

"Kiddo," Solly barks, "Did you get my drift? Porky flied lice? Or are you queer for men like Izzy?"

"That's enough," Izzy growls. "*loz im op.*"

"Come on Solly," Little Sam adds. "My kid don't bother you so why do you bother him all the time?"

"Because he just eats tar, and he's got no friends. Always hanging around us, like a bad smell...."

"So do you," shouts Peter. "In spades!"

"Peter *loz im op*," goes Izzy once again. "*Cumbaya!*" And then his father can be heard echoing: "Behave!"

1947, and the war being over now two years, all the men are looking to make a killing (making up for lost time, as Izzy says) except for a couple who are dead, and *vai iz mir* Alvin Gruberman has this angry red scar across his belly.

A lot of the others are also stitched up, bald, big heavy globes of the world, whereas before they were like little Jack O'lanterns. Saved from the *Malech-hamoves* they touch themselves with oil, cry out "*Dorten!*" Their least words seem Holy to them, even their farts. God speaks through a burning bush, a windy tush, same difference. The ashes of other Jews in Europe are like incinerator cinders wafting across Eastern Parkway toward the Grand Army Plaza from Canarsie and Jamaica Bay on dirty pigeon wings: Sheol...Gravesend...The Cropsy Avenue landfill *vyimru*....

Those pictures of bodies piled up high for bulldozers in the newsreels made Peter cry out in his sleep....He's really all alone, even now, inside his head up here on Tar Beach, eating tar, and *cockymun* this stuff tastes good. MY T FINE chocolate pudding with a skin on top. So deep and dark it's just *umfatu*, the Dead Sea, with a salt stink.

Shiny stuff's my favorite. A *shmeck* like ages past, ages gone by, in his mouth, from all this tar. Even Sam said, "I never saw the like of it. A kid should be eating tar. Man's inhumanity to himself. Blackjack chewing gum, or Mason's Black Crows, nigger babies. Tar. Feh...."

From ages gone by the stink is a blackness sticks to the fingertips, and to my *gummeh*, and then I have to bite them all the way down beyond shiny to that thin pink line where hurting starts. Maybe even to blood....

Always here between the bricks of Tar Beach with that smell of such a long time ago. Sometimes men and women smell just like that. Kids smell more like cheese, maybe Muenster in a slab, but they also have got this other smell too, like something cooking on the stove, squash or yams, patty pan with molasses, acorn or butternut, rutabaga, turnip, stale.

Izzy says Rostok smells just like his aquarium at home. *Neshomeh.* Tar peeling everywhere leaves these spots like that time at Bide A Wee Home when they gave back his dog, Felix....

I wish I was seven again. Uganda is so dusty in summer you can't hardly stand it for an hour, much less a whole long day in the sun. Nearly eight like me is no better off. Can't hardly see over the edge unless Izzy he holds me up there like this or that. The way he holds me high, doesn't really dangle me, makes Micky Rivlin cover up his eyes.... So nice when Izzy does that, or in the steam room close. "Get an eyeful kiddo. You'll swear by it someday." Then all the little green bushes and dusty open spaces are black glistening patches.

"Hottest summer since Spain," says Izzy. He glistens so much, but he never really seems to sweat, or even smell of sweat. He smells like the Bond Bakery on Empire Boulevard, like baking bread, that Izzy. Never gets too sticky that Izzy, the way he shows me everything, a whole wide world down below: Bed Stuy and Fort Green in one direction; the ocean with Coney Island and Rockaway; Manhatten like the bristles on my toothbrush. *Umgazu*... his body just as warm as bread....

At certain times of day in a certain light everybody up here looks crazy, like in the movies, but down there the whole lake is Prospect Park, nice smoothest black....

Peter stares at shiny black rivers and little ponds and picks and pulls. Gar...At nearly 8, I'm much too discouraged, basically bored. All I've done all summer long is cry, eat tar, eat shit from grown-ups....I swear I never did it for real. Umpapa says, "It's not nice anything like that. Very unsanitary. This is just not nice a boy should do."

"Not nice anywhere anyhow," says Memsahib Lillian. Tossing back her twilight hair so her face shows blurry red, she adds, "If you do that ever again, I'll have to send you to Dr. Brady, the talking doctor." "I don't want to talk to no talking doctor. He's crazy! He says I'm crazy? Well I say he's crazy...."

A problem, even worse, for Peter. *Pesi Pesi*.

(O God thou art my God, not their God. Please help me!)

My brother Benjamin he stayed in camp when I got thrown out, and he writes me postcards all the time. "I'm fine. How are you? So write me...."

"Now we play a lotta ball and swim in the lake."

Benjamin stinks so much I never believe a word my brother says. He stinks on ice. He even makes the ice stink that Benjamin. Says, "We're even learning to pray at camp.

If I forget thee Jerusalem if I forget thee...."

May my *punim* turn to pudding. I'm stuck here, that's the problem. Turning into salt. The roof of my mouth and the meditation of my prayers full of Flatbush Avenue trolleys. Busses....If I forget thee, neglect thee, I should have to spell out
  TEKLE APHAR
Can't spell on these bricks without more spit. Mouth so dry need sodey. Tar does that to you sometimes. Stinking hot sun on me *buckrah* skin twelve floors up.

Up here is just like heaven, Rostok says. He peels and segments a blood orange, talking as he eats, with specks of blood orange on his face. Heaven, he repeats. *Heaven*.

(Have a heart, will you fellas?

Have a heart, will you, big shots?)

The sun boils pale orange and froths in and out of skimpy grey-blue cloud puffs. The sun sits in a frying pan sky as Rostok and Harry recline sunny side up along the deck.

Garry Briskin had a big fat ass and a thimble dick, and he was wrong to call me "stupid little prick face" July 4th at the fire works. Nobody said he couldn't stay on in camp. I shot him with a beebee where he sat. So what?

Then it seemed like the whole world was against me, except for Izzy. He always was a good guy, like Winston Churchill, a big smile, only blacker, from the sun, because he truly likes me. "I'm sure it was an accident," he says. "Mistakes do happen...."

"Don't I know." Sam's looking right at me....

Sweet Izzy in the shower, when he soaps himself all over with the Creco liquid, the top of his head comes to a fluffy point like a big Charlotte Russe. With his eyes closed he can't see me, can't see anything. Asks, "Are you there kiddo? Did you wash yourself real good? In *hinten*? Everywhere?"

Izzy makes my face tickle when it feels like iron.

Last Saturday I wanted to pee in the shower, but I didn't want to get caught because it makes all the big shots angry. Little yellow beads of water dangling from their schlongs, and when they see me copying they yell "UNSANITARY!"

Izzy made jokes: "It's so little compared to you Rostok. What's a few drops, more or less?"

If all I ever had to deal with was Izzy. Umpapa was ashamed of me. He said I'm honestly ashamed of you Peter.

He stood under the shower with eyes closed, belly jutting forth, hair sawtoothed on his forehead, on bandy legs, a little dick like a cocktail frank, kicking at the water pipe with the side of his bare foot to get it running again. "Ashamed," he said "I'm ashamed...."

Then he starts arguing with Harry: "This part of Brooklyn is doomed Harry. The handwriting on the wall. *Shvartz* ....Put your money where my mouth is...."

The usual talk: money money money! All he talks about while I walk around without pockets: FHA, the Dime, the Fed, Chemical Corn Exchange, Fanny May, Purchase money, promissory notes...A man after my heart, Rostok once called him.

He could drive you crazy at dinner when he used to be on the phone all the time with Rostok. Even Mammileh never liked that. We all got to eat quiet while Mr. Big Shot Little Sam talked *vi fil* this and that, and me with lockjaw ...and then no more Rostok calling at dinner and he's even worse down in the dumps....

Mammileh saying we mustn't give Little Sam a migraine. Not to disturb Mr. Big Shot. He's just lost his precious client. "Don't worry we won't ever starve," he told Memsahib, but it sure felt that way....

I wish I had a friend my own age this summer, some nice little kid, boy or girl....Everybody's interested in everything except me. Dopey Benny. Momser. Zip. I get all the abuse. The way Sam's feeling about Rostok puts words in his mouth. A blister on his tongue. Bad taste against his gums.

"Sure," Izzy says, "because he's your father, kiddo, he loves you. He don't really mean nothing he loves you just the same. Why worry? It's just a bad time...."

With a wink Izzy thinks he's making things alright for me.

"Dad's are like that sometimes. It don't mean they don't love...."

Izzy also says, "Always remember you and me are men, and Man is Man, kiddo, that's all there is to it. You can't trade love for love. There is no other Uganda. *Herszt?* Good for the goose is good for...."

"Uganda Izzy!"

"That's my Petey boychick. Kiddo...."

Like Izzy also said two weeks ago when I told the *shlepper* Solly Cohen he should wait until I grow up someday. "I'll get you Solly Cohen."

"*Herst* Solly," Izzy says. "He'll get you? Got to be more careful around kids like Peter...."

Izzy saying, "*Herst* Solly? *Herst?*"

And I said, "Umpapa I can be good."

"Good for what?"

"I'll behave I swear just don't let Mr. Cohen pick on me anymore...."

"So don't pick on him," Umpapa says, "that means you Solly, and you too boy...."

"I won't pick if he don't," Solly says, but the kid shouldn't be here with us. He's queer in the head. Gets in the way...."

"Look who's talking. LSMFT. Mully Mully Booga Booga...."

"You see what I mean Sam?"

"Look who's talking Umpapa. I ain't made of cellophane...."

"THAT'S ENOUGH FOR NOW! BEHAVE!" Sam says.

Izzy holds up one hand: "JAMBO kiddo. SALAAM!"

Thou did wax fat! Grow thick! Become gross!

One hundred fifty feet, maybe two hundred, from where he now squats, Peter imagines the Regional calisthenics class at Temple Eretz Uganda leaping, chanting:

    WAX FAT

    GROW THICK

    BECOME GROSS

Ver Veis, first in Yiddish, then I think in African, finally in Swiddish, the newest language in the whole world, because it takes a little bit of this, and a little bit of that, and a little bit of the other, from all sides of the lake, and from Swedish, for the United Nations volunteers.

"We got to have our own language," Izzy said, "a way of speaking on the QT, you and me. *Herst*?"

Izzy found Swahili on one of his old Paul Robeson albums

and for Yiddish, as he says, nobody ever had to teach him
that. "It comes with the territory kiddo," pointing down
to where he was cut at eight days old.

Izzy says a lingua franca and I think of French tongue,
like French toast Sunday morning, the *Times* sticky with
maple syrup.

Izzy says Swiddish is best for calisthenics:

FAT

THICK

GROSS

SWAK SWASS FRASS

Sawa sawa! Very beautiful, up and down, and *pesi pesi*.
(Burn burn bright sun with figures loping far away across
tar sands.)

FAT

WAX

FRASS

GROSS

Up, down, and *pesi pesi*. (*So far so very far away*, like
the new library, 160 feet, maybe 200.) For all I can see of
them naked they could be on the other side of the moon.

He brings himself a little closer. As Memsahib always
says, Peter has "a very vivid imagination," and now he can
just barely see more, cocks and cunts, tits and ass, and I
have none of these things myself, am flat, brown, skinny,
hairless, hardly a semi-boner, shiny dark moon for a face.
SWAK....

Flesh slapping flesh, feet splayed, hands reaching heaven-
ward. I'm always staring down through these big brown
eyes to where smudges between the bricks make ground,
and bush, and veldt. Here's Uganda and here's the lake and

Kenya and my nose is like fried skin, a blister, black....

(O little face of Peter, pasted beneath the sky like a grin.
When you look down at tar the sun's eye has a wink on
one end makes you want to cry. It leaves its sheen.)

All summer long big tears have washed across his eyes.
He has asked Little Sam why just because Memsahib had
her "nervous breakdown" he has no brother anymore this
summer, and Umpapa says, "Benjamin will be away in
camp, away in the Green Mountains, two more weeks, be
patient, Peter...."

"And the Memsah?"

"She was in Loch Sheldrake recuperating, on the other
side of Tar Beach. She shouldn't be bothered every minute
of the live-long day."

He also has told Umpapa all about cocks and cunts. The
calisthenics....

"Cock and cunts?"

"So why don't we all sit together like people?"

"Close your eyes next time," Umpapa says. "Don't
look!"

"Why not?"

"Don't give me a hard time Peter my son."

"I'm not Rostok. I asked you this question."

"Someday maybe you'll know."

Sullen: Sam's puny nakedness trapped like a boat with
cardboard sails inside the bottle of his anger.

"A boy your age I can't even discuss such crazy business
with...."

"Nothing like boys and girls together," Izzy blurts.
"What's the problem?"

"Leave it to your uncle Izzy," Sam says. "He'll really screw your head around about *nafkeh*."

Always putting Izzy down for being nice to me. Last Saturday in the steamroom the men were talking *ferd*.

Izzy said, "That Murry Buxbaum is built just like a *ferd*."

"Not in front of the boy Izzy!"

Then Harry asked, "*Ferd* is *ferd*. Whatsa matter Sam you embarrassed for your little peanut?"

"It's big enough to serve the purpose Harry. I don't have to look like no horse...."

"No use in comparing fellas," Izzy said. "Enough is certainly sufficient and too much of a good thing is socialism."

That's when Little Sam made me leave the steam room.

When I forgot to dip my feet in the chlorine bath outside the door, Rostok grabbed me, a towel around his waist. "If you don't keep sanitary you could lose your whole business from athlete's foot... Everything would just fall off..."

"My whole damn *shlong*?" Peter covered himself with both hands.

"Your toes... your feet and then all the way up the line," Rostok said.

"Don't give him such *meinsehs*," said Izzy, coming out of the *shvitz* just then.

He made me dip my feet even so, and afterwards we played under the waters of Victoria Falls in the shower together: Mr. Izzy I presume *Henayni* ....

"Fat
 Wax
 Swack"

Dollars to donuts somebody falls off this roof someday.

Little Sam's in a terrible mood. He almost got in a fistfight with Heshy about nothing in particular. A glob of zinc oxide on his King of Spades.

Days like this with his father always, his mother all summer long, and always a look like a fist, the shrugging shoulders, that sad wilted look. Izzy says a good woman is the best tonic of all. Sal Hepatica. "Occupy yourself," Sam tells me.

"Go find somebody to play with Peter."

Little Sam means stop bothering me and my friends, Mr. Mistake, but for crying out loud there really isn't anybody except for you and Izzy. Micky hasn't even got a full tank....

The little brown boy with the moon face really thinks he's been working hard all summer long at being nice to his father.

Telephone calls inside Peter's head. One extremely sour buttermilk message is heartbroken.

P.S. You wanta be my friend?

He turns again to face Umpapa in person:

"Bwana Sam?"

"Sssh."

"I'm hungry."

"In a little while Peter."

"Now!"

"Go talk to Tobias in the swimming pool. Don't bother me now please."

Rousing himself, Peter tries Swiddish:

"*Mapapa*!"

The air is wet and warm like a lick, except where the

sun gives it teeth.

With a mighty hand and an outstretched arm, Sam slaps down a black three. Izzy says: "My gin card, *vez mir.*"

"Papa, *Mapapa*"

A six of diamonds, big black nine.

"*MAPAPA!*"

"Peter, you're too old for baby talk, and don't interrupt!"

"I'm bored Papa."

"So go and take a swim. Be rational...."

"I'm bored swimming. I'm stuck to all this tar like a god-damnte waffle down below...and I'm hungry. Food, *Mapapa. Matooke...Anpesi....*"

"*Gotenyu,*" his father slaps a thigh, "that kid of mine he picks up the funniest expressions. Uncle Izzy, did you hear that? Already you got him talking like a Greenie...."

"*Zognisht.*"

The Bwana has a lot of phlegm and gravel in his voice, for once in his life. He shrugs and picks a cinder off the white stuff on his big black nose. Cross-legged, he squats opposite to his squatting chum Sam, and their greasy chub bodies ooze, perspire, threaten to slide down off the sundeck, and maybe off the Tar Beach, down into the veldt.

Over the pile of rummy cards they have scooped a deep well of shadows. Where the tips of both their delicate cocks touch the hot grey wood in a sort of wobble slouch, Peter stares like a detective. It hurts him so much just to look. He wonders if it doesn't burn them a whole lot worse. His scrotum feels like a balloon would carry him off the roof.

Once again he tries to get his point across to Sam, Izzy, whichever:

"Papa?"

"Peter if you bother me one more time...."

"Your cock is a sight for sore eyes darling."

"PETER!"

"*Zognisht* Sam! I wish I had an orange," Izzy says. "You'd like an orange kiddo, sure you would...."

Greedily, the boy nods, as though gnawing at the air which separates them.

"Go ask your momma. She has...and tell her one for Izzy, too...."

"Got ya!" Sam announces, laying down his cards, in threes.

SWAK! He knocks with one.

Scared for every part of his body that's visible, Peter moves rapidly, far away from the gin game down to the other side of Tar Beach, toward the promised orange, beyond a partition marked

WOMEN

Two

FROM PHIZZY IZZY

Boy of mine, says Bwana Izzy Berliner, to himself, a little later, you got your whole life ahead of you boychickle. Don't spoil it with a bad mood....

Even for one minute, he thinks: Don't. Not worth it. They're not worth it. We're not worth it, nothing is....

His own son, Sigmund Karl, dead now more than a decade after meningitis, Izzy still grieves softly, from deep down inside his chest—like a wheeze, a summer cough— even as the light froth of air in his head, warm sun upon his body, lulls him once more into an affectionate regard for this seed from his own loins grown so far astray as to be Sam's boy, so help me, Sam's own son now. This frail brown waif, Petey....

Sometimes, during a hand of gin, how he wishes he could halt the play a moment to say: "I think of you as my own son, too, kiddo. I like to think of you that way...."

Except for Sam, he might, and Lillian. The boy would benefit in the long run, he is sure: a bargain, two dads in one, or vice versa.

Who am I crazy or something? Touched?

Exasperated with himself, Izzy announces to his own head his certifiable condition, and then he discards a seven of spades: I could never get away with saying things like

that. *Meshugeh*...Better to say, like I almost always do, I'm
your friend, *Farshtayen*.

There's really no doubt about this boy to Izzy: it's his
son alright, this Petey boy; and seeing this replica of himself
in miniature hotfoot along on those dark red bricks on large
flat sensitive duck feet—so like his own walk, he thinks—
toward the high grey metal partition, and the corridor
beyond, dividing the women's section from where men
like him happen to be sunbathing, Izzy's eyes water up all
over again.

A certain wet curtain of loyalty to his own, an admiration
of the result, though putative and problemmatical to others,
has him running like a faucet from *beide eyeginner*. For the
sin which I have sinned, he murmurs, and with a rush of
heat to his face thinks someday it must all be clear to
Peter, and the rest of the gang here: that this boy will bear
his mother's face, but my brown eyes, and my build, too:
couldn't be helped, he thinks, love, you know, love demanded such. And so on....

He remembers way back to the summer before he went
off to Spain when it happened, after an early morning
swimming date at the St. George hotel in itchy wool suits,
just the two of them in a room at the Bear Mountain Lodge,
the two of them on the Storm King in the Pontiac, a summer
storm, and then he flashes to last Sunday, holding *sheiner*
Peter close to his clammy sweet body inside the steamroom.

Soft wet layers of vapor and steam bowed their heads,
and bent their knees, as he grasped the boy close as a clam
four floors below this place where they would never be
seen by all the rest of their detractors. Sam would be at

the hospital all day; Abraham Abraham was dying a year now, and Izzy was in charge, the baby-sitter; they were dripping on each other like Popsicles.

The boy asked, "How old is Abraham Abraham...?"

"Very old," Izzy said. "I am young by comparison. When he was a little boy there were no cars, and radios, and motion pictures...."

"Bathrooms too?"

"Bathrooms maybe...outside in the cold," he told Peter. "I'm really not too sure about indoor toilets which flushed...."

"That must have been a long time ago."

"1863 he was born," Izzy explained. "Hitler was a bad dream in the night. Abraham Lincoln was our President...."

"He never told a lie...."

"That was Washington. Lincoln freed the slaves...."

"Like me?"

"What did you just say Peter?" Even Izzy was startled.

"I'm a slave."

"You're a child Petey...a boy...not a slave. Children aren't slaves no more. They're kids...."

"Same thing." He spoke to Izzy with words all flattened out like metal. "If Hitler was still alive," he said, "I'd be dead."

"So there. See how lucky you are. Other kids...."

"I don't care about other kids," Peter said. "I just want to be happy, and all they talk about is *gelt*...."

"I'm sorry kiddo. That must be tedious...."

"And I don't happen to have any myself," Peter explained. "Otherwise...."

"Otherwise?" He was teasing his son.

"I could buy my own things. Be on my own, *ale mitvoch*," Peter said, "just like a grown-up. Maybe to buy you something too Iz. On account of I don't have anything of my own and I have to stay up here on Tar Beach all the time...."

Izzy liked to sound like a reasonable man. "Slaves don't have synagogues with swimming pools Peter. They never did. They were made to work hard all day long in the fields...."

Izzy knew he sounded pretty unconvincing to a child of middle class parents like Sam and Lil: "You have your problems it's true I won't deny...overprotected...misunderstandings...."

He cleared his throat, as though to change the subject: "You're a child Petey...a boy...nobody's slave...anybody mistreats you, tell me...children are just little people...."

"Same thing I said, slaves...."

"Well," Izzy added then, as if he still had lotsa snow in his throat had to be shovelled out, "as I been telling you, kiddo, that was just a long long time ago...very...before FDR...."

"Before Churchill?"

"Even before," he said. "Before Stalingrad...before radios, and televisions and the Blue Network...."

"So long ago?"

Their sweats are running together. The boy's buttocks slide against his naked lap. They have never been so close as in all this close sweaty air.

Izzy kissed his "son's" moist brow, and, when the boy squirmed away, pecked at him again.

Then Peter asked if Izzy knew there were such things as

angels in those days. Sure there were, Izzy said, and there probably are even now, because angels are the emissaries of the Lord God of Hosts.

"What does that mean?"

"God knows," he shrugged. "Not Izzy."

"So?" Peter asked, "Why did he have two names?"

"Who had two?"

"Abraham Abraham? Why?"

"All little boys have two," he said, making a joke of it. "And thank the Lord for that, I suppose... *qu'est que c'est that N'est cafe*...."

"Names," Peter went on. "Why two? Why Abraham Abraham?"

"Why Peter Pintobasco?" he exclaimed. "It's a name is all...."

"His parents came from Germany a long time ago," Izzy explained "before the War...before there ever were wars ...before Uganda. They got rich here in Brooklyn with a department store. Like Namm's or Loeser's. The name Abraham Abraham means his father was Mister Abraham and he named his son Abraham...."

"Like my name is really Ben Shmuel....?"

"Ben Shmuel...Ben Israel," Izzy shrugged, feeling almost queer for the boy. "And your brother is Benjamin...."

"He stinks."

"A brother doesn't stink," he explained. "He's flesh and blood, mostly...and can't help what the parents do."

"Benjamin doesn't like me...."

"He likes," Izzy said, "and he can't really help. He's kinda just a kid himself...another victim...of the mis-understanding...as I been telling you all along...."

"So why did he stay in camp when I had to leave like this?"

Wasted motion. A boy feels so sorry for himself.

"Why?" The air smelled close, like sulphur. "Why is not a brother," Izzy observed. "Benjamin stayed because he was not sent for. You were sent forth. It happens. You mustn't hate Peter. Don't hate. Brothers shouldn't hate."

"Hate?" He really didn't act as though he knew the word. Probably just the feeling.

"Resent," Izzy explained. "*Amacha*...."

"*Amacha*?"

They were playing Uganda again.

"*Satope*," went Izzy.

And Peter became overwrought: "*Hinny Hinny Hinny Izzy Hinny*...."

For lack of other words, in their common patois, Izzy pointed out to his son it was standing room only in Heaven right now, on account of the recent war in Europe, but he would just have to try to find Peter an angel to look after him for the rest of the summer, and this angel might even be a playmate too. "All in fun," he added.

"With wings?"

"Lox wings," Izzy said. "You'll see or you won't...the rich call it Salmon P. Chase. Wait and see. A little angel's gonna be at your side when I can't be with you, from here on. You'll see, *na na*...."

He gave Peter a little tickle in the ribs had him hot all over suddenly.

"*Na na na na*," the boy said, mixing dubiety with hope, next to his "uncle" Izzy in the steam room.

Then Peter asked, "What sort of angel?"

"*Malech*...a cherubim," he sang: "Cheri Berri Bim," as though hoping to change the subject.

"And the name?"

"Cross my heart if I know," Izzy said. "It could be anybody, a mouse, a cockroach in disguise. Maybe even one of the yentahs on the other side of the roof. Beelzebub or just plain Bubbeleh...."

"Do I have to sit here and listen to all this bullshit from the peanut gallery?"

From a cloud of steam the voice of Solly Cohen, all sweat and bluster, salt, ice, steam, wrath.

"Leave this kid alone with your malarky Izzy, and kid this is a place for adults, grown-ups, big people. Bad for a little kiddie's heart...."

"OK Solly. OK Moloch...."

Izzy hugged Peter close again, and his lips kissed his brow one last time. "Now go boy and don't get in any trouble. Go! *Herst?*"

"An angel hubba hubba," Peter was saying; and he left Izzy, with Solly, behind a cloud of steam....

Where to?

Goddamnte *Kurveh*. His natural mother, my girl, Lillian.

Izzy, naturally, has always thought of his son as a *shayne*, a *ziss*...pretty boy, more like when I was a kid. The look on dead Sigmund's face was pure Eggy Brammstein: a *halbe* Eggy and a *halbe* Etta. But Peter's angelic....

Out loud Sam declares: "Gin!"

Izzy says, "You win a fortune!" Caught daydreaming again, he discards a single trio of threes, so that all the rest of his seven cards will have to count against him: maybe fifty points, not counting boxes. Maybe even more.

"That's all for me Sam," Izzy says. "I'm cleaned out, just like Ex Lax. Won't have anything left to take Etta out to dinner tonight...."

"I'll run a benefit for you Izz. What's a matter, you didn't have a good week? No commissions. Fancy women....?"

"It was all right. Please Sam...." Izzy's head is cast down. "I just need to be with myself, alone, a little while...."

"Suit yourself, Temperamental," says Sam, sliding down off the deck to douche himself briefly under the cold shower. "Just remember how I got you on the schneider and I'll collect later...."

Shaking himself down like a puppy, Sam wanders over to the klatch of other men at the far end of the bench. "Suit yourself," Izzy calls after him, sadly.

"*El Male Rachamin*," he adds, glancing up toward the heavens. "God full of compassion gave his friend Sam a knack for gin rummy and a draft exemption during the war and, in return, has made me into auxiliary cantor for the High Holidays."

Izzy Berliner is a lost man, but not ordinary in his ways. Not ever! More like a lost battalion of selves and in the center one small doctrinaire socialist. He's always been strong in opposing the exploitation of man by man. Never mind women....

Izzy believes in angels the same way that he believes in the Masonic Hall of Double Truth, in ghosts and spectres, such as that "spectre haunting Europe." He believes whatever comes to mind willy-nilly must have some basis:

The Trinity and Relativity, the Laboring Day, Surplus Value, Reconstructionism, Existential Psychotherapy (but not for him). That Mozart was Jewish, and so was Hitler maybe, way back when, and George Gershwin, and Mezz Mesrow, General Franco, LaGuardia's wife, Ivy Litvinoff, Barney Kessel the guitarist, Ra and Akhnaton. Blood love and blood hate and universal brotherhood....

When not sunbathing naked, or losing at gin rummy, maybe a little four wall handball, the self-same Jacob I. Berliner runs the sportswear showroom at Fancier Frocks, near Paddy's Irish Clam Bar, on West 34 Street, not too far from Macy's. Before that he was for many years with E. G. (Eggy) Brammstein, Inc. Resident Buyers.

He knows how to talk to strangers, and he's a crackerjack at selling, with women, particularly if they're out of town buyers. Also certain overweight models. He knows production, and he's got a flair for design, is easily distracted. On some weeks he takes home triple his regular draw, maybe even more, and some weeks he slumps, and fools around an awful lot with *mieskeits*.

Can't be helped, anymore than with Lillian, for what happened between them once, what goes on even now, sometimes; and there's a certain loving admiration he has, plain and simple, something just a *bisel* special for Lillian and, of course, the boy, Petey....

"*Adonai bin nachalats*," be then my possession—as thus cast from my seed, Izzy addresses his girlfriend and son, silently. He adds, "In Uganda, for peace and friendship among peoples...*Ohmein*."

So now, eyeing what they once made together (so naked

and frail and brown) and so vulnerable to every slight from
his legal father, Sam, Izzy Berliner thinks a *kapores*, a
scapegoat, that's all we ever made together, you and me,
Lill. See the father won't really accept him and we can
never really accept that situation, can we darling? Nor can
he, Petey. Never, poor darling....

Bubblichkeh, he thinks, a case for Solomon, or a *Gallech*,
rabbi, or priest, or judge. A true mess: Izzy pines for what
Sam has and doesn't want and what can he tell him? Say?

Loz im op Sam, Izzy says: That's all. Ever....

Accordingly, Jacob Israel Berliner scoops a gob of Noxzema cream the size of a Sunsweet prune from a large blue
jar beneath the deck with his long index finger, as he smears
it like a war paint all down along the bridge of his nose,
making such a cold white streak he shivers.

A *kapores* plain and simple, he decides: a boy must be
accepted by his father and he never will. The birth of
tragedy in the making....

A memory of that first date between the sheets with
Lillian less than ten years ago has rushed back on him again,
a slightly more reverberant shiver....

He'd been upset for months about the purges and then
Spain, not knowing which way to turn, and should he
volunteer, and she was the distraction who appeared when
Sam was down in Washington with a client, and suddenly
there was no turning away from her. On the same day
he went with her he bought his passage to Spain on the
liner Primo De Rivera from Montreal with the McKenzie
Papineaus.

His fingertip stayed by the fleshy tip of his nose, so aquiline and fine, Izzy recalls the hot sun of Valencia and Alicante. It stings him again just a little, where he's had so much heat his dark cheeks are wrinkling. Too much glare on my face and heat. Too much recent history. Too much under the reflectors, he thinks. Blotches....

I'm barbecuing my face. He recalls the chickens turning on spits outside the cafes on the Ramblas, parrots squawking, bombs, and more red everywhere than he has ever seen in his whole life.

Etta will surely complain if so much sun puts me to sleep at ten o'clock tonight. Frankly she puts me to sleep, but can I tell her that? (Too little sonny boy, and too much sun, poor woman.)

Poor Izzy, he corrects himself.

With his finger resting so, on his schnoz, Izzy fancies he must look just as thoughtful to the world around as Buster Rostok, Gonuv, as he calls him.

Regular Man of Distinction Izz can sometimes be, when he's wearing a good suit of clothes, a Schenly ad. Long gone the *tummler* who helped tear the swastika flag off the Nazi liner Bremen when it came to dock on the West Side. It's this medicinal Noxzema smell, he decides, makes him seem that way, even naked, like a doctor, physician, medicine man, not somebody who just writes orders and plays *chazen* in the Sanctuary annex: so many dozens this or that for Christmas, Easter, for inventory before the High Holidays.

In his other life, Izzy hangs around with good friends of Paul Robeson, and Vito Marcantonio, or did, for awhile, downtown at the Cafe Society, though sometimes, nowadays, he can't always pay his bills, and if not for Etta bookkeeping part-time at the Board of Education....

In clothes, however, Izzy thinks, I still look like a million bucks, in that grey sharkskin for example with the lounge jacket and cross-stitched lapels...more like a certain actor than a doctor, to be sure. Even naked, there's still a certain charm, and maybe it is from my skin and what I treat it with.

Again he can hear Lillian's voice: "A skin like that deserves olive oil with saffron Iz...."

"Maybe baby oil?"

"Baby oil, of course, baby oil," she says: "What else?"

Pity for the weight I've gained around the midriff. Even handball doesn't melt that away, a week in the *shvitz'* winter camp in Beacon. Nothing...but I get so hungry, and sometimes I just gotta eat and so on....

And moreover, he adds, it's them lunches, Izzy decides, and laughs his silly laugh, as lunch usually means, in his lingo, a date, a matinee, a hotel room maybe, the Company flat, a private room above the Russian baths, maybe tea and cakes with cimbalon music at Moscowitz & Lupowitz after, and, if the Company is paying, a Broadway show, the best seats in the house. It's called working late and it means figuring out a way to excuse himself afterwards to get home to Etta, while still remembering to write the order, topping last year's, if possible, and keeping a stiff prick for Etta, after so much lunching...and *shtupping*.

Such an operator you are, Izzy. Oy. Izz the Phizz, healer, one-time devotee of A. D. Gordon's agrarian Zionism, later C. P. militant, and now specialist in melancholy women. To cure Lillian's chronically lugubrious nature, Izzy had, of course, prescribed some poems of Kenneth Fearing, after Catullus, and tea and cakes at Lucullus on Church Avenue, Kropotkin's *Mutual Aid*, Canada Lee in *Native Son*, Sorel on *Violence*, and, finally, his own special marathon course of sub-cutaneous injections in Bear Mountain.

Result: *tsores*, namely Peter, and angry Sam rejecting him, Lillian's later breakdown, some cure, a *tsaddik's* nightmare. And now she won't let me go, not for love or money, Izzy thinks.

Izzy thinks the fact that Lillian still pines for him is only proof of how inappropriately he has behaved toward her, and, almost inevitably, such guilt stiffens his prick.

The last time he felt so guilty and randy was at Ronces Valle on the French Border when he was about to cross back over after failing to enlist. Met an Irish girl with a red beret, claimed to be a cousin of Michael Collins, and what they did together for two days and nights in the inn of the Carmelite Fathers made him feel even guiltier.

Maeve was her name. We made love right above where Charlemagne's army lay buried. Well she said she'd come with me to Paris, by train, but I left without her, and, in Paris, met Hedva, Etta's schoolmate, and I was trying to keep that friendly too, only that was hard to do in her little *atelier* off the Observatoire.

Abruptly he hears his friend Sam again: "I've got college educations to think about Izzy and I'm not saving a dime...."

"It's hard," he tells his friend. "Everything costs."

"Maybe I need to speculate," Sam says. "Something volatile. Feed grains. The French and Germans are feed poor, it says in my Kiplinger...."

"That's big time stuff," Izzy says. "Stay well out of it. The margins could kill you...."

Is that really the best advice he can give?

"What could I lose? Lill's pin money?"

"Lillian would like you in one piece altogether," Izzy points out. His friend doesn't seem to realize, rich or poor, nobody wants a corpse as father of her kids.

"Remember Murray Pullman?" Izzy adds. "He had bushels of some kind and then one day they called in his margins from Toronto and when he couldn't cover he jumped off a roof...."

"Depressing..." Sam says, but personally he don't seem that worried.

"Went right off the Graybar Building," Izzy says, "and then he'd forgotten to change all his insurance policies and a lot of the money ended up with the Party in Chelsea. Worse still, he hit a Checker cab so three people went with him, passengers, Sam, margins...."

Izzy's own dad went broke the first time in the Taft bear market of 1906. He always said William Howard Taft made him a radical. He never finished high school, took night school courses at Jefferson, and once upon a time enjoyed reading. Thought he might even try to write something someday.

An egoist he wasn't, he decided in the end. Just to make a good living, have something left over for playing around, a few bucks here and there for good causes, such as the *Hashomer*, Willy McGee, the Textile Strike. To be a regular person, a *shmutznik*....

His friend Sam is so different. He still imagines he could

someday be Rostok. Less is poverty to Sam, a grind, a grudge, humiliation.

They've walked off together, beneath the crash and splash of the shower, having taken turns wetting down. Now they will dry off again, like raisins. He hears himself cautioning Sam about margins.

"The big guys always have the edge," he tells his friend. "Remember?"

Sam changes the subject: "Being President of this institution will also cost a pretty penny...."

"So don't run. Take Lill to Florida this winter. Have some fun in the sun with your money...."

"It's strictly business with me," Sam explains. "Being Temple President brings in business. Lillian and I aren't getting along too hot anyway...she and me...."

"Don't I know?"

Wet from Sam's hair drips down his brow and high cheekbones, and curls along his high florid brow when he frowns. They are matching shrugs like different gabardines hanging from the same closet rod.

"It's not what you think Iz." Either Sam's got pink eye, or he's gonna start crying on me.

Izzy keeps staring at his naked friend like a frayed collar. "What are you trying to tell me?"

"I'm no piker Izz...."

"Whoever said you were...."

"She just has no affection for me. It's hard living that way...."

"Why not leave?" he asks. "Worse things could happen."

("If you want exclusive possession you can marry me," Lill had said only three days ago.)

Now he adds, "A trial separation maybe...."

"Not so fast," Sam says. "There are children."

"You'll see them," Izz says. "She can't deprive you...."
But he knows he's going much too fast. Is he recommending
for Sam, or for himself?

"Nowadays," Izzy adds, "the psychiatrists do wonders.
You two could be very happy together with a little help...."

("Liar!")

"There's someone else. I know there is. But I don't
know who, or how? *Why*?"

"Sam," he says, "you're making things up and only
making yourself miserable. I can't help you so leave me
alone, for a little while...."

"She cries out in her sleep," Sam says, "but I can never
make out names."

"Please," Izzy says. "I'm not Lillian. Don't bully me.
Be President if that makes you happy. I'll vote for you.
Just leave me alone...."

Izzy Berliner feels pretty bad for his words, though they
keep the worst from being divulged, until the next time
with Sam.

Guilt makes you anticipate, he thinks. I am guilty and
fearful all the time, like a hard-on I don't want.

Izzy also feels all soggy wet in the crotch from all this
heat, and there's a cold frost of sweat all down along his
Noxzema streaks as the boy once more comes into his line
of sight, conversing with that old faker Zuckerman.

Izzy thinks the rabbi is a show off and a fool. He
wouldn't even be able to hold down a job if not for his wife,

Nahoma's charms. An utterly fierce woman. *Moyredick*, scary, like she knows all about you. Izzy calls her "No pasaron" because who would want to make a pass at her?— She reminds him of La Pasionaria, even to wearing black all the time to services.

Just look at Zuckerman now, trying to make friends with boychick.

What can the old fraud be asking my son?

Under the shower Zuckerman seems truly diminished, salt licked by the sun. Dried up old worm he's got up down dere is an empty spigot; a beard like dirty water hanging off his chin. Izzy knows his worst secret: he can only read Hebrew transliterated in the Roman alphabet. Terrible! Izzy can't do any better, but he's an amateur.

He tells himself he saw Zuckerman with a pony inside the open Torah last Sukkoth. How is he going to teach my boy anything?

And watches Peter's dark face go lank, the buttocks flexing, a little colt, when he moves hot-stepping along, with not even a white towel draped about his waist.

My beautiful son, he thinks, my boy, and they spend all their time making him unhappy.

Last Sunday in the shower room, when the boy had questions to ask about men and women, Sam made him feel so bad.

Now he ain't got anything to say to anybody. Talks to himself, like me, or is fresh, a hooligan....

What can a man expect? The boy's a hostage, not a slave: Lillian's hostage; Sam's hostage, too, and I—who know better—who am I to talk?

What can I do?

Lillian, he groans out loud, our son is being driven crazy...and I don't want to lose a friend, a wife, to be embarrassed...?

He shakes his head to chase away the thought, the feeling like a stab to the heart, and the gap separating Peter and himself now growing larger, a space, a pang, a yearning hurt such as he only felt maybe one other time in his whole life, when they brought him in to see Little Sigmund, with the eyes closed shut, so placid, like he was only fooling around, playing dead on his face, and then he said, "Don't fool around please, Sigmund, my son. You're not really dead...."

"My son, my son," crying out then, "Sonny boy don't. Don't fool around...."

On that day at the Caledonia hospital, ten years ago, Izzy never really knew what hit him like a brick wall.

He collapsed.

So now, back at his bench, staring down at 10 brand new cards dealt out by his friend Sam, without even a by-your-leave, Izzy's surprise is adumbrated when he notes that all the threes, and jacks, and nines, triple up so readily, and there's even an extra nine left over.

He's got

"GIN," Izzy shouts. "I'VE GOT GIN!"

"And about time," Sam says. "All month long I've been killing you. If this had kept up...."

"Sure you would," says Izzy .

Tears of joy surprise him in his sorrow.

Gin is good and God is great. For a change. The chambers of his heart exude a happy gas; Deliverance must be near at hand.

"Just leave me a couple of box seats at Ebbets Field," Sam says. What's that look on his face?

Izzy's ears are ringing: "I got a break for a change. What's with you? What's the score?"

"You're off the schneider 160 points, and you're a liar...."

"About what?" He's feeling a little too much heat. Did Sam set him up with this win?

The face on Sam makes Izzy cringe. He feels like Abe Rellis halfway out the hotel window.

"It's not like every day in the week is my party," Izzy says, "So temporize a little. In the long run you're way ahead."

"Deal," Sam says. "Enough advice. I want revenge!"

DO NOT ENTER WOMEN

Red glass letters hanging down from a black metal two-way sign in the passageway, which separates partitions like armor on a battleship's gun turret: DO NOT ENTER WOMEN....

Stopping himself in mid-step to hold back, Peter touches an oily warm spill, dripped off the slippery body of a handball player, or sunbather, and anoints himself on the forehead and along each of his bony shoulders, his fingertips fragrant with Little Lake Albert.

He's been standing here like this five minutes, maybe even more, feels beaten, beaten for the light, with pure oil olive, or scented *shvitz*, and if so, what so? You ask for a little thing like an orange and someone says pain in the ass. Just looking makes him feel a little better, hiding....

Am I now anointed, like King David?

I'm only being childish again, he decides, nerves, as Mammileh says. From being knocked from pillar to post and back by Sam, by Solly, Harry, and the gang, I could honestly die. *Mord*, he thinks, die..."Who's a queer? I like girls," he says, "girls...."

Atterhu, he says, to his shadow, in Swiddish, meaning after you. Nice to soften the burning on my shoulders with a little grease. And still he holds himself back, *yetz*, not to enter where his shadow wants to flow ahead of him, like a dark river.

Somehow he has skinned his kneecap and there's this tiny stiffness, a clot.

Blood, Peter thinks: Do not enter women period!

As simple as *ane kimoshy anu*....

Which he would translate as *krasnoy*!

He thinks of a mouthful of tart pulpy orange streaky with blood. "Talk. Don't spritz," Memsahib says.

Sometimes he thinks his life these days is just like a song Peter really used to like from Hebrew school: "Who is like unto thee Mammileh, *tatteleh*, Fairest of the fair...Transplanted from old Europe's shore...Religion of our fathers' awe..."

Words like that. To that effect. *Moriah?*
Setanu
Cement Mixer Putty Putty
Oobop Shabam
Shazam!

On all those parts of his body that jut forth, he has anointed himself with pure oil olive, and maybe a *bisle* wintergreen...He believes he must also shine forth a whole lot; and there's a meatloaf odor wafting at him, faintly, from somewhere afar....

Peter thinks I will now present myself to Bathsheba who does not know I've been watching her bathe her *naynays*....

He's also hungry, and that's not the only reason why he would very much like to enter and see what's cooking with the Memsa' and all her women friends. A certain need to hear her voice, sit on her lap. She's been mostly absentee

Mammileh all summer long....

On the floor, where his feet are splattered flat in shadows, the oil spreads a dark film, and there's kestrel song, and keening.

"When I'm like this," he hears, just as a police siren from twelve floors down below interrupts and fades. "When I get this way," Mammileh shouts, even louder above the jangle of trolley wheels, her voice a heavy prophecy, like sparks along a wire going off, Rachel crying for her children. "Dead from the neck down," she adds.

Somebody else he recognizes interrupts: "The same likewise, Don't I know Lillian?"

Yetta Sternglass, whom Lillian always calls Thelma. "Crazy Yetta," says his father. "You know Yetta. That's just like her."

Peter thinks it is unconstitutional on account of he wishes it were Etta Berliner, with whom he sometimes gets along like franks and beans, just like with Big Izzy, or his Cousin Muriel.

Slippery things course through Peter's mind: Izzy's "eggs," Lillian's legs. Her sleek jet black hair when wet falling across her shoulders to dry as red-brown as she makes up her face to go out, the strong high cheekbones. Indian cheeks, Peter calls them. The brilliant green of her eyes, her figure, her smell of dusting powder and heat....

Mammileh again: "When I'm feeling so bad I could scream," her voice lifts so as to compete with that goddamnte siren again (an afterglow to his own tarred up aftertaste), "all I can really take is maybe a little lukewarm camomile tea...."

"*Ohmein.*"

"...A two cent plain Good Health, cold borscht with lemon...."

"AZOY," Peter repeats, his words thundering against those grey metal bulkheads as he hears the crash of the shower from that side also, crescendos of falling water: *"L'hadlich ner shel Fox's U-Bet...."*

Like God Himself, he thinks crazy stuff like that. Faced with that DO NOT ENTER WOMEN he thinks a grown man you tell don't. A little boy like me is still a *kalb* of a different color *komoshy anu. Moriah....*

As Izzy says, they got more to hide, kiddo, simple as all that. When you get a bride someday you'll know.

In fact, he knows already: so much fulsome rounding of flesh in bunches and bounces and a dark pink slit like a cut peach between the legs, except the Memsahib has a small waist, big bubbies, a fine straight back, a clear brow, and that other thing, too, which he's seen only once when she was painting her toes on the toilet seat and he walked in uninvited....

Who me? I didn't see a thing, he protests....

Dead from the eyes down....

"They're like a fist to my stomach," the Memsahib adds, "and I have night sweats, terrible...they don't ever let me do much else...."

"I can't even breathe sometimes," she says, "when its hot like this...."

"Double in spades," Yetta-Thelma says, "can't work... can't eat. Maybe a cold glass of tschav, a tuna fish sandwich...."

"OR DEVILLED HAM WITH CHOPPED UP GERKINS AND MAYO...."

He has thundered again so his Mammileh inquires:

"Who is that there?"

"An eavesdropper," Yetta says.

"...NAISE," adds Peter. "The Underwood brand for sure, red devil with crossed pitchforks, a Horlich malted milk, not any buttermilk feh. My rocky belly and my *shaine ponim*...Cookies Lavagetto...*Jambo*!"

Last time he crossed over Memsahib told everybody about Memphis when she was a little girl and the big muddy river, and a large Canaanite woman stood under the shower, bubbies bouncing beneath the small drizzle, an ass, astounding, in high heeled clogs, legs—O wonder...the whiteness....

Yette-Thelma again: "Whoever that is over there eavesdropping actually isn't being very polite...."

And Peter replies: "*Henayni* woman. I am the Lord thy God who brought thee out of bondage...out of the house of bondage...."

"Who can cook?" asks Mammileh. "If he has to eat I'll ask Sam it don't have to cost a fortune: that Chinks, near the Cameo Theatre, or Dubrow's, or Garfield's...I hear they're redecorating...."

"A mosaic marvel," Yetta-Thelma says.

"Anything else," Lillian adds, "and I'm almost sure to vomit. Can't hold down a thing. Seems like I'm flowing night and day...."

"Day and night," sings Peter, "Under the heart of me...."

To which Yetta-Thelma declares: "Dubrows ain't got fresh." There's a luncheonette on Avenue J from Cookies where they got a decent smoked fish salad...a bargain...."

"I don't like smoked fish," he rumbles forth. "It tastes bad breath to me...."

Beneath the shower big fat woman pulling down the shoulder straps on her bathing suit bra to soap her pelt with Lava.

From behind him in the Men's Rostok calling out to Izzy: "Little Mr. Stalin."

"*You didn't have enough dead Jews from Hitler Mr. Smartaleck Berliner?*"

"You tell him Uncle Izzy," Peter shouts: "*Bandera Rosa!* Suffer Tuffa Umbriago....*"

"Kiddo please...."

His Mammileh calls out: "Is that you out there Sonny boy?"

"Who did you think it was? Winston Churchill?"

"Fresh! So fresh...."

"Spoiled," Lillian adds. "I am afraid I spoiled...."

"A disturbed child," Yetta-Thelma insists. She teaches second grade in Pelham. "Such a pity for you Lill...."

"*Gai Kucken ah fen yam Thelma!*"

"Peter," says his mom, sharply. Then she has the *chutzpah* to add, "That's just because we spoiled him, Sam and me...we spoil him good...."

"It may be true
for all we know
but it sounds so
mighty queer.
So take your crap
to another chap
'cause we don't like bullshit here...."

Thelma saying, "What's with Old Lang Syne?"

Still and all, the boy in his mom's life hasn't yet made

his appearance, sticking out so hot and stiff, in his metal decompression chamber; and they're talking about him like he was a piece of fish, sable or white. When he knows it's different. Not fresh, nor spoiled. A case of the crasses, just permanent boredom.

"Horshitsky," as Izzy sometimes says. Camp again, or an orphanage for me, he thinks, with a lot of other *choleryas* just like me.

As Izzy would say, *Kapores*, meaning Zum Zum Baba-reebop....

Leora, though, the light he sees through ventilator pin-holes in the metal is like early morning light on grasslands, a little softer maybe except in the sun where there's so much glare. Peter hopes, presumes, on another glimpse of that fleshiness.

Women vermin *atterhu*.
Um sissa, Peter thinks. *Zim* Izzy....
As he takes two steps forward, beyond the cool shadow of the bulkheads, flash of a shower rushing down, and such big pink knockers...hoyda hoyda!

To enter, with eyes more or less wide open, where all those pink splotchy blotches sag, then bounce, or jounce, beneath cloth, in halters, or, even, God help me, entirely without, a swelling, a *swali*, or *sevali*—for sure....

Peter feels the deck as slippery and has to steady himself from wobbling.

UMSWASU

Overcome with unreasoning curiosity, and blush again, his face and ears burn, as if they are all coming to the same point directly at the end of his penis, which juts frail, though ever forward, a midget's battering ram.

How he wishes he'd worn his bathing suit now.

So embarrassing to be without a blank in front.

This thing he has all the time over here, a true boner, Izzy says, tiny knight's lance from King Solomon's Mines, not at all like those big fellas, what do you call them—Watutsis? Little forest folk, or pigmy *shvantzen*, pogoing out so much it hurts. They sit right on top of the world. Not me....

He has found the eye of his Mammileh where she sits *der nayim naket*, shoulder straps down around her waist, bathing suit skirts hitched up high across her meaty white and strawberry thighs, hint of a bloody bandage jammed between her legs, her plug, the sweet raw gravy putrid smell.

On the hot grey deck, next to her friend, surrounded by other women equal in nakedness, or distress, Mammileh squats like a lot of bad weather, a summer storm over Long Beach....

Sometimes they talk books, or fashion, and the movies, and sometimes current affairs, but Peter has walked in on body functions, the basic unit course of their boredom.

A million cows are also lowing about inside his head, while they munch at the grass of the afternoon. Still he can't get either of the Memsa's liquid green eyes to look his way. Time for a song, he decides, some merry melody, of course, to get her wall-eyed attention, dissolve the soft collodian of her stare.

Jutting a little further, the boy commences:

"Rose O'Day

Rose O'Day
You're my binamaroosha
skinna matoosha
ballsy wallsy....
(Whereupon protagonist always steps forward and rubs
himself down with the palm of his hand in the *beytsim*)
     ...ballsy wallsy
     Boom-toodey-A...."
Embarrassed laughter, and tomato faces everywhere.
Such looks. You'd swear Gary Cooper just took his pants
off.

Yetta-Thelma Sternglass exclaims, "John McCormack?...
Dennis Day?" with seemless seeming delight.

Peter points at himself: "The Rising of the Moon?"

"The nerve of him," Yetta says, cross now, "coming into
here like this, saying things to us like that...."

"It's just childish talk," the Memsa' declares, "Singing,
all kid stuff...." She's suddenly feeling little joy at seeing
her son like Izzy and defensive about that, too, a throbbing.
"Izzy says he has talent...."

"Some judge...They're both big show-offs," Yetta-Thelma
Sternglass settles back into her permanent state of grudge
that Izzy Berliner should have chosen Lillian over herself
to be his tootsy.

"Izzy is no expert on anything anyway," she says, "and
no friend of mine, for sure...."

The boy is standing in the sun like a melloroll.

"Well," Lill says, "he thinks I should give Peter singing
lessons...."

"Singing? Like that? At us? Wait until he's grown, why
dontcha? His voice hasn't even changed...A little peewee,

Lillian...."

"And that's the only reason why I ever let him cross over," she explains.

"But he's much too big for this," Yetta says. "Too big to be coming over here without a thing to cover himself when we're...like this...."

"A big boy like that," she goes on.

"Make up your mind," Peter says. "Am I big or little?" He feels himself decline.

Yetta ignores him: "It's not right...Not the way at all. You should scold, chastise. He's no baby anymore. Tell Izzy that...."

"Tell him what?"

"He's such a big bozo," she says. "The way he treats women...."

"Me or Izzy?" Peter asks.

"Listen here boy," Yetta says.

"What should I tell him really?" Lillian demands.

"Why tell him it ain't right."

"Don't I know," Lillian says. "Don't I know?"

ROSTOK DREAMS

Rostok dreams, thinks Peter, beside Lake Edwin in a sun stupor, this sun drunk hippo.

Actually he just dreams. Punct! Dreams in the sun. Dreams sun dreams, and that he is playing cards in a cool Arab tent on a patterned rug with blind Piggy Baer and winning all the hands.

"I could play you blind," he says to Piggy, out loud.

Rostok dreams the sun is no more cruel than an inoculation in the buttocks, from which he once fled, when on Army service, for the Provisional Government, without his pants, onto the nearest steamer leaving for New York, with his parents, but arriving only in Baltimore, to work their way North, he found himself in his dream, an orphan suddenly, under the East River, where his own crew of sandhogs lurked, soldiering on the job.

No smoking here *tattileh*. Pee in the designated areas. Smell of mouse shit and cinnamon from a sunken barge. "Jesus, it's the boss," his foreman, Mergantiler, said, as Rostok fled the White cossacks on ice skates.

Deep beneath the river, he walks *yetz* with Proscauer and Manny Tilt, the asphalt man, and the Sicilian crowd, and wakes up again in a garrison along the river Bug in the company of Vladimir Jabotinsky and his Jewish self-defense force. They are both wearing campaign hats, and Jabotinsky has a camel tethered to a telegraph pole outside.

"Vladimir," he asks, "how did all this come about...?"

"Because you are such a jabbering *buttinsky*," says the famed Litvak orator.

He wakes with the Pintobasco brat staring at him, no more than a few feet distant. Bug-eyes. Or, perhaps, the boy, noticing Rostok awake, suddenly materializes, like fungus on a crap house wall.

"Your humble servant, Colonel," Rostok says. "A Jew isn't safe here anymore...?"

"You were making such noises out loud," the boy observes. "You sounded just like rusty plumbing...."

"What's it to you?"

"So I want to know who is this Mr. Jabotinsky?"

"A great hero of his people," Rostok says. "A man of action...but your friend Izzy over there doesn't like him, so why ask?"

"Just wondering."

Peter backs away a step.

This brat is a little sissified, intense, Rostok thinks, with eyes like cupping saucers. Huge, and shiny. The mother's eyes but Izzy's face...*NO'KHTAM*!

"Can you make change for a dollar?" Peter asks the millionaire.

Rostok waves him away like a fly: "I got no pockets. Go away boy...."

"You're not being friendly," Peter says. "I came over to look at you because of my father...."

"That's certainly none of your beeswax," Rostok says.

"You hurt his feelings bad," says Peter. "What you did to him. Mine too...."

"That was just business," Big Sam says. "I don't talk business with kids...."

He's looking at his own knees, heavy with water, as though they were big Jersey beefsteaks for making a vinaigrette. Delicious. Who can tell? As the old joke goes, "Looked so good I ate it myself...."

"Mr. Rostok?"

"What now?"

"Please...."

"What's up doc?"

"There's something I gotta tell you...."

"Make it fast, I didn't get much sleep last night."

Rostok opens his eyes on a finger pointed like a gun. "Bang bang you're dead," Peter says. "I hate you. I don't think I really like you... You scare people...."

"So?"

"People like me," he adds. "Little kids."

"What I had to do I did," Rostok says. But he's flinching. "Your father never really wanted to set the world on fire. That's a problem, in my line of work. We're the 'live wires' ...Big business...Don't point that at me," he adds, between clenched teeth.

"You're a big shit-ass schmuck," Peter says. "Bang Bang again. Bang Bang Bang!"

"Peter *loz im op.*"

Umpapa and Izzy pushing the hot air his way. They hold themselves back behind him. A naked thigh against his buttocks. He hopes Mammileh and her friends can hear him now.

"Some way to talk," says Rostok. "Did you teach him that Pintobasco?"

Sam starts to speak, holds back.

And Izzy says, "You're a big shot when it comes to little kids Buster...."

"O shut up Berliner...I could say a thing or two about you...."

"I'd like to see you make him try Mr. Pooh-Pooh head," says Peter.

"*Loz im op in spades*," says Izzy. From across the barrier he hears the high piping of Lillian: "Peeter? Sonny what's going on?"

Izzy grabs Peter and pulls him backwards, as though he might be struck. "You gotta admit," he says. "This kid ain't shy...."

"He's either crazy or a quart low." Rostok says. "But you would stick up for him...."

He shuts his eyes again, perchance to dream. Ella, his wife, has combed out her lustrous black hair before the mirror. He comes upon her seated in front of a vanity, her fine naked back and slim waist erect along a startling curvilinear. Such *shaykhes...Toyer...* They are at an inn in Brody, near the Austrian border.

He has an erection...it doesn't happen so often.

Izzy says, "Mr. Rostok wants his privacy...."

Again the brat speaks: "It's got a head on it like a Jersey strawberry...Mr. Rostok, that must hurt a lot...."

"What....?" The eyes open again. Sag and wilt *nebuch*!

"I was just thinking with all your money you should wear a jock...."

"Wha....?"

"Come on kiddo," Izzy says. "This is no way to behave...."

Rostok sees Ella on her bed of childbirth pain. She labored so long to produce a fly, his sissy son, Georgey, a fly, a flit...who he got into West Point from a foxhole in Belgium, right in the middle of the Bulge.

Kid still won't go away for love or money.

"Maybe you don't know it," Rostok says. "It's considered rude to stare?"

The fall of his glance, pout of an underlip: "How rich are you anyway?" Peter asks.

"Rich enough."

"How rich is that?"

"Plenty...plenty!"

"How much? Just tell me," the boy says. "Please...."

"I could buy and sell the whole roof, all these guys," Rostok says, "with plenty to spare...."

"...I built this place you know, my own crews working overtime...."

"So?"

"I also make up the deficit every year," he says. "I'm not no Walter P. Chrysler, but I am a multi-millionaire kid...ask my accountants."

"I'm sorry for you," the boy says.

"Why be sorry? Why me?" he asks, amused at last.

"You just don't know any better," the boy says "...your poppa *hot gelt* before you, *you'd* be nothing without him...."

"A lot you know." Rostok is getting angry. Whether he likes it or not. Watching the boy walk away, Rostok quakes disparagement at the father, a laugh followed by a grunt for allowing such behavior; and then closes his eyes again, so he looks like his own big brown LaSalle, parked in the lot at Lundy's for Sunday lunch. "Goddamn kids," he mutters.

Rostok hocks up some phlegm. He doesn't spit but swallows, a grin of distaste, bitter pre-cancerous look. He thinks of Ella in a mausoleum near Scarsdale with the Rostok logo chiselled in stone, Ella and his Setter, Biff; his parents in Staten Island in the *Varein* Cemetery with all their friends—A *mispocheh*, and he alone living on, alienated from his only son, George, the remittance man.

As soon as he can doze off, he commences to dream again: of his new accountant's sister, who is also a part of the practice, and taking a bath in a bowl of big party-colored tapioca like they used to serve at Joe's Court Street Grill: pink, blue, yellow, green. Of bubbles and bubbies he dreams *bonkes*. Of a woman used to shave herself so close down there he gave her a Yardley gift pack with wooden shaving bowl and beaver brush for St. Valentine's Day....

Rostok dreams his grown son, George, that sissy, went into business with him under the name Warner Baxter.

Now the dreams are unwinding from their sprockets, fast and jagged, Coming Attractions. He's wooing Pintobasco's wife, Lill. He's thrown this brat over the roof and has his fist raised high at Pintobasco....

He's on the D & H with a girl heading North...and
Jabotinsky enters the Dining Car...and they are making
plans to swim someplace....

"Here's one I just heard," says Izzy Berliner. "A British
Lord is speaking in Parliament...."

"That's a long way to tip a rary?" Solly asks.

"Naw," says Izzy, "this is different, a faggy shag
story...."

"Shut up you guys down there," Rostok yells.

He wakes amid lingering reveries of his testimonial last
spring when the Governor came and, afterwards, friends
took him to the Montauk Club to play bridge at fifty cents
a point. He took the hatcheck girl home with him, and
did she really tell him off. "Pig, moron. Mr. Big Pockets!"
She was just about to have her monthly. Later, though, for
$200, which she said she was saving for Night School in
the Fall, dame practically sucked him dry, and he returned
the compliment, so she didn't mind one little bit....

Izzy with his fakest mocky accent: "Frankly, I was thinking
how we're losing India...."

A lotta laughs from the kibitzers. Don't they know anything? Peasants....

Rostok thinks of his two hundred dollar *byale* with cream
cheese and novey, a Greek olive, at the hatcheck girl's
flat....

What's $200 anyway to Big Sam? A day and a night in
Boca Raton on the beach....

As Mushy Cohen always says, "Rostok is as rich as
Nesselrhode pie...."

He wouldn't mind saying so himself, if you asked in
the right way, not like sonnyboy over there. A whole

lot better with money in the bank than when he was
a shlub on Keep Street. Look what he did for Georgey:
a house on the beach in Sarasota, a portfolio of blue-
chips. Let Georgey have a good time with boys if he
must. It ain't what he does so much as his contempt for
me bothers Rostok. I struggled, in my own way, he tells
himself, and he....

"Boggles expectations," he declares, out loud, to the sun
and the wind, eyes open wide again.

He thinks back to the time last year when they offered
to sell him the Dodgers, if he would only build a bigger
stadium with more parking out by Mill Basin. The City
said it would condemn the land special for him, too, and
there would be a subsidy, and a good price on the Ebbets
Field parcel for an apartment development, but Rostok
was involved with other matters, *Yisrael*, as he calls it,
raising money to buy arms, ship refugess. "I got enough
on my mind" he told the city fathers. "Why should I want
to be a sportsman?"

Suddenly Rostok sees the handsome black face of new-
comer Jacky Robinson who the Dodgers have brought from
Montreal, and he shouts, "Go away please!"

It's one thing to be a credit to your race, and still another
to be coming to Brooklyn...where they never even tried
to find a Jewish boy could hit, or pitch, or play second base
for the fans...A million and a half Jews between here and
Cropsy Avenue, and Hank Greenburg's still with the
Detroits....

There must be one or two somewhere else, he thinks,
If not now when...that fella Trosky played for Pittsburg

maybe...?

"If you don't go away," he suddenly announces, "I'll do something you'll be sorry for the rest of the summer...."

"Prove it!" says the brat. He's staring at Rostok's gas bag belly. It's a straight look down to his fine straight calves. What's that supposed to prove anyway?

Rostok stares at the brat like poison. In a minute he'll blow off in all directions. A hydrant on this summer day. "Go away boy. Go away," he says. "You think you got troubles now? What till I get ahold of you...."

He lurches up from his bench.

"*Bullshit makes the flowers grow*
Rostok plants them row by row."

The boy runs off quicker than his shadow, leaving Rostok standing in the sun with his fists clenched like a twin standpipe, the diamond solitaire on his pinky finger ablaze in sunlight. Aloud he says, "The kid's got *beytsim*. Though no tact. I'll say this much for him Pintobasco...."

"He certainly isn't shy," Izzy repeats.

The phlegm is coursing in Rostok's chest again, he hocks and spits and hocks, and woo—over the roof as the brat quickly ducks behind a knot of men down the other end of Tar Beach near the shower with the pull chain. "Nevertheless," says Rostok, "Kindly keep that kid out of my hair ...will ya?"

"Look whose talking Baldy," Peter shouts. "Tall bald man with a smell...."

Rostok hocks and spits.

"I can't help myself," he proclaims, "when I got a cold...."

"You should be ashamed," Peter says, "even so. This is

a religious institution...."

"The same for Mr. Izzy Berliner over dere," says Rostok.

He hoops and coughs, viscous, starts to spit again, but swallows. Ech...

Rostok blinks his eyes shut once more and he is dreaming —of Cal Abrams and Jabotinsky with the Rabbi, of Wilna, in collaboration, in a toy factory, a colloquy, a concentration *lager* outside Kishinev....

"Vus er gesucht?"

"What's your problem?" Peter interrupts. "A man of your means. Unsanitary. In the subway you'd be arrested...."

"I built a whole lot of the subway," Rostok says, "And when I'm spitting it's not a good idea people should be walking down below."

Peter asks, "Don't you have any respect?"

"Ask your mother," Rostok says.

"You're a big bluffer. You don't know anything. Just spit...."

"You little son of a bitch," Rostok says. He keeps his eyes shut, will not face his accuser—so like his own little Georgey once upon a time—until, at last, knowledge that he's responding to the interrogations of a mere sprat burns on Buster's face, and in his meaty chest, and down across his loins.

He's lost control of himself. With some kids live and let live just don't work. A good wallop is the only answer. Though he never had much stomach for it.

Rostok doesn't believe in hitting, liking is another story. This permissive new type way of doing things is Bushwick.

He hears the roof door swinging open and then slamming

shut again, rolls over onto his side, falls sound asleep.

No more noise, or nightmares. *Gornisht.* Regular blotter, soaking things up.

"Goddammit to hell," Rostok roars, as he rolls over onto his side, and wakes himself again.

THREE

ON BEAL STREET

Izzy sings to himself: "On Beal Street...met her on Beal Street....Brown sugar woman with the big bare feet...."

Peter has come back to him again, huddling almost under his armpit listening, his cub.

"That you boychickle?"

He blinks awake.

"That you boy?"

"Sing me some more Uncle Izzy."

"Drather drink muddy water
live in a hollow log...drink muddy water
live in a hollow log...."

When Izzy sings black, he don't exactly niggerlip, like some. You know it ain't white talk by the feeling he shows, not because he's making faces like Eddie Cantor. Banjo eyes and Mammy loving lips, "Izzy sings with a lot of expression," his Mammileh says, "just like Lawrence Tibbett."

"Sing *Cumbaya*", Peter says.

"Na...You want Peat Bog Solders? You want Irish?"

"Whatever you say Uncle Iz...."

He pulls the boy even closer under his slippery folds. His shiny flesh heaves. He's short of breath. A smell like rolled beef, spicy, pickly.

"Here's one I heard just the other day...."

"Sing me Izzy please...."

"On the green banks of Shannon, when Shelah was
nigh

No blithe Irsh lad was so happy as I...."

"Sing something else...."

"When we dead awaken

Jews will fress on grits and bacon.

Fancy lox and smooth sliced sable...."

"Get your elbows off the table," Peter shouts happily, and
Izzy nods, "Fine...a not quite erudite contribution...what
else...?"

"Save the gravy for the Navy?"

"Wonderful," Izzy says. "Esenin the poet could not do
better...."

He cups a hand around the boy's neck and squeezes easy
and soft: "If we're so smart," he adds, "why ain't we also
rich kiddo?"

And Peter just says, "Zum!"

They are sitting some yards away from the card sharps
so Izzy feels pretty comfortable about singing out again:
"The pale moon arose on the great purple fountain..."

"Mountain," Sam corrects him, out of the side of his
mouth, from afar.

"Mountain fountain...."

"Its a mountain all right," Sam says. "I promise you...."

"Listen to your friend, the Chiney," Mushy says.

"Not too fond of 'The Maid of Traleen' are we?" Izzy
stops in mid-sentence again, gawks about, glares like a
comic in the mountains when they start serving in the
middle of his act. "Ingrates," he announces, "all of
you...."

"Sing! Izzy sing!" Peter urges him.

"The only maid I like," says Sam, "does floors and boils up my hankies in a big cast iron pot...."

"Never mind, Umpapa. Sing 'The Wild Colonial Boy,'" Peter says.

"Pull my sheleileh," adds Solly.

"O shut up guys," says Sam. "Let the man sing...."

And Izzy does in a voice so sweet and thick as melting toffee in that hot Tar Beach air, and even pigeons stop their shivering throbbing restlessness to listen; and Izzy, singing, knows his sound will carry across the partition to the Women's side where his lady love Lillian Pintobasco will be pining for him even now, and maybe to the sleeping dead in Greenwood Cemetery, Pinelawn, *Shari Tefilla*. He wants to be heard....

"There was... a wild... Colonial boy...."

"All these Irisher songs," Sam observes, rudely and loudly, "they have so much character compared to our Jewish whining...."

"Not all Jews are whiners," Izzy interrupts his pursing lips. "Remember the Warsaw ghetto, and Bar Kochbar... Benny Leonard," he adds.

"I'm talking about singers, not boxers... or killers," Sam says. "Eddie Fleischer is a whiner from first to last...."

"For shame Sam. I never knew you to be such an anti-Semite...."

"I never knew myself," Sam says. He stares hard at Izzy and his son, a couple, it seems. All they'd need is a canopy. "If I had any guts myself I'd be in Palestine fighting...."

"Marvin Glauberman and Micky sure weren't whiners," Peter says. "They fought Hitler while you were 4-F on the sun roof..."

"Because I had you and your brother to support," Sam adds. "Ungrateful kid...."

He's looking bloody murder at Peter: "Did you know your uncle Izz fought in Spain? He fought for the Republic...."

"Not really," Izzy nods. "I got there a little later than I'd hoped. Got there too late...but I did see some of the country."

"Did you kill anybody?" asks Peter.

"Not so I recall, and I'm sure I would if I did...."

"A beautiful place Spain," he adds, "even in wartime...."

He pats Peter's shoulder and draws him closer. "Wonderful brave people...."

"Not like on Tar Beach...huh Izzy?" He gives him a little elbow in the ribs.

"You never can tell about people," Izzy says. "People do what they have to do kiddo. You mustn't judge...."

"Umpapa says Micky Rivlin got shell shock in the Solomons."

"Poor Micky," Izzy explains. "He hated Hitler so they sent him off to kill Japs. You figure it...."

"And Umpapa never went anywhere at all."

"That ain't fair," Sam protests. "I volunteered as air raid warden and for the draft board. I would have gone, honest, if they had called on me...."

"Never mind that stuff Sam," Izzy says. He reaches over and touches his friend on the shoulder with a finger and turns back again to Peter.

"Life upsets your old man sometimes. He isn't Mr. Rostok up down dere and he isn't sinking on the destroyer Rueben James on route to Murmansk with some lend-lease tanks...."

"I don't really get it," says Peter.

"A father doesn't really have to be a hero," Izzy observes. "He can just be ordinary, a striver. An ordinary fellow, like Sam here, or me...."

"Maybe we should all be a little nicer to each other," Peter says.

"Thanks a lot Izz," Sam says. "Thanks a whole lot...."

"Come on Sam," he says. "The boy understands. He loves you Sam...." Peter is shrinking away from him he can feel it. "Kiddo," he says, "your father is a good man, an ordinary man, a *mentch*...."

"You've got your foot in too deep already," Sam points out.

"Suit yourself," Izzy says. "*Loz mich gein....*"

And again he starts to sing:

"Flow gently, sweet Afton, among the greenbraes
Flow gently, I'll sing thee...."

"That's Scotch, sing Irish," Peter says.

"OK...OK...."

"On Mountjoy one frosty morning
Just before the break of day
Kevin Barry gave his young life
For the cause of libertay...."

"Quiet on the roof!"

Rostok's is awake and roaring at the sun.

Izzy falters a moment. Then:

"Just a lad of 18 summers...."

"SHEER CRAPOLA!" From the across Tar Beach Buster's voice, hoarse with sleep, dooms him once again to silence: "That's just 99 and 44 hundreds percent pure crapola. If either of you'se guys ever saw a real revolution you'd run like there was Cossacks on your tails...."

"Now I'm trying to nap, and unless I can get a little peace and quiet around here," Rostok threatens, "I'll start taking my business down the Parkway to the Jewish Center and they'll close this place up for lack of funds and you guys will have to play in the Knights of Columbus."

He's hyperventilating, a bad recording, angry.

"Excuse us," says Izzy, with some exaggeration. He'll keep quiet all right because he really isn't at all surprised by the rudeness of Rostok's interruption.

He leans close to Peter and whispers sotto voce beside his ear: "Kiddo, only in America can such a sorry excuse for a human being end up breaking bread with Newbold Morris...."

"I'm sure sorry Izzy," the boy says. "I really am."

"Nothing to be sorry about," he says. "Mr. Rostok is a great dictator with his dictaphone, in the office and out, and even though I ain't really his personal secretary I'll let him have his way just this once. *Alevei....*"

The other men nod their approval, even Umpapa. They know who Buster Rostok is and who they are. It's a stacked deck up here on Tar Beach. They sit there, stunned by too much heat and sun, and after a while, Sam Pintobasco finds his deck of cards and begins to deal out another hand of rummy.

"Same as before?" he asks Izzy.

"Not for me."

"Then how about a swim? A little handball?"

"Later...."

Sam is still staring at him as though later is no answer at all. The boy seems to be dozing. They could slip away

from him for a while. Leave a note, a message with Mushy.
The afternoon is beginning to drift away from Izzy. He'd
like to see Lill again, touch her hand, to say just one or two
words, comfort her somehow that the worst of her feelings
have come and gone and she'll be happy again, with or
without him. To say "I adore you." Or even, "How are
you Lill?"

He closes his eyes and mutters to himself the words he
cannot speak aloud.

"What's that you just said?" asks Sam.

"I got just as much right to be on this roof as Big Mr. Rostok
over there," Izzy improvises.

"Serves him right," Sam replies. "Now it's so quiet he
can hear himself think...."

"Rostok doesn't think," Izzy says. "He reacts."

"Fuck it," says Sam. "Lend me your reflector...It just
may do me some good...."

He lies back and claps the set of aluminum panels open
at an oblique angle to his face. The sun is like something
out of his masonic bible: A plague against the face.

All of a sudden Izzy starts to sing again, in soft low
sibilants:

"Sweet and low
sweet and low
wind of the western sky...."

"It's sea, I think," Sam murmurs.

"Sea sky," says Izzy.

"Sweet and low
sweet and low...
I don't know...."

"Sing something sexy," Sam says. "Sing a Lillian song

...like your duets...."

"Duets?"

"At Mel's party. "The Gypsy Girl's Dream." Remember?"

Izzy is embarrassed. Mel's party was such a long time ago. He and Lill were just fooling around in those days. How should he know it would ever get so serious? How should he know a Lillian song? But he sings a song from his childhood, anyway, on and on:

"In dreams I kiss your hands madame
your dainty fingertips.
And when in slumberland madame
I'm dreaming for your lips...."

"Is that a Lillian song?" Sam asks, incredulous.

"It happens to be one of Etta's favorites," Izzy says. "Can't you tell?"

"Yea, I suppose so...."

Izzy lies back next to Peter who is flanked on the other side by his father, Sam.

"...I haven't any right madame
to say the things I do...
but when I hold you tight madame
you vanish with the light madame...."

"Some business that," says Sam. He feels himself dozing and so is Izzy, he thinks, and Peter, and suddenly he croaks so only he can hear:

"In dreams I hold you tight madame
and pray my dreams come true...."

Interlude

Rooftop Words
From Rabbi Elias Zuckerman
Standing Beneath The Pullchain Shower

"Just so long as the sexes are kept separate. A man may be aroused by his own parts and if he manages to conceal this from others he is virtually blameless. Otherwise I recommend counseling, or if it's real serious, like the Pintobasco boy, Dr. Brady can probably be helpful."

A lot goes on here I don't know about. They don't pay me to be a policeman. I'm for spiritual guidance. The rabbis say we do not need to look at sin; it accosts us, and bemuses us.

That time Micky Rivlin tried to kill himself by falling asleep on the top perch of the steam room I was the one who found him there, and saved his life. His pulse as slippery as a fish beneath my fingertips, he was dehydrating rapidly. I got old Doc Baer out of the shower and we carried Micky to the chaise in the card room. We made him drink warm Cola syrup. When I tried to suggest he'd just been over-tired and fallen asleep, he wasn't having any of it. "I really tried to kill myself," he said. "I've been trying ever since the Duration. Hard work."

Speaking of spiritual lows that was the worst for me. His whole face looked cooked. That Port wine stain from Okinawa was two shades darker. My heart went out to the boy.

Micky, I tried to say, when bad things happen it's not by design.

He looked barely awake. "That's nice of you to say Rabbi."

They told me later he could have had a heart attack or a stroke. Maybe two hours he was baking....

I'm going to be brief and cogent in my remarks at the dinner tonight. One great Jewish leader of the congregation passes, and new leaders spring up. The Earth abides ...I can't say a thing about his habits, as they were all filthy. Once he had me to dinner in the Heights. The woman looking after him was a slut. She served us dinner in a moomoo low cut around the bodice.

For the funeral I'll let that be, of course, and talk about pioneers, the people who came here a hundred years ago and made a synagogue where none was.

Should be very effective.

They promised me a new contract by last Pesach. Mr. Abraham's dying isn't helping things.

The earth abides; the fullness thereof. It would be nice to have Rostok's resources, but that's out of the question. Nicer still one of those new congregations in Westchester.

It's probably not appropriate for a rabbi to stand like this soaping himself in front of his congregants. If I stay away and never take exercise they complain the rabbi is distant, not a regular guy, and if I stand under the shower just like everybody else they're making dumb jokes, comparisons, of all things.

I don't understand how some people get away with the things they do up here. Well they don't ask my advice anyway. If I were to say what I thought of the goings on up here.

During the war I wrote a letter every week to the boys in service from our congregation. Some of them I hardly knew. A few wrote back, a few died. It was appreciated my writing but they still said I should be doing more. Maybe Chaplain at my age? There are little lights next to all their names on the placque in the back of the synagogue and I had special stars made. I don't remember any of them very well except for Micky. He always seemed such a lively young fellow, and good to his mother for as long as she lived. But when he came back at war's end after so many landings and battles I hardly believed it was him, and we never spoke until that day I found him there in the steam room. Dave Marcus says he was a hero. Well he should know, I guess.

"You have to believe," I told Micky, when I made a pastoral visit to the VA, "All Mighty God is against self-murder."

Maybe he heard me; maybe not. Two weeks later he tried to climb the parapet and jump.

I have his best interests at heart when I say it would be an embarrassment to the entire Temple Family if Micky killed himself in this sanctified edifice.

Think I'll begin tonight: Mine is a high honor and rare privilege...Better yet, Each anniversary a milestone. It helps us look back to measure the distance we have travelled, while we pause to look ahead at the road before us...

Hoping Micky won't show up. Hard enough to say such words to yourself. Worse when you have a guy like him in the audience. And those Zionist thugs. Every event is an occasion for their propaganda. Surely I support the Jewish Homeland but not at a Congregational Dinner. If they crash the ballroom I'll have them ejected. Better still ask them to sit, have dinner, a blessing, and give them maybe five minutes, no more, to talk to my people....

If I'm very serious I'll lose my audience altogether. Let me try again: a synagogue more than bricks and mortar. Abraham Abraham was the *sine qua non* of this Community, more than the sum of his parts...No! We are all diminished by his death. No. Strike that. They wouldn't like...We are all in his debt...Too literal, when you consider the mortgage, and his interest in the Bank.

With the passing of Abraham Abraham an era comes to an end. Let no one say he was faultless. When God placed Man and the son of Man little lower than the angels he made allowances for this and that...and Mr. Abraham took advantage of every one of them, and will shine forth forever as the *emmes* in the annals of this synagogue: *Shemah*....

Cut the Yiddishkeit. Too many flourishes. Strike that...."

FOUR

REFLECTIONS

The red Indian staring without eyeglasses into Izzy Berliner's black batwing reflector, Sam Pintobasco, has always regarded himself as a feisty beetroot of a man. Having collapsed into self-regard, in hopes of putting a little maroon back into his cheeks, he nonetheless appraises his face for what it is—ordinary. Plain ordinary. No angel wing eyebrows like Izzy. The face of a man who does not mind looking on himself with kindness, though he's unconvinced others do.

Broad and full, with a small sharp nose, Sam's face looks waxy to him, the shine and hue of an Edam cheese. His thin lips pout beneath those high ridged cheekbones, as though the sun picked him out personally to saute, whereas it was Sam's choice, as we've just overheard, to shut his eyes and opt for this flood of hot glare over supervising anymore of Peter's activities.

Let Izzy worry about the boy, Sam thinks, in a swelter of witch hazel aftershave and limbering-up balm. His sinuses are killing him and the sun should help better than that sinus mask for his post-nasal headaches Izzy gave him a month ago to wear to bed like Zorro...wires coming out of both temples.

"Whatsa matter *chaver*? You look just like the Pimpernel. *Lui meme*," Izzy told him, two weeks ago, when he tried it on the first time.

"I could electrocute myself in my sleep," Sam explained.

"You never can tell Sam," Izzy told him, with a wink. "A little charge like that might help...."

When the sun gets downright excruciating, Sam blinks open his eyes and there's a little nervous paper cut from shaving curled against his right nostril. A fetish mark. Sam can hear Lillian from bed: "Don't tell me. Let me guess. The masked marvel...?"

"Well, I thought we'd try something a little different tonight Lill."

"Sam, you don't have to act for me," she told him. "A face like you got...."

"What's wrong with my face?" he found himself shouting.

"It ain't nothing to write home about hello ma I've just been kissed by Ramon Navarro...."

They both had a good laugh over that one. Sam was peeved all during their lovemaking, and she maybe sensed it too. *What's so terrible about the way I look?* he kept thinking. *Who is she thinking she's with right now when we're doing this?*

Besides, it's my face. Ordinary an ordinary face...and his longing for undivided attention got the better of him so that he came approximately two hours and twenty minutes too soon.

Sam adjusts the reflector, making himself squint, a frying egg. Off and on, and off again. Just so. A coddled egg. Feels sorta good with the breeze interrupting. He fans himself with the aluminum-coated cardboards....

Sam always knew he was sort of physically repulsive to Lillian. What was the big deal? He never pretended he was Frederick March.

She told him once you look like something the undertaker forgot.

At Abraham Abraham's viewing this morning she was even more apropos. Before he crashed over Ploesti, Lill used to go with the Abraham's only son, Royal. She had a huge crush, they say, as he was a Harvard Law School man, and when he crashed we were on our second honeymoon at Lake Placid and she positively sulked for a week. So, this morning, peering down at the old man's face, stuffed out with cotton, I heard her say, "There always was a family likeness...."

"One corpse is very much like another. They don't budge...."

"Don't make jokes...."

"The deceased oughtn't to be here...It's not even Jewish...."

A sign of respect," she says. "Abraham Abraham's family were the founders...."

"So what's wrong with Garlic Brothers? Or Riverside? Even the Academy of Music? As a trustee, it just don't seem right like this...."

"Too impersonal. You wouldn't like it if that happened to you...you'd want to be among your kith and kin. Friends. Colleagues...."

"I wouldn't even know the difference."

"*You* probably wouldn't...." Then she gave me that look again, as though I'd cut myself shaving clear across the jugular....

As though I looked so gross and crude, my feeling all squeezed up inside a head fit to bursting. Some unsightly sort of whitehead pimple maybe....

No wonder she always turns away at night. *Where does she go? Who really wants to kiss such a ponim?*

Once again he peers at his reflection in the shiny foil. With sun enflaming his nose and cheeks, Sam looks so different from the haggard grey face which will never quite meet with his gaze in the bathroom mirror every morning when he shaves, or brushes at his teeth.

He has begun to think lately he has some terrible slow consuming cancer that puts these folds and bags beneath his drowning eyes. If so, even the sun, and lots of Briosci, won't keep his illness secret for much longer.

An ordinary morning washup for Sam is a post-mortem. The Kolynos powder tastes like Barrium. Shaving, he biopsies each cheek....

Maybe, he thinks, I should get myself one of these little gismos, except you could get sun poisoning. Even worse. Never any harm to Izzy though; he wears his nose-plugs, breaths through his mouth, lets the sun make a brisket from his face....

Can't always be borrowing. At Cut Rate Drugs they sell them, ten bucks maximum, and a jar of Noxzema, too, maybe two bucks more. Worth every penny, if you make sure to grease the skin first with lots of lanolin, then Noxzema, Zinc Oxide, other *shmalz*.

Last Sunday at the Dubrow's, after Tar Beach, Etta Berliner told him he sure looked like a movie star with "so much color" in his face and his new Hawaiian shirt open at the neck.

"Anyone in particular?"

"You know who I mean," she said to Lill. "That character actor...."

"It could be anyone," Lill shrugged. "How should I
know who?"

And Izzy made a joke: "Lionel Stander? Lugosi? Laird
Cregar?"

Maybe I should buy myself a medicine ball, too, Sam
thinks: something to keep me trim. He's seen Zuckerman
lying with a 20 pounder on his belly like a big tumor.
Seems to help. Flattens out the abdomen. Though maybe
not...the lifting, with my back...look what happened
with what's his name when they put him on that crash diet.
Heart failure....

Finally, Sam just has to assure himself that, considering
all his troubles at home, and with his law business, and with
his mother in Far Rockaway, and investments, and this
goddamnte kid, Peter, he's looking OK, for a man his age
and height. Not too much hair left, but enough to make an
appearance, a little puff pastry belly that doesn't show if
he wears his double breasted, and no jowls yet, or sags of
any sort beneath the chin. He will be changing to tortoise
shell glasses, at the recommendation of Murry Kourcik's
receptionist, Sharon, and maybe a few deep knee bends
every morning....

Please don't be calling the sexton yet fellas. There's still
time, he tells himself, time.....

Why Barney Braverman in Joe Trunk's office, we went
to Southside together and, in those days, all the girls wanted
him, not me. Now, when I see him, so many liver spots

between the wrinkles make me think I must be looking at
a scrotum for a face....

   Funny way to put it, Sam thinks. Like son like father.
He's laughing...the joke's really on Barney. He screwed
himself silly with other women when he was married to
Katey, the Irish Catholic girl. They're separated now and
I bet Barney can't even get it up anymore...probably needs
a feather....
   Did Sam ever screw around? Well maybe once—or was
it twice?—with Roni Leibergold, because she really used
to admire him a lot—and, believe me, that was no
freylechkeit....
   Once she even told him, "You're such a sweet-natured
person Sam. Shows all over your face if a person cares to
look...."
   Sam Pintobasco is always surprised when his own kindness, or another person's, interrupts us on our course
toward death. When, for example, Izzy took him to that
lecture at the Jefferson School a few years back, all the
women seemed as interested in him as in Izzy. More...
They all said, "An interesting man, a smart man...with a
conscience...."

   It was just so different with Roni Leibergold. She, whom
he usually calls Miss L, has been his office manager and
secretary 13 or 14 years; and the rest was just a bad
mistake....

   Woman with such a dry smile her lips looked peeled,
and those dirty dead blue eyes, a slave's eyes. Where her

legs met, under on the El, he thought, he'd ride all the way home to Brooklyn by morning, for sure....

Still living with her mother somewhere down near Van Sicklen Avenue, the last stop on the New Lots. Poor Roni. Got a law degree but never bothered to pass the bar. Being a woman. So fearful, I guess. Well I pay her a decent wage. She just can't bring herself to live any different. Depressed. A flat tire....

Once, when they both had to stay late to go over a contract for an early morning closing, Sam said you've earned something special and he took her to Leon & Eddie's for supper, and then straight up to bed in the Commodore Hotel.

A waste of money. Roni had no nightgown. No toothbrush. I showed her how to use a damp wash rag, but she didn't want to kiss me, me kissing her. She blamed the onions on her steak, said her breath embarrassed her. Money down the drain....

Embarrassing...just spread her legs wide and leaned her knees against my shoulders. Closed her eyes like she was kicking against the tide. She'd been had before, I suppose, but not so you could notice, and not much fun, I gather. Lill gets hot but that's about it. She, well, it took maybe a minute, with that look on her face, no more....Lukewarm like someone's leftover glass of beer. A cough, a sneeze, takes longer....

Sam shivers: And when I wanted to try again, a little bit later, after I bought the bottle of Johnny Walker Black from Room Service, she asked me, "Does Mrs. Pintobasco know about all your extra-curricular activities?"

Try and convince her it's the other way around.

Sam simply said, "Mrs. Pintobasco is the mother of my children...."

It so happened Roni wouldn't stay the night, so he had to give her cabfare for the ride home to Brooklyn, and the next morning off.

The lesson Sam learned from all of this was sex, even with women who are not whores, can get very expensive, if you add up the dinners, hotels, everything else. A little gift later for her desk in the office.

And sex with someone from the office is also an inefficient way to run a business. Better go to a hooker. Less problems. You're off and running, like the meter of a cab. It's tax deductible, too, if you're smart....

When they tried once more, a year or so later, Sam couldn't even get it up the slope unassisted. And that took so long to come about because the looks Roni always gave him made him think, *eppes*, she had such longing for him she would kill him for what happened between them once; and now he was supposed to divorce Lillian just because he'd been with Roni one night out of a lifetime.

She told him once, "You came pretty close to ruining my whole life one evening in the Commodore Hotel."

Even so he never fired Roni. Just kept her around the office as his reproach....

Men like me are like that, Sam decides: so self-absorbed. The truth was, as he well knew, Sam couldn't bring himself to fire Miss L because now she had something on him.

When Lillian called the office, Miss L always took messages. And she was always making excuses for "Mrs. Pintobasco" if he called home and Lill was out.

"Maybe she's downtown shopping. Or is it a school holiday? Could be she took the boys to a stage show in New York...the Capital, the Roxy, Radio City" etc. etc....

Roni seemed to live in the various corridors of his unhappy domestic situation. If she still had a crush on him, as her looks sometimes said she did, she was also his critic, and would have liked him DOA first thing some morning. Whenever he complained about Lill's negligence, or other behavior—and usually he tried to make a joke of it—Roni would say, "Don't you think you're being harsh on Mrs. P, under the circumstances?"

"What circumstances?"

"I believe you know exactly what I mean Mr. P," wetting down her lips with her tongue.

Sam's waking glance is the swollen red silver face he sees in the triptych panels of Izzy's reflector.

"They seek him here.

They seek him there.

Those Frenchies seek him everywhere...."

He plops himself down on the bench, buns up, so he can feel the heat across his shoulder blades.

The prime of life, he decides, really ain't so good as it's cracked up to be.

Ask the man what owns one....

Peter is nowhere in sight. Izzy and the bunch he's talking to couldn't care less.

He decides he'd better take a look, gets off the bench, and with his wang beating time against his thighs, walks over to where Izzy holds forth.

His favorite topic: Russian war losses. Izzy points to an article on the front page of Rostok's abandoned *New York Times*, pushing his finger against the columns of smudgy print, as Solly, Mushy, and the others quietly listen: "If Mr. Arthur Krock, or Mr. Churchill wants to know why The Soviet Union behaves with such concern for its security," he says, "they should consider those losses...none of the industrial nations suffered such a terrible devastation. Russia wants buffer states between it and a revanchist Germany...."

Lousy bunch: House listers! Block-busters! Red-liners! One glance at the newspaper, like a census tract, and then a glance at Izzy playing Henry Wallace, and all nod their agreement, or impatience, Sam can't tell for certain which.

"Have you seen Peter anywhere?" he demands.

Izzy points to the corner where the boy sits like drift-wood with his back to all of them. Only his hands are moving. He seems to be playing with something, but he's certainly not bothering anybody. Doesn't even seem to hear Sam talking.

"I see you had a few minutes on the horizontal," says Izzy. "Good for you...."

"Don't let me interrupt you," Sam says. "Even though I've heard it all before...."

"It doesn't matter," Izzy says. "You know the way I get sometimes...."

"Sure I know."

They stand there gawking at each other like crows.

Sam asks, "Peter you want something to eat?"

The boy doesn't look his way. "I had an orange, a banana...."

"So? That isn't lunch. You asked before...."

"Can't you see I'm busy? Do you like being bothered when you're busy?"

Goddamn smart aleck kid, he thinks, but he asks, "Maybe later Sonny?"

"Later sure later. *Loz im op....*"

Sam's hanging by his own pecker. Standing there balls adangle, as Izzy would put it, and everybody's waiting for him to say something, now that he's interrupted their conversation.

"Well I've said all I'm gonna say," says Izzy. "I'm still fairly optimistic. If I said it once I said it twice...when there's another war, Russia won't start it...."

"Change the subject," Mushy says. "I've had a belly full of politics...."

"Let me tell you something that happened to me a while back," Sam suggests.

Only Izzy seems disappointed, probably because he thinks he knows all Sam's stories, but when the others say go ahead, sure, he nods along with them, and they climb up on the *shvitzbench* again to hear Sam's story.

SCRUPLES

"Some people are real foxy," Sam Pintobasco says. "Always are, always will be...."

The blank he's worn in front of his face all day long up here on Tar Beach is fixed of a sudden with the dumb startled stare of Micky Rivlin, a deer caught by bright headlights.

Never says anything. Not even a nod. Just stares, a flash-back during a movie close-up. A few weeks ago when he tried to jump off the roof and Buster and Zimmerman held him back, he gave a speech like Hitler, one hand raised high in the air to shield his eyes.

"You got no right," he said. "If I wear galoshes in the steamroom none of you can stop me...."

"This ain't the Russian Front gents," he shouted.

Piggy gave him a phenobarb, I think, or seconal, I can't remember, and he was just as right as rain the next day, after Buster's chauffeur drove him home, but Jesus he was quiet then. An Emerson with a bum condenser. Nobody could get a rise out of his tubes.

"So don't leave us hanging," small-eyed Harry Halpern says, massaging his bad ankle with Dermaheat. "What you got on your mind Sam, if anything?"

"A war story?" asks Micky. Where he's charley-horsed you can't rub liniment. Last time he ever heard Micky say anything remotely coherent was when Rostok talked about serving on the draft board. "Which was more crucial to your war effort, Buster?'' Micky asked. "The Draft? Or buying hot tires?''

Rostok yelled galore galore and I don't think Micky's had another word, good or bad, to say to anybody until now.

"You were saying Sam,'' Mushy puts in.

"I was speaking foxy,'' he says. "About certain foxy types. The world's full of them.... In our business you can never turn your back!''

"For instance?'' Izz says, cueing him.

"For instance when you say times change Izzy you got to realize time really ain't what it used to be.... It's a small world, if you got friends, and enemies are easy to find anywhere.... For instance,'' with a deep gulp of breath, hoping he won't flub more of his lines, "fella came to see me once when I was on 60 Court Street... as I recall, it was some months after Pearl Harbor... Japanese gentleman, regular swell, dressed from Finchley, or Weber and Heilbruner....''

"That's such an old one Sam,'' says Izzy. "Why not tell the guys something new, hot off the burner...?''

"Well I never heard it anyway,'' Mushy puts in.

"Me neither,'' Solly says.

"O all right,'' says Izzy. "Tell if you must.''

"Much obliged,'' Sam replies, trying to remember where he left off. He closes his eyes....

"The Finchley Jap?''

"The very one,'' says Izzy.

"So,'' Little Sam Pintobasco nods, "dressed he was, as I say, like a million bucks and had manners like the Duke of Windsor. I mean it guys... and, get this, he says he wants to put down 150 thou cash into a parcel we're syndicating

on Broad Street, Newark, near the old Mosque Theatre...."
"The Proctor Building?" (Good old Solly always got to
show he knows everything).

Sam turns himself around on the deck to face Solly like
they're at a pow-wow together, opposing Indian chiefs.

"The very one Solly...Proctor's. Only the old theatre
was now an Associated Supermarket, with bowling alleys
up above 24 suites of offices...Mostly Charley Rheinfug's,
from his bootlegging days...."

"You don't have to go into all the grizzly specs," Izzy says.

"Now listen," says Sam. "I'm telling and I'm telling all
and if you don't want to hear...."

"Tell all ready. Just don't make it into such a big deal...."

"Thanks a lot Iz...." Micky's eyes are glazing over. Stewed
prunes.

Sam turns toward Solly and Mushy again. "In those days,
time was if you had that much cash you could have picked
up the whole square block, including two taxpayers on the
corner, and a parking lot. Now times are changing, if you
know what I mean.... This was considered a distress situation...."

"You keep saying that," says Mushy. "But I don't see
anything so different...."

"It's a different world entirely Mushy. Believe me. There
was a war on. Prudential held the mortgage on this particular
parcel, and they were thinking of getting out of Newark
altogether. They always are....So Murry Garbowitz from
Trunk's office and I had this plan to sell the whole building
to the government OPA people which needed space...since
who else would buy? It was tight money in those days
too...."

"So?" Mushy's eyes are fluttering, impatient, opaque with incomprehension.

"Well it was right in the middle of the goddamnt war," Sam blurts out, "with our boys dying in faraway jungles, from malaria, and worse...."

He looks toward Micky who is staring at a horsefly wandering across the meat of his right leg. "I wasn't feeling awful friendly to no Japs, believe me...."

"Absolutely, as they were our enemies," Mushy says.

(A brain like that should be served with capers in a brown butter sauce, Sam thinks.)

"You get the picture."

Suddenly Micky stands up, right in the middle of Sam's story, and he points with his arms like he's holding a rifle and walks over to the ledge and peers out at the City, and he starts keening like a strange bird. Like some savage in the bush: "Ooooooeeeeh oooo. Baroom! Baroom." His body trembles. He's weeping, then he backs away again, sits down apart from everybody. He's crying....

The other men are as surprised as if he'd taken out phylacteries and said his *mahriv* prayers right there. When Micky had one leg over and was yelling at everybody down below in Brooklyn in Japanese nobody saw except Buster. Now they are all watching him out of one eye as Sam continues, not wishing to alarm anybody in any way, but keeping an eye fixed, in case Micky has it in mind to do something foolish again. You never can tell, Sam thinks.

He looks everywhere except at his audience. Izzy has his eyes closed, Solly examines his toenails; only Mushy seems actively interested.

At the other end of the roof Big Sam Rostok, supine,

spreads like an oily spill across the pages of his *Wall Street Journal*. Little Sam doesn't know if he wants to be overheard or not. The big man is always so critical.

"It felt to me nice manners and all," Sam says, "This Nip could have been fronting for Nazis, maybe even worse, who knows...Right? So I had this old friend, Nat Klug, went to work for the FBI, right after law school, as he couldn't get a decent position no place else, it just being the tail end of the Depression, and he was also a CPA, a tax expert of sorts, but that's certainly another story...."

"...I hope you never mentioned me to your friend Nat,"adds Izzy.

"Come on," Sam says. "You know better...."

"Even so."

"O shut up Iz! I never would do such a thing. But as a patriotic citizen I felt I did not wish to be misunderstood, so I called Nat and I said Nat, something troubles me about this deal. Something's fishy. If you ask me it stinks on ice. 150 thou in cash from a Japanese gentleman in a grey chesterfield topcoat with velvet collars, and when I ask where the money's coming from he introduces me to his ward from Smith College, a very pretty young woman, very, and she's making eyes at me...."

"Don't sound too fishy to me," Solly says.

"It sure does to me," Harry, with a snigger.

Sam hot-faced, blushing: "Name was Yamahare...her name was Green Tea Garden...some damn slant name like that. Girl with slit skirts all the way up her legs and all...So you know what my friend Nat the Klug says? Guess...."

"I can't imagine," Izzy puts in, with a poker face.

"Nat thinks I should get what I could from the slash and

then take the money and he would investigate and if anything was fishy he'd arrest them both...."

"After all he told me, we'd share 50/50 and it was either you and me, Sam what am, or the IRS...."

"No kidding, says Mushy. "Jees...."

"Only man on this roof who ever passed up ginch for his country," Solly points out.

"Never mind that! I could have really used the moolah, but you know what I always say, 'Corruption finds its own level....' So I was not about to sell out my country in time of war. I said to Nat first you investigate and then you make an arrest and if worst comes to worst we got a deal. Because not all Japanese are traitors you know Nat...."

"Even I think you're a shmuck Sam," Micky says, and he starts keening again, but Sam gives him a look, like water boiling, that shuts him up.

So so much silence after that is embarrassing. Let the walls come tumbling down, Sam thinks. He's burning up.

"That's just what my old friend Nat Klug told me, But I guess you got a point Mick." Sam shrugs at his shadow, splayed out across the deck below his feet: "But you know fellas with our boys dying I just couldn't take a dime under the table that way. I had my conscience to live with...I would have lost sleep...."

"With that kind of money you could have made it up *shtupping*," Harry says.

Izzy laughs: "Sam here thinks of his Uncle Sam, first last and always...."

"Shut up Iz!"

"No I won't. You think you're good Queen Esther. Well it ain't so...guys always take advantage of other peoples' *tsoris*...that's what Capitalism is all about. Look at Big Sam over there...."

"Words words words," says Micky.

"Big Sam War Profiteer," Izzy shouts.

The titan grunts as if stung by a horsefly, and rolls over onto his side, a log.

"I've heard enough shit on this roof today," says Rostok, "to plant strawberries up here...."

He suddenly sits up like his own tombstone sculpture: "I'm losing my patience guys...I'm getting really pissed...."

His underbelly bloats, an enormous whale of a figure, slicked with the cold seas of his own sweat.

Laving in effluvium, Rostok calls out from the far end of the deck: "If my former counsel and his friend down there think they can embarrass Buster Rostok, they got another think coming...."

In the sun, with his squint, he looks blinded, like Piggy. A big wounded Rhino with a ferocious jaw...grey hairs tufting his chest....

"You lost my business, counselor. You want also an eviction?"

"Easy does it," says Izzy.

"...I'm no piker and no cheat," Rostok says, "and never was, to my recall...married 42 years to the same woman ...to the day she died who here could match that record?"

"But you always were self-righteous as hell," Izzy points out.

With a flinch Sam adds: "I'm sorry Buster. You must have misunderstood. I don't attack you. How could I anyway?"

"Bygones be bygones fellas," Izzy says.

"How could I," Sam repeats, "when I worked my fingers

to the bones for the palooka...."

"Devoted," Izzy points out. "Absolutely. A public servant...."

"Poormouth," Rostok points out, "never got Big Sam his way in life...."

"Izzy you shut up," says Sam. "You're not my spokesman...."

"Turn on me," says Izzy. "That a way Sam. Make believe we're not friends no more."

"Well all right then," Rostok says. "You have your differences with him and I have mine. None of it is worth spoiling a day in the sun on Tar Beach."

He subsides again, seems to slide down a little on his bench.

"Horshitsky,"says Izzy. "Have it your way, again, and again, and again. Rapacious...."

He gets up and starts to walk away toward the parapet.

Little Sam feels he's all alone, though he's surrounded by the rest of his gang. It's a feeling he always had whenever Rostok looked at him in that way in the office, or at lunch somewhere. A loneliness, nakedness. Defenseless....

"I'm truly sorry," he adds.

Rostok: "Forget I ever said a word Sam...."

The way he spreads out again, in his oily fulsomeness, Sam observes, is more like I'm seeing some big slab of Novey, or belly lox, coral pink, just ready for a slicing. You could slice up all Rostok's largesse very thin and parcel him out to the Community in quarter and half pound portions on greasy white paper they should only get his brains and guts, the cunning bastard.... He had me scared the day I met him, scared every time I sent him a bill for 'services rendered' it would come back with a big NO scratched across it....

The only Republican on this stretch of Tar Beach, Rostok knows everybody in the City counts: Herb Brownell and J. Russel Sprague, Democrats too like Bill O'Dwyer and Myles MacDonald, Hymie Barshay, Krock, Merman, Lippman, Dewey. I used to count on him for the future until that day when he told me, "Don't you think you're in over your head Sam?"

That was at the "Gay 90s" costume ball here at *shul*. Rostok came dressed as Diamond Jim Brady. I was P. T. Barnum, but, Lill, naturally, was Lillian Russel...who was Izzy? Maybe the big *shvartza* Paul Robeson as Othello...The band kept playing "Frivolous Sal," and Buster kept hogging all the dances with Lill. I kept hearing him call her that, also whispering little things into her ears....

You can bet I knew about his reputation so I cut in.

Interrupted, he said, "You're over your head, Sam, this ain't no Roseland Ballroom...."

"Over my head?"

"Over your head," Buster said, "and under our feet."

I took Lill away from him then, just danced her away toward Izzy and the service bar, and we haven't spoken a friendly word together since.

The next day we had lunch and he told me he needed better representation. Somebody a little more high class, he said.

"It's all your fault," he told me. "The lady was dancing with me as a smokescreen. She wasn't interested and I wasn't either. It was just a smokescreen, and you made it into a red herring...Don't you think," Rostok said, "I could have your wife anytime I wanted her?"

"Maybe I already have," he added.

Of course, Lillian denied all that, which never stopped Rostok.

"Women," he said, "they sure know how to sell a guy like you a bill of goods."

I wanted to kill him. What would that prove?

Even Lill she got angry when I told her. What did that prove?

The band was playing "Our Gal Sal," he kept dancing. The next day at lunch when he fired me I told him, "Buster, if you ever bother to touch my wife again, or say things like that, I'll clobber you. Knock you from pillar to post...."

"Do me something," he said. "*Tu mir Epes....*"

"Your wife's no dog," Rostok said, "but she lacks style...."

Even Lill got a little put out by his talk when Sam repeated some of it to her over dinner. Such manners, too, that hot proprietary air.

The band was playing "Sal." Rostok said women sure know how to sell you a bill of goods. I said, "Buster, if you don't leave my wife's reputation alone I swear I'll knock you...."

"Little Sam the killer," he said. "Do me something...."

So you end up paying for their funeral with yours, Sam reflects.

He recalls how after Rostok's second bankruptcy, Big Sam was still in big trouble with his stockholders, the Abraham family, and so he made the deal with Niggy to build Pine-

haven Gardens out near Cropsy Avenue, and then the
Dewey Commission got on his back about labor racketeering
and a few other illegalities, so just then, lucky for him, his
wife Ella passed on, and he paid off and recapitalized with
her money, and built Hillside Terrace near Avenue J, only
Peter Pizzarelli's boys had to do all the pipe fitting and
terrazzo work or no deal....

It was Sam who got Niggy and his boys from Bergen
Street, Newark, to consider the deal, and it was Sam
through Anselm Esposito who arranged the Pizzarrelli
connection. When Buster Rostok needs you he snaps his
finger, and when he don't he retains somebody else and
takes over your wife to get you to make a scene. He loved
calling me small time. Made him feel so big. *Azoy*!

How Sam wishes he could be like the rest of his lodge
brothers on Tar Beach. Be one of the Rostok claque again.
Not a care in the world today except handball and cards,
and maybe an early death. Or some highbrow speculations
about where Hitler really is these days.

　　"They seek him here...
　　They seek him there...."

Izzy says the Russians for sure know he was burned in
the back yard of his bunker in Berlin by the SS, but Mushy
thinks he's in Argentina, and Rostok says he heard through
a lodge brother he's living with the Grand Mufti in
Jerusalem under the name Ali Akhbar Thingamig....

"Where'd you get that one Buster?"

It's maybe the first time we're talking since he started in
on Peter. Where is Peter anyway?

Heshy: "I read the same article in Colliers I think it was

by Ben Hecht...."

"It's well known," Rostok says. "Ask anybody with a brain. It's logical...."

"Not for me it ain't," Sam says.

He spots his son, in a corner, entertaining himself again by pulling tar. Better that than trouble....

"When I joined the Pythians," Rostok boasts, "that's when we started building this temple. The fellas used to call me Solomon...."

"Well I call you a son of a bitch," Sam says, not quite under his breath.

Why did I have to say that? Rostok heard. They've switched topics on me again. Mushy's going on about some dirty novel his wife's reading. Thank God, Lill don't read such trash. She prefers shopping and the like. Matinees ...Give me the theatre any night in the week also: A musical, or the Lunts maybe. Katherine Cornell. Serious woman. The Maitre d' at Longchamps seating you at a banquette is just about all the culture Sam can really stand.

Burt Lahr Bobby Lewis Willy & Joe Howard, Louisiana Hayride...Stop looking at me like that Buster!

"Ethel Barrymore," he says, aloud. "Guissepi DeLuca ...Caruso...now that's what I call Culture...."

"Caruso's long dead and buried," says Izzy. "All the big boys they're long gone...John McCormack...Galli-Curci ...Rosenblatt...a good novel, though, hangs around your bedside table and your library. If you read more good literature, Sam, maybe you'd recognize yourself and stop with all the...Stop trying to impress people...."

"Look who is talking," Sam says. "He brings Checkhov to the roof but reads the Worker and Walter Winchell every chance he can get...."

Solly interrupts: "Bull...Izzy...My wife just took out *Forever Lover*. What crap? A love story...."

"A love story a war story they can be good or bad," Izzy says. "It depends on the art...."

"Art?" Mushy is making faces again.

"Like restaurants," Izzy explains. "There's Tofanetti's, for the tourists, and there's Peter Lugar's...or Voisin, which is an acquired taste just like Checkhov and Hemingway and James Joyce...not to mention Sholokov...."

"Who?"

"Some Commy writer," Sam says.

"That's not fair," Izzy points out.

Solly says, "This *Voi San* must be pretty special...."

"A good chef can make any food delectable," Izzy says. "It don't need to be fancy, with atmosphere. The Little Oriental on Pitkin Avenue...."

"Just so long as it's within your means boychicks," Rostok adds.

Izzy: "I'm speaking food, not consumption, or showing off...."

"Who said anything about showing off?" asks Solly.

"Big talker," Rostok says. "Give me the Corned Beef hash at 21 any day in the week...."

The other fellas murmur in agreement, although they've probably never been.

Sam wants to help his friend if he can. He says, "Izzy's talking philosophical. He means Book of the Month Club. It's for women like your Sandra, Solly, not for the connoisseur. No insult meant, but it's not good literature like "*Crime* and...what do you call it Iz?"

"*Punishment, Punishment* Sam."

"Izzy means punish....."

Rostok scoffs. "Hearing you palookas is punishment enough."

Not all the men seem to agree. Sam just may have turned the tide. Least he could do. After all, Izzy is my friend, something important to me, not just toilet paper. When Rostok said those awful things about Lill was when Izzy told me not a chance. "A virtuous woman," he said. "Who shall compare?"

That's friends, I think. I just don't walk over to the Montauk Club and shake hands with all the *shkotsim*...A friend could be for life...Forever...Izzy and me...No matter what....

Even Lill says our friendship is important. She really likes Iz. Always asking me what he said and what he did about this or that....Once Sam saw them talking together next to the credenza, and they looked just like two good friends talking so he left them on the rug next to his mother's best dishes, talking like that.

Even a wife needs her privacy sometimes.

If there's someone else it ain't Izzy for sure. She wrote in her diary. "I am surely someone else with him." Can't be anyone from up here on Tar Beach.

Probably she was just worried about me, or feeling unwell herself, needing to talk to a friend, and there was Izzy. He always asks a lot of questions and he would tell her not to worry. Pressing her face close so I couldn't hear a word....

Sam is speaking now of that time he calls "before her
breakdown," when Lill used to cry a lot, but she would
try, at least some of the time she was trying. In those days
when he wore handball shorts she called him SAM THE
MAN

MY FRIEND SAM WHAT AM

So now who am I to her anyway...? A bad taste in the
mouth.

A schlechten tam....

He's been feeling so shrunken and sad lately, foreshortened,
like a paragraph in a miser's will.

It must be he has cancer or something. Feels as though
this sun will make stale bread out of me, Lill, all of us, but
it isn't really the hot spell we've been having. It's his
domestic situation. House and hearth...to be living with
such a sadsack woman, always turning away from him, no
matter how hard he tries to be nice....

...That new silver fox jacket he got her with the little
heads in lieu of a fee from his client, Buchhalter, the furrier
...and the gold bangle bracelet she lost somewhere. Cost
a lot...and she never said how...or where? Then I learned
she gave it to her sister....

What's happening to us? Sam wonders. Why?

Are Izzy and she up to something?

Nonsense!
The whole crown of his head feels waxed over like a big
bald turnip. He's nobody's fool.

*Disaster may walk all over you, but there's always
tomorrow....*

Rostok is going on about all the high rollers in the back room of Ben Marden's and about a certain deadbeat comedian who owed a bundle until Rostok helped him on one condition: he should find a more congenial line of work and no more jokes. You ain't funny! Never were! Never will be!

Sam turns away from Rostok, the Zeppelin Zeckendorf they call him in the *Daily Mirror*, and squints at almond-eyed Mushy, so content to be just himself, with his *zaftik* wife and set shot from the corner; and then he feels the totally cynical glance of appraisal he's getting from Mongol-faced Solly, and thinks maybe they believe I am but I am certainly not anybody's fool....No deadbeat....

Forget it fellas....

And then he shifts one slippery buttock to the other and makes a tiny skin fart against the hot deck from his own friction, and gives a *kvitsh*: "Peter...."

"Here I am Umpapa."

The boy behaving, bent over his tar, a face like a chimney sweep, but minding his own business for once.

"In a little while," he tells his son, "in a little while maybe lunch...."

"I told ya Umpapa I already had. Izzy gave me...."

"That's no lunch for a growing boy...In a little while. You'll see...."

"In a little while Umpapa...."

"That's a good boy...."

"Sure Umpapa *gib mir...geshrei*."

"Stop with the Africa stuff already," Sam says. "Which reminds me...." He turns back toward his friends again: "When I was with the Title Company I used to see quite a lot of Police Commissioner Valentine, and even Al Smith. Big shots. Lloyd Paul Stryker, Arthur Garfield Hays, for that matter. I saw them all the time when I had lunch in Joe's, or Dolly's Place, Nicholai's Court Cafe...."

"Seeing ain't really knowing," Rostok points out.

Sam never said it was. Today at breakfast Lill told him, "No matter what you think I'm proud of you for making something of yourself against some very heavy odds..." Made him burn all over like a light bulb. So tonight he's running for President, tonight at long last, and he wants votes, just wants to spritz a while longer, for the legend of his knowledge to spread across this sunny pond.

"So *neshomeh* lunch I'm having one day with the Gipper Shumlin and Nat Holman from City College uptown, you know, and in they all walk with Ruth and Gehrig coming from some Cardinal's mass uptown: Smith, Proscauer, Jimmy Walker, the ball players."

"Musta been Bishop Laughlin or Malone," says Solly, "as Spellman ain't that old...."

"So it was Malone, or Sheen. How should I know? I was still a kike in those days...."

"You're no longer?" asks Rostok.

"You know what I meant. You guys must know," Sam says. "Rough edges...."

"I thought we was talking celebrities," Mushy says. "Now suddenly its religion...?"

He's thrown drowning Sam a line and he reaches for it desperately. Skin farting again.

"Exactly that's my point Mushy...It so happens there was also this guy in the restaurant all the time from Vaudeville and he was an acrobatic tap dancer, as I recall, only he was also deaf and dumb, you know. Couldn't say a word, so he spoke sign language all the time, and in Yiddish. He was famous, well pretty famous I forget his name. What do you think of that?''

"Yiddish," Rostok says, "cannot be transliterated...for the deaf and dumb...."

"I saw an eye chart like that once. Maybe he was stupid," Izzy says, "and never knew the difference...Real signing or not. Just dumb show...."

Sam grabs again: "Not every Party member worked for Moscow you know...."

"Thanks a lot," Izzy says, who really doesn't know how they got all the way back there from deaf and dumb.

"I'm thinking of this guy Fogel, Manny Fogel. Had a wooden leg from the Somme, and a medal, and when the war was over he came back a big hero and the Communists put him in the rag business. He was beholding to them a good deal...and was even obliged to furnish some of the comrades with models from his showroom. Well, when Hitler and Stalin signed the pact, he sold everything and moved to Miami. Just like that. Thanks a lot fellas...Opened up a chain of franchise Piggly Wigglies. Made a bundle...."

"If you mean Eggy's former partner Harry Fogel," Izzy says, "he went bust on 7th Avenue, and the Party took a shlonging...."

"Anyway," he adds, with his hand raised, "Stalin was no fool. He knew what was coming from Hitler. He just wanted time to prepare...."

"So some Jews should die by him and the rest from Hitler," Rostok says, slyly.

"How do you know?"

"I wasn't born yesterday Berliner. At least I was born. Think about all the babies, *they killed babies*," Rostok says. "You think the world is a better place now than the way it was when we were kids?"

"When you were a kid was pogroms," Izzy says. "Life was hard. I ain't being defensive, the Russians have their problems. Sure! I don't want to talk about any of that... and Sam I don't want you talking about things you don't know anything about either. People could get hurt. Good people, just like you and me, with different politics...."

"People are getting hurt every day in the week," Little Sam says. "Don't tell me you're still Bolshy Izz?"

"Don't be silly Sam. Don't be a jackass...*Me?*"

It's his look that shuts Sam up, a pleading, like the oven door closing on the *cholent*. He doesn't want to talk such things in front of Rostok and the guys; it embarrasses Izzy.

Sam's always admired Izzy's "courage of his convictions," even though he don't really like such people himself. He remembers that sudden holiday Izzy took from the showroom and how frantic Etta was, and when he came back from Spain Izzy looked like a prophet. A beard. A little red beret. Sam lent him $300 until he found work.

The trouble with Izzy and me, he thinks, is we're defensive about altogether different things. I wouldn't be caught dead with some of his women, and his politics never put bread on the table of anybody except maybe Earl Browder....

Nevertheless he doesn't like to see his friend ganged up on because basically Izzy is as *hai mish* as they come, just another *boychickle* like me....

Pintobasco decides he has an announcement to make and he better make it quick: "We should all please leave Izzy over here alone...He ain't no Commie...Progressive person...with different experiences than you maybe...."

"The closer you two guys get," adds Rostok, "the more I start to wonder who is the fairy and who is his patsy?"

The big shmuck stares at Izzy like a walnut he's just cracked open: "But I really know better, Mr. Berliner, don't I?"

Izzy can no longer restrain himself. He's up, then down on one knee like Jolson. Now he's Paul Muni at the Dreyfus trial.

"This is infamous," he shouts. "Infamy!"

His lips are coated white with Noxzema, and his burnished pelt glows mahogany. Looks like Al Jolson playing a Zulu in the National Geographic.

"Buster has it I got eyes for women. So? You all know my likes. I like women. Any news there for the Camel Caravan? Women are my good friends. I don't usually tell off-color stories. Don't put them on pedestals neither. But I am happiest in the company of some women. I like being held and holding someone. If you ask me," he goes on, "buying and selling don't count for nothing compared to love...."

"Sex too," he adds. "Making nice. Compliments. Touching (Izzy isn't thinking of Lill at that moment, but of Spain again, the girl with the red beret, a million other faces he has passed too, shoulders brushing on the subway, hidden glances in the showroom...)

"Women always have been pretty wonderful to me and I got a kinda knack. Anyway, if you ask me, it pays to think I have...."

"He gets more, I know, and it sure ain't because he's got

a lot of money," Sam says. "Izzy's really from the old school...He doesn't live for it, but he really isn't in business just to make money every day in the week, ain't callous, or crass. A worldly person, but believe me fellas he don't mean no harm to anybody...."

"Well you oughta know," Rostok says.

"There you go again," Izzy says. "Try to have an open mind will ya...."

"My mind's open enough. It's my business I keep closed...."

Puffed up by his claim of good behavior, Rostok turns the other way on the bench and his claque follows like a lot of puffins catching the sun. "Berliner advocates open minds through open flies boychicks, especially in the company of your ladies...."

Izzy and Sam seem virtually alone again inside the same weary shrug.

"The price of understanding something is beyond their means, I think," Sam says. "Buster's full of himself these days...."

"Bluster Rostok," Izzy says.

"You mustn't mind any of these kibitzers."

"Where's Peter?"

"Where is he?" Izzy asks, a second time.

Sam points toward the corner where the boy still sits in an abandonment of tar patches.

"Are you sure he's OK?"

"He looks OK to me, but maybe we ought to check...."

"Maybe." Izzy nods. "I promised to do some things with him later...."

He lowers his voice to a cajoling whisper.

"Speaking confidentially Sam, maybe you ought to spend more time with him. Take him to a ball game, for a picnic. An outing...A boy wants to know his father like a pal...."

"He knows me," Sam says.

"He's still a boy now, but he'll grow up much too fast...."

"We don't get along that well...."

"Don't I know? But he needs you. The mother...."

"Change the subject," Sam says.

As usual, Sam Pintobasco wishes to be confidential without giving away his feelings.

"Frankly, I wish it were different. I don't think I really understand that little kid. The brother is so different...."

"You mean you like the brother better?"

"I mean I just don't feel loved. He makes me so crazy ...so angry with myself...."

"But he's just a little kid...."

"I don't understand. I never understood...."

Sam shoves the reflector off his lap toward Izzy, as though it was a library book he's returning.

Got broken glass in the corners of his eyes. He peers at Izzy through a squint. It actually hurts him to talk and tonight he's gotta be on his best.

"If Lill were less the way she is," he says, "I could be a different man too, with the boy, with everybody...."

"Do yourself a favor Sam. Do it for the boy, not Lill...."

"O shut up Izzy." He lowers his shout to just the way it was over Abraham Abraham's bier: "You're supposed to be my friend...."

"Na? What do you think I am? *What*?" Izzy demands. "*Na*?"

Sam says nothing, looks like nothing now. He's backing away from what he thinks he just learned to bake inside suspicions.

"Maybe I will take Lill for another vacation someday...."

"Sure. It couldn't hurt...."

"You'd really like that, wouldn't you?"

"Me? Don't do it for my sake...." But Sam's accusation just won't disappear. "It's for you I'm saying all these things...for you and the boy...and Lill...."

"You're such a big philanthropist?"

"I'm just like everybody else. I have my faults...."

"A good heart," says Sam. "That's why all the women love you, including my wife...."

"I get a lot of the spotlight with my singing." As he says the words, Izzy is looking out over the plains of Brooklyn cut by rivers of traffic and swaths of green. Izzy feels Sam staring at him. He won't look at his friend. Izzy feels cold with his face all hot.

"When you sing a lot of sentimental songs like me the ladies just naturally fall for you, but they don't mean nothing. You know that. I know that, too. In a manner of speaking it's just behavior...They fall for crooners, too, like Sinatra...."

"That's different."

"*How? How different?*" He looks catty corners at Sam. "*My wife really loves you, not Sinatra...Izz.*"

FIVE

LIFT UP YOUR VOICES

Forty minutes later in the sun Lillian feels her heavy breasts swell against her arms. Such a burden. She can hear and feel the beating of her heart.

Cumbersome as she feels, she is also unencumbered, having released the bandeaux around her neck so that her breasts are swaying, more or less dropping, loosely free. Nipples as tender as teething gums.

Yetta-Thelma went down for a swim twenty minutes ago, and she's alone in a terror of wonderstruck aloneness, except for all the mah jong players, and Mushy's wife, Helen, the *shikse*, nursing her infant son under the shade of a large blue and white beach umbrella.

Lillian has a lot of respect for women who nurse, but she never tried with her own children. It's an inconvenience and here on Tar Beach it shows a lack of propriety and respect in some women's minds...and it could make the breasts sorer. Helen is low class, a Greek woman. Mushy isn't going anywhere in life and she must figure she don't owe anybody anything, not even for formula....

Lill thinks of dressing early, writing a note for Izzy, leaving it in the cantor's box where he'll be sure to find it before the dinner tonight.

"Dear Mr. Berliner

The bank called. You neglected to make even a small deposit this week. For shame...."

"Dear Cantor Berliner

I've learned some exercises in my voice class would help you clear your throat sometime...."

"Dear Izzy

I miss you so much. Just to talk, hold each other close...."

Other people use the same box. Can't be done!

"Dear Izzy Berliner

Can you arrange to see me sometime about the Women's Auxiliary luncheon? We'd like you to sing...and there may be special requests....

Thanks in advance

(Mrs.) Lillian Pintobasco"

He'll get the point....

Abruptly Lillian feels herself poked, or budged, by Etta Berliner: "Can't you make him go away? The other women are embarrassed. We're all embarrassed...it's not right...."

Peter has reappeared to play slap ball against the retaining wall that hides the water tank. And he's singing again as he moves:

"Bouncy bouncy *beytsim*

Bouncy bouncy ballsies...."

"What can I do Etta? Sam's supposed to mind the child...."

She's always saying things like that, and never doing anything. Telling Izzy we could go away somewhere and when it was time there were the boys, her sister's daughter's wedding. Sam's testimonial! Masonic weekend at the Tamarack Lodge; her life a spittoon with Sam and the kids spitting into it whenever they pleased.

Nevertheless, when it happened the first time, I was surprised. Jesus, I said, when he kissed me that first time in my own flat. Now I'm in trouble....

And when he ran away to Spain I was worried for him all the time, even more than for myself with the baby....

When he came back I thought this is crazy but it happened again with him when I was six months pregnant....

Three times it happened like that after Peter was born and we never went anywhere because Izzy said he didn't want any more lies to Etta, more excuses.

Lillian has glanced away from the brown stick figure of her naked son to Etta Berliner and asks herself the question of her life: Does Etta know?

Izzy came to visit me in the hospital and I asked him then did Etta know? He said Etta knows lots of things. *Does Sam?* I wanted him even then...in the hospital....

Pitiful the way a woman like Etta loses her looks.

She just don't care, she never took proper care, a scorched pot.

Izzy says it isn't true *it was me*, not Etta lacking anything, but I still think it has a lot to do with her. I wanted him to like me for other reasons besides.

Izzy brought me daisies and lilacs to the hospital. He gave Peter a little silver kiddush cup from Holland.

I loved him like the father of my child because he was
A pudding of stones Etta gave him
So? Why should he want?
When they lost that boy it was all over between them
Curtains

Drapes

"You'll see," She says to Etta, "He'll exhaust himself
and quiet down again. He'll go back over to the Men in
a minute...."

"You know I love Peter," Etta replies. "But it isn't even
good for him. He's over-stimulated...."

"That's more than I can say," Lill laughs.

Etta is overweight, her jaw a bit underslung, a chicken
comb beneath her chin. Soft burned out eyes like ash.
Even in their younger years, Lillian never found her friend
and rival much competition. What hangs off a mop handle
for hair, big spaces between the front teeth. It would take
a brave man, she thinks, to make Etta truly happy.

Seated with her friend on this sunny *shvitzy* day, she
inhales the fetors of Brooklyn and Etta in one breath, a
warming body smell she can't deny, and Lill finds herself
stopping her breath. Nauseated, she is also aroused, excited,
embarrassing when she recalls those women in lumber-
jackets Izzy took her to see last winter at Romany Jane's
in the Village....

Kind who only love other women. Was it thoughts of
Izzy, or Etta being here, so close, next to her? She's thinking
of a pretty woman with a parasol who wore wing tip shoes
and a double breasted man's suit? ...Such a wholesome
pretty face. Strange...downtown at that time it didn't
make much of a spark in Lill, though she had to admit she
was curious. She wanted to ask, "What exactly do you do
with each other?" But, as she didn't wish to lead the
woman on in any way, she put the question to Izzy over
a second round of drinks.

He was pleased with her, and amused, she could tell, the way he took her hand, played with the fingers, a little tickle in the palm, licking his lips, smiling: "You'd be surprised Lill how inventive human beings really are...."

"With fingers?" she asked. "Carrots? How? Tell me?"

"I'm not the *maivin*," he said, "but it's not so different from you and me lover...tongue in cheek, lickety split...in short, these girls make love every which way, as best they can, and some say even better than you and I...."

"There's no law against it in the Bible," he added. "For men there was, sure, but not for women...."

"My education is now complete," Lill said. She wasn't kidding either. Her intimations of suddenly being one of the illuminati had come to her now after a sheltered childhood, and adolescence, and young womanhood, during which she'd done plenty, but always with wise guys, hoods. Those sweet Southern boys in Memphis—they'd always been perfect gentlemen. And Sam was a decent livelihood, and not much else.

Now she squirms thinking of women with women, Izzy with women, women and Izzy doing things with other women doing things with Izzy...and then more women ...*Phooey*!

Hot!

Lill tries to break the spell she feels with conversation.

"Etta, is Izzy singing anywhere lately?"

"Singing?" As though she don't know what I mean.

"Your husband. Come on Etta, Izzy...."

"He has engagements now and then," she tells Lill, "frankly he'll never be another Richard Tucker...."

("And if he ever were," Lill wonders, "if ever....")

"Izzy sings beautiful," Lill reminds her. "He sings wonderful. When he does Kol Nidre on the High Holidays in the annex...."

"*Kvell*," Etta puts in, supplying the word for her friend as well as herself. "Me too...I *kvell* too...." She wipes her forehead of sweat with the flat of her palm. "I would never put my husband down, you understand, but being an artiste is such a...an undependable way of making a living...."

"O sure."

"He'll always have to do something else for his bread and butter, my poor Izzy, in a showroom maybe...."

"Poor Izzy..." Lill wonders why Etta can't help out more. She works part-time only, and there's no children. She was born with two arms and two feet just like everybody else....

The last time they were together Izzy's feelings were hurt. At Fancier Frocks they wanted him to sing, "O You Beautiful Girls," while the models paraded with the new line. He'd refused. "My voice is my one gift," he said. 'It's not part of this job. I will not prostitute myself...."

Izzy was embarrassed. "I won't use my voice to sell *shmattes*. The dollar just doesn't mean that much to me, Lill...."

But not everything embarrasses Izzy. She'd come looking for him in the robing room on the second floor at *shul* after a wedding rehearsal. Izzy was in a handball game and nearly forgot all about the rehearsal. At the last minute he'd draped himself in his cantorial gowns and rushed downstairs to sing the cues for "*Becuase...I come to you....*"

Everybody said he'd be just marvelous and, afterwards, when he was all hot and sweaty, in the robing room on the second floor, Lill lifted up his cantorial robes and took him in the mouth.

Izzy told her, "After many a swallow Lill it's spring again with birds on the wing again...." And then he was glum and told her about the showroom. "Izzy," she said. "You done right." And he kissed her, right there in the robing room.

Etta's got her own problems with Izzy, but they ain't mine: "Before Sigmund I always worked full time, Lill, in offices as office manager, but Izzy meant well, only he didn't know what was up and what was down in the business world. He said a mother shouldn't work full time, and then we could afford not to...I'm talking when Izzy was number one man at Eggy Brammstein's. There was plenty of money...and now I couldn't find full time even if I wanted to...They all want younger women. Izzy says I should go back to school, maybe take a degree in something...."

"Whatever's right for you, of course," Lill ad libs. "Sociology maybe...?"

Etta's no fool. She could find good work. She just don't want to. Home she can keep an eye on Izzy, more or less, Lill thinks.

She says, "If Sam would let me I'd work...I worked before for the wine people, Altschul. They were bootleggers and then they went legit. Felix, the son, was a good boss, but he also wanted to be my boyfriend...and that was almost a tragedy in the making...."

"What happened?" Etta asks.

"You know he thought I was easy," Lill explains.

"It happens." Etta shifts on her bench, brushing against Lill's hip.

"When I got pregnant with Benjamin Felix sent me long stemmed roses to the hospital...."

"That was nice...."

"The nurses asked me was he my boyfriend...." Lill laughs.

"Was he?"

"Don't be silly. Not even when I worked there. Such a face he had...and he was a killer...They called him icepick, corkscrew...."

"Sounds like a difficult man."

"Yes, but generous. He had beautiful hands like a pianist...." She's blushing she knows it.

"I'm very sorry for you," says Etta, glumly.

The weight of her words sinks on top of Lill. She's been lying, of course. Felix got what he wanted from her and then she ended up with Sam. Does Etta know that too? She has to find some way back to her advantage.

"Etta why not try again you and Izzy...?"

"*Try again what*?" Her friend's peevishness hides her knowledge of Lill's meaning. "It's not possible anymore trying again...The doctors all say so...."

"Doctors?" Lill meant some other way, adoption maybe.

"We would have to apply to an agency," Etta explains, "and Izzy really don't want me to. He says he don't believe blood is thicker than water but he also don't want someone else's *tsoris*. He's happy this way. He says he would take a DP child from Poland, or Hungary, one of those countries, if there were any...but I don't want such headaches, honestly Lill. Not now...."

"Well it's a hard decision." Her friend shakes her head so the sweat drips off her chin.

Izzy always says, "Etta has a broken heart that's permanent and she can never make up her mind about anything except that...."

Lill doesn't like hearing such things from Izzy anymore than she likes hearing Etta now: "You don't really know Izzy the way I know him," correcting herself. "He makes a good living one week and the next we're eating groats. Sure he has his draw," Etta points out, "but that just covers basics. He's a dreamer, an idealist, not a provider, like your Sam. Some weeks he makes his commissions and some weeks not...."

"I'm not planning to marry him," Lill says, with her false hearty laugh.

"Good..." Etta replies. "*B'shalom.*"

The other woman's scent wafts at Lillian, sweet with talc, and pungent, from body salts. It's really her own smell, Lillian realizes. The air congealing with odors from herself, from Etta, so that Lillian finds herself aroused with intimations of her own body's chemic mysteries.

"*B'shalom,*" Lill repeats to herself now, as her loins shudder on her, recalling Izzy's words to her the time they met and she was feeling like *drek* of a *shpendel*, like she did almost every month, and he treated her so nice with wine and caresses it was so wonderful. Something Sam would never do. Izzy didn't mind at all the way she was.

Later, when she asked why, he said, "Maybe because I

have Rumanians in my family. Bela Lugosi was a cousin. Between a vamp and a vampire, what's a little blood?''

She hears Etta again:

"Looks like you were right about sonnyboy Lill. He's having quiet time...."

She glances across the expanse of hot red bricks to where Peter squats, drawing with his spitty finger on the bricks.

Didn't I tell you so? But Lill is truly surprised. Unlike Peter to play by himself for hours on end like her Benjamin. It surely won't last, she's sure of that... The boy's hyperactive, according to Moe Glass, her pediatrician. Maybe he'd like a game of tic tac toe.

Lillian arises, hitches up her bra, and across the hotness waddles over to her son, as though wading through a river of her own exuded grease.

Great block letters scrawl and spread, connected by loops of drying spittle, and sweat. There are whole areas already beginning to fade, though others seem unearthed with streaks of tar, like an ancient text from the windy grit of Tar Beach. What holy terror is this?

SCUM BAGS

BIG FAT COCKSUCKERS

FUCKING ADULT CHEAPSKATE NAZIS

OHURU!

Her hands spring out before she even thinks I will beat this child, my son, and she feels the flesh of his face and then his warm shoulder blades sting against her palms....

"You little monster...." Wam. "Holy terror...." She can't believe her own rage. "Juvenile Delinquent!"

"Mommy," he's shouting back. "Mommy!"

Her hands are wet with tears and sweat.

She slaps at him again. "To call your own mother such things...Calling me filth...."

"They're just words mommy please just words...."

He's on all fours and he's scampering away from her blows as she slaps at him again. "Holy terror! Monster!"

"*Wait till I tell your father... Wait till he hears. I just can't wait....*"

He's escaped her again, through the partition to the other side where the men are, and when she stares at the work of her hands again, they burn, and when she stares at the work of his hands, all the letters fade out.

"What did I ever do?" But she's shouting into the wind, through a metal divider which she's forbidden to cross.

She feels so foolish in the sight of all the other women. It was such a shock to see such filthy cruel tramp words from the hand of her own child....

Lillian hears his voice: "I'm sorry momma. Please don't hit me anymore. I'll never do it again. Please don't tell Umpapa...."

"What did you say?"

"Please don't tell. Please...."

"Did I hurt you?"

"It's OK ma, honest. Don't tell please...."

She knows he's cowering behind the barrier. Knows she has him frightened at last.

Lillian isn't sorry for that.

"What did you say Peter?"

"I'll behave myself now."

He's weeping, she thinks, big crocodile tears.

"I didn't mean it Memsahib. They were just words. O
please...."

In the shade of the grey metal structure, she feels a little
faint. She could collapse right then and there from so
much shock to her system. Life is such a trial with this
child sometimes.

"Please please...I'm sorry. Never again...."

"Go to your father!"

"I really mean it Peter," she adds, "one more time and
I really will tell your father...."

"No more fucks and no more cocksuckers," he whispers
back loudly. "Honest."

Despite herself, she's smirking, turns away, even as the
sweet smell of Etta's fleshy presence intrudes on her senses.
What kind of *khazeyrim* is this? When she hears the boy
pad away, she feels a hand touching her shoulder, and when
she has opened her eyes again there is friend Etta, not quite
so homely now, her face dimly lit with the only real emotion
she ever feels which is pity for herself and others.

"It's not so terrible," says Etta, "it's mostly all gone
already...and your friends don't judge you one way or the
other...."

She looks so much like Lill's mother when they used to
go together to the baths on Essex Street, after they moved
up North from Memphis, and then Lill would tell herself
she would never let age and wrinkles and fat happen to her.
Lill loved her mother, the sweetness of her smile, smell of
her flesh, the pity in her voice: "Come darling come here
and I'll hold you." Esther would say, when they bathed

together. "Don't look at these other women. It's a shame the way they look...."

"Come darling," Etta tells her now. "It ain't so bad as you think...."

Sobbing, though she does not wish to, Lillian rocks against her heels and falls forward toward this solid naked woman so that she feels the sag of her slippery gooseflesh breasts against her own body.

And she is held, and quieted, for awhile, in the heat, in the smell, in the sobbing, by those hands pressing against her back, of her lover's forlorn wife.

"Help me," she says. "So help me...."

And Etta continues to hold her close, their bodies warming together, hair touching shoulders of each other, rocking back and forth in the heat, standing there like that, God willing....

ON THE STEAM TABLE

Half an hour later Etta feels like a leftover on life's steam table, hot and dry outside, soggy within.

She's always been a down-to-earth person and she'd thought a good talk now with Lillian could do them both no harm. Her friend took, but what she gave back after they finally let each other go was more like reproach than acknowledgement. "The girls are looking at us. I can't stand here like this...."

Lillian squirmed.

"So don't...."

"I'm feeling so uncomfortable," she added.

"No harm done anyway," was all Etta could say as she went off to play cards with some of the other women.

She'd always known Lillian was a little cold, indifferent to most other people, and their feelings. Always resented being stuck with Lill here on weekends, like Izzy's baby-sitter. That she kept on trying to make some emotional connection with her husband's *maidel*, his "girl," as she liked to call Lill, was as rational to Etta as being kind to Izzy's maiden aunt, Ida, who lived all alone in Brownsville. Somehow Etta was convinced that if they ever talked as woman to woman she could convince Lillian for everybody's sake to break the affair off...but after they'd embraced Lill seemed flustered and so did she. Lill said, "You're really very kind...."

Etta replied, "What did I got to lose?"

She rarely misrepresented except by sarcasm. What she'd lost she knew she could never recover. As they parted and went to their separate places on Tar Beach, Etta announced, "So this is what they call a vacation girls...."

She wouldn't have come here today, or any other day for God knows how long, if it weren't for Izzy. The man liked to see his friend Sam, and the boy, and to play a few games of handball. When she wanted Atlantic Beach with sea breezes, where her friend Helen Dorner keeps a cabana, Izzy said, "I'm not up to strangers if you please...."

"You really like to bake here on tar?"

"I don't know what I like anymore," Izzy said. "For sea breezes I flush the toilet."

"Breakers don't appeal to you...."

"Etta," losing his patience, "I'm drowning just the way I am on Seventh Avenue...."

They can't even sit together up here, and afterwards Izzy's so *shvitzed* out from handball and the sun, and the steam, all he wants is cold soup, and a movie, and he always falls asleep in the movies, just as he does later in bed.

"Golly have I fallen asleep?"

"It was only while you were making love," she reminds him.

Fardrait, chagrined, Etta turns to her partner, Bonny Pofftstein. A gauzy net of stars and sequins shapes Bonny's ash blonde do about her feral face, the total result is not unattractive, a bon bon hidden in fine tissues, or foil.

Bonny is a dresser; season after season she gets compliments at synagogue for her hem lengths, and furs, her exquisite gold jewelry, her scents, subtle skin tones. Certainly not for her *moykhes*. No brains Bonnie! On Tar Beach she seasons her pelt with special Helena Rubinstein concoctions of walnut oil and civet only long enough to play a few hands of rummy, before she's off to the showers and the workout room.

"*Seykhl al filete pomadoro*," Izzy always says. "Brains of a tomato."

Bonny's husband, Marcel, the eye doctor, left her, with a substantial settlement, for a veterinarian from Farmingdale; and then she got together with Xray Fivel, the cancer man, whom she almost never brings to Tar Beach.

Bonny must be Etta's age, although her breasts and double chins are probably younger and newer. She had them uplifted in Switzerland right after the war, and ever since, Izzy says, "she presents herself to one and all like the blue plate special at Rattner's."

They say she took special embryo injections in Lucerne to look young again from the same man what treats the Pope in Rome.

Etta also knows Izzy had Bonny's pants down once or twice, years ago and she has long since forgiven the world for that. If she held that against every woman on Tar Beach, she'd be even lonelier than she is.

She asks Bonny about her Holiday plans. Sometimes she and Fivel take the children off to Atlantic City....

"Will I see you in *shul*?"

Bonny replies, "Your bid Etta...."

"I'm sorry." She throws down a black seven.

"I brought tickets, of course," Bonny explains, "only

Fivel says he don't want to . . . He don't like all the talk about Palestine . . . ."

"It's important no?" A red sequin glittering at Etta's eye makes her squint a little.

"Fivel says we're Americans, and we should all stay that way . . . ."

"It ain't for us. It's for the others . . . ."

"Fivel says that's just mockie talk . . . ."

"Don't we all gotta have compassion?"

"Well he gives donations through the hospital. He just don't like all the malarkey," her friend points out.

"What sort of malarkey?"

"Fivel's an American born and bred, and he says if the Rabbi wants to preach Zionism he should do it someplace else . . . ."

"I see . . . ." She throws down a red three. "Fivel's got real strong opinions . . . ."

"It's not your turn," Bonny points out.

"I'm sorry."

"Personally I don't always agree with Fivel, but I like peace in my house . . . and when he says they're nothing but terrorists over there, in the Holy Land, I guess I gotta agree . . . ."

"I guess we all gotta do what we gotta do," Etta says, "and so do you."

"In the court of world opinion maybe, but Fivel says it could cause trouble someday for all of us here in America . . . ."

"Maybe." Etta has her cards all mixed together in her hand and starts to rearrange.

"I'm afraid I'm no great shakes at cards today. Can't even

concentrate...."

"It happens. You want to quit?"

Etta nods, and they throw in their hands. "I owe you one," she says, gets up again, and pulls on her bathing suit hard so that it stretches across her buttocks. She can see a little of her stomach bulging lightning blue in front of her eyes as she starts down toward the sun deck where Lillian lies flat-out and prone, her knees browning just across the edge.

Etta sits down alongside her husband's girl. She won't say anything, for fear of waking her. Yawning, she recalls, not for the first time, the weekend the two couples spent together at the Tamarack Lodge when she caught Izzy and Lill holding hands together in beach chairs beside the pool.

Sam was on the links and they didn't see her coming across the pine needle lawn behind them. She stood a moment and listened to their words. They were talking about Sam. "He couldn't care less," Lill said.

"Don't," Izzy told her.

"I don't know why I even bother waiting up for him," Lill said. "He's always out to lunch...."

"It can't last forever," Izzy said. "So maybe someday...."

Before he could finish, Etta gave out an Indian war whoop such as she'd heard in the movies, and made a running dive into the pool. Such a big splash. It almost made her forget, and if they seemed startled, they also didn't choose to wonder how much she'd overheard.

Well she was always a bit of a clown, and maybe Izzy just thought she was showing off for him....

Etta yawns, and stretches out flat on the hot wood

alongside Lillian.

The sky is so blue it could kill you, she thinks.

"Days like this" she says, "I wish I was at the Ocean...."

"That you Etta?" Lillian knows.

"The very same... Etta Loretta...."

"No more cards?"

"Who can concentrate in this heat?"

"You got a lot on your mind," says Lillian. "Like me."

"Enough, I guarantee...."

"More than enough." Lill sits up and faces out across the roof toward the Knights of Columbus. "You know what I mean...."

"I'm not sure what you mean Lill."

"What's been going on," she says, as though swallowing words.

"I don't know what you're talking about Lill...."

"Izz...."

"Don't," Etta warns her, sharply. "Please... You could spoil a good friendship...."

"You don't want to know?"

"We're not Catholics up here," Etta says, "why confess?"

"Etta I need to talk...."

"Talk about what?" She's sitting up herself, but Lill has gone down flat again, and she has her hands over her eyes.

"There must have been others," says Lill.

"No competition darling believe me." Etta turns away from her own sob. "Please everybody stop trying to drive me crazy," she adds.

Lill touches her friend's wrist and then her shoulder, gently: "I'm sorry. I truly am. I wish it had never happened...."

"Liar!"

"I mean it...."

"Well don't be silly," Etta tells her. "I'm only sorry because I can't say I'm glad. Better you than a tramp...."

"The other tramps can all go to hell," she adds. "At least there's love between you two...?"

"Etta please."

"Why deny? A man has needs he shouldn't have to buy. A woman too, I think. You know you're not sorry. So why say sorry? The boy is beautiful...he's a beautiful little boy ...and Izzy loves children...."

"True...."

"Be sorry for your husband."

"He really don't know how to love," Lill explains.

"He could learn...."

She has a headache and she wants to cry so bad but not in front of Lill.

"You really love Izzy?"

Despite herself, Lill is nodding.

"You love *my* Izzy?"

"I was desperate," Lill explains, with a look likc strangulation on her face. "Try to understand...."

"I understand, and so will Sam some day...."

"He doesn't even care."

"O he will someday," Etta says. "When he has to, when someone says your hen just laid a goose egg."

She's laughing, almost cackling.

"You're indispensable to Sam, absolutely, I can tell, only he's shy...The two of you are some pair. So selfish...."

And she rests against the wooden slats again.

Moments later, when her eyes close, she's in bed. Izzy, propped against the pillows, reads a Russian novel and sucks on his pipe.

"Did you think I was blind?" she asks that part of herself she calls her husband Izzy: "Are there two faces like that?"

"I'm really sorry," Lill says. She gets up and moves off the bench toward the edge of the roof.

"Be careful how you stand," Etta says, and to Izzy she adds, "That Peter is your son just like Isadora Duncan gave a son to millionaire Singer. Mary Astor and George Kaufman ...It's page 4 Daily News stuff...Such an Izzy...."

Etta gets up and begins to pace and now she talks to herself and to Lillian: "When Izzy went to Spain I also was going crazy with worry. Do you think I ever told him about the sales conference at the Statler with Eggy Brammstein...?"

A car horn honks.

What's to remember? A good time was had by all. I suppose. So what? It was hardly Tristram and Isolde....

"Izzy," she says, "This must be love between us. You see how we treat each other?"

But love is Izzy and Lillian and if she thinks about that she'll want to jump right now. Be furious....

"O Iz, Eggy was just a fuck...A one-night stand which lasted for a weekend. Sex...no more no less...And Sigmund was your son, just like Peter, only he resembled me...."

She's weeping, tears rolling slow across her cheeks, and turning cold.

Izzy speaks back: "Lillian was also a one night stand that could last me for my whole life Etta...Her, me, the boy...."

She says. "I don't want to be left with Sam...."

"Let my people go Etta."

"I like kids. I could help out. Babysit. Look after things. You know...."

A chill breeze moves suddenly among the cinders. Lillian stands next to her again.

Izzy sings, "It may last a day
and it may be forever...."

Etta folds her arms across her chest.

"I was just thinking."

"So was I," Lill says, "with such a heavy mind."

She comes in front of Etta and holds her by the shoulders. "I'll never take Izzy from you. Whatever else happens I won't ever run away with him...."

"Say that for your sake darling," Etta tells her. "Not for mine...."

"I'll write him," Lill says. "I'll see him. I'll tell him...."

"Do what you like."

"I'll do it," Lill says. "I promise. You wait and see...."

Lill seems so much lighter to Etta for saying so that she leans over again toward her friend and pecks her on the shine of her cheek. "Just don't hurt anybody anymore darling," Etta says, and turns away again.

MUSHY CHEATER

Mushy really can't remember the last time anyone ever called him by his proper name, Maurice. Ever since he was 14 years old it's always been Mushy: on the streets, in the flat, the courts, in business, and here on Tar Beach, just as his little brother Daniel was always Dushy. "Mushy Dushy give it to me give it to me quick," shouted big Howy Weiner from beneath the boards.

Quick-handed Mushy sometimes passed, but give-and-go was never any good. Better a set shot from the corner, fake and underhand the lay-up when the guards fall back to protect the post. They called him "Mushy" and "Mushy Cheater" because of his hand fake and his hip fake. A small man has to make his own odds, Nat Holman used to say.

Once Solly Cohen said to him. "Sounds like shit your name. I wish there was something else I could call you...."

"What's in a name?" shrugged Mushy. He had trophies and watches and gold and silver medals: the JWB, the JCC, you name them. He played with the best: Katzoff and Schlomo Baum, and Boycoff, and Big Stu Kolodner....

He could have made the Pros if he had a couple more inches, but Mushy isn't that much taller than the Pintobasco kid, and he's prematurely bald. As Shtummy used to say, "A shiny star but not anymore with the TV cameras and all...."

Mushy went into real estate in partnership with Dushy

and their old friend, Arty Kessel, but Arty and Dushy they were aces, and Mushy wasn't holding his own so after a while he left the firm and took a job with the Trunk Organization. They liked to hire jocks for PR. His office-mate was Buster Kinneret of the football Dodgers.

With the new baby, Mush figures he's just about keeping up with the others at Trunk, only you never can tell. The Old Man Trunk likes Mushy to greet all the new listers, but he also reads the sale reports, and, according to those, Mushy dribbles a lot while the other salesmen are knocking homers.

He's prepared himself for the worst. If he doesn't start making money soon, he's going to move the family to Florida. A Chinaman can make it in Florida real estate, the Old Man Trunk once advised him. And Buster Rostok says, "Nothing beats the Beach."

He's flat on his back at the moment like a pullet watching the Navy planes descend toward Floyd Bennett Field. During the War Mushy played USO basketball throughout the East Coast, and his brother Daniel, who had two boys, was a volunteer air raid warden. Sometimes Mushy liked to visit with him on the roof of the apartment building during blackouts. They'd share a beer, a cream soda, shoot the shit about the Duration....

Now that it's all happened at last he's still nowhere again....

He's ashamed for what happened earlier about the cards. He could make a pledge, sure, tonight, but will he be able to pay up when the time comes? Checks like his make good tire patches...if they called him "Mushy Cheater" again they wouldn't be talking about set shots....

He has $1000 in a special account at Amalgamated, but doesn't want to dip into that, if he can help it. That's for emergencies. Maybe Sam will understand if he talks to him in private...It ain't as though he's stealing from people....

As he makes his way across the deck to where Pintobasco and Izzy sit together over cards, Mushy remembers the first time he gave $100. Such a good feeling, and he got nothing back from the other guys except a lot of thank yous. Sam Rostok took him to the set up bar and personally fixed him a rye old fashioned. "I know I can count on your vote," handing Mushy the drink.

"I wouldn't be at all surprised."

"That-away," Rostok said. "Close to the vest...." And he gave him a good hearty slap on the back.

Suddenly Mushy felt he was one of them. He thought he would be going on from there to an apartment on Plaza Street, a Buick Regal, nothing less. He could imagine cashing in his GI insurance and putting a down payment on a house in Flatbush, or Marine Park, near his brother, Dushy, a two family semi-detached with a tenant, and a garage.

Then came Trunk's FHA foreclosure, and everybody in the office had to take a cut. So last year he gave $200 and it really hurt. He gave until it hurt. Not this year, Mushy thinks. I can't put up a front when I'm wearing a suit with a canvas back...Maybe if I told Pintobasco I would vote for him...He approaches with caution, not wishing to set off any booby-traps.

"Hey guys." Aloud.

"Hey...."

"Sorry about the fuss before...."

"What fuss?"

"You know what fuss," Mushy says to Sam. "About the cards...."

"Forget it. If you don't want to give, don't...Just holler out a number when your name is called and we'll talk it over afterwards...and compromise. I just wouldn't want you to discourage other people...."

"But I would never do that."

"Why not? Do it," Izzy tells him. "This ain't Nazi Germany...."

"How could I?" Mushy says, "It ain't right. It wouldn't even look right...."

"Looks don't matter when you can't pay your bills," Izzy tells him.

He nods, and backs away. Now they all know how bad things really are, Mushy is thinking, they're not likely to get any better. At least, when you look like you're doing OK, people have confidence in you, and business picks up....

Mushy says, "Maybe I'll go play some ball...."

"Anybody want a game?"

"Later," Sam says. "We got things to talk about. Limber up a little. It will do you some good...."

"Take your mind off things," Izzy adds.

He agrees with the suggestion, but as he backs off Mushy wonders if this is the way things are going to be from now on. You don't pay you don't have players to hang around with. He's sort of out of the picture from here on in unless he can find the jack to make a pledge and redeem it. "See you down there guys."

"Sure Mushy sure."

"See ya," Izzy adds.

"Sure," says Mushy. "Soon I hope...don't be long...."

"Sure...."

"Well I hope so."

"Enough already," Sam says. "Leave us be...."

"I just hope," he goes on, "nobody thinks less of me. Because if I had it you guys know it would be no big deal for me...."

"How could we not?" Sam asks.

"Sure," another time. "Because that's the kind of guy I really am...."

"Sure," Izzy says.

Mushy still isn't sure what Sam meant by his question and that icewater look. "It's not as if I didn't know better," he adds. "I'm just as disappointed as you guys honestly...."

"Sure enough?" Sam adds.

"Well I'm glad," Mushy says. "And I'd be sorry if you didn't...."

"Don't ever be sorry about a thing like this," Izzy says.

"Sure...."

"Frankly," Sam says, "Your $100 won't make a difference, one way or the other."

Mushy walks away feeling that, at least, he's making an effort and nobody knows better than he what an effort that is, but when he enters the dark stairwell and the acrid odor of perspiration seasons his nostrils he thinks he probably should be looking for another place to work out. Maybe down the Parkway at the Jewish Center. He could still

play a little ball, if they needed him to, in return for a reduc-
ed family membership.

Regular give-and-go he'd offer them, maybe even a little
coaching of the teenagers.

Mushy-Dushy give *it to me quick*.

SIX

DARK NOW

A dark echoing stairwell surrounds Peter like a mummy case in the museum.

In the old country, on Eastern Parkway, where the box leaned against the museum wall, the golden goddamnt door to the case was always kept open. You could look inside, crappy old bandages and all....Here in Uganda death is *eppes* a regular daily business like taxes and real estate. The way people talk. Dropping like flies...first Roosevelt then Hitler. "I could die thinking about you," Izzy said once on the phone when I probably was not supposed to be listening in. It's all Micky ever thinks about. War, Death....

"As I live and die...."

Peter thinks of dying, his own someday oblivion, and that of Abraham Abraham downstairs in the Sanctuary. The first time he ever missed a *harabee* was to die? Imagine....

They dig a hole about six feet deep and drop you in with worms that creep....

When he thinks of dying himself the room is always dark, he's in bed, his parents on their knees beside the bed, and he is begging their forgiveness....If we loved each other would this be happening all the time? Or was it because love made death so sad? He didn't always know he loved his parents except when he thought of dying. Then death was unbearable. Love was all he begged for....

He thinks of a hole in the ground somewhere all the way out on Long Island, and just laying about down there forever and ever, with nothing left after a while except bones and dust.

Maggots too...?

Or else he thinks of being wrapped inside those crappy old bandages forever and ever like a sore thumb. A hang nail.

Henayni!

No heaven, no hell for Jews, Izzy says, but awful things even so: ants, beatles, terrible like that. Like waking in the dark after dreaming something terrible....

Christians go straight up to Heaven if they're good. He could never be that good, no matter how hard he prayed and even begged.

Peter grabs for the cool bannister rod, and takes a few steps further down, his feet echoing slaps. Dark here dark now....

When Grandpa Pintobasco died the box was closed up tight, and when Peter asked his cousin Muriel what grandpa looked like now, she told him it didn't pay to look at Grandpa. Not now....

"Your poor old grandpa was just skin and bones in the end," she said. "He wasted away to nothing Peter...."

"So quick?" He couldn't believe it all happened to Grandpa so quick.

"On account of he was so sick," Muriel explained. "It just happened...."

He goes a few steps further down, and the air feels chilly and damp.

He used to dream of beatles and ants and when he told Umpapa he said, "My father lived to be 96 or 97 and his father before him lived a long time too...."

"And then?"

"That's the way it is boy. We all gotta go someday...You won't know the difference when it happens. I promise...."

He laughed gently as Peter called out, "Not me. Never!"

They don't ever speak about the subject anymore and Izzy always says think about life kiddo its a lot more fun. The joy of life by which old Bwana must mean Shere Khan and Rikitikitavi as well as Shaneys too, of course, but Lillian, she says, "It's nothing I talk about with my little boys. Death....a pretty sad business...."

Once Peter told them, "Anyway I'm not afraid. Christ will lead me up to Heaven...."

"Christ?" His parents making sorta weird funny faces: "Where did you hear about that boy?"

"On WOR on the Rosary hour," he explained. "They were having a *harabee*."

Memsah echoed. "On WOR on the Rosary?"

"We don't happen to believe in Christ in this house Peter," said his father.

"Praise the Lord Christ is Love," he said. "Our salvation. King of the Jungle I believe...Our Father who...."

"Say that one more time and I'll give you a licking," his father said.

So Benjamin said, "Peter just said the word again...."

"O Christ loves us all, and you can crucifize me for all I care," Peter responded. "I really think God is a girl, a

woman anyway. Izzy says they got the plumbing for it,
kiddo, not like us...."

"Peter just said God's a girl...."

"Don't be snotty," said his father. "Don't be a wiseacre...."

Peter turned away toward Lillian: "Holy Mother full of
grace...."

She gave him a lopsided look. "Be sure you wash your
face and hands before dinner."

Turning away, she walked back into her kitchen to lay
hands on the meatloaf before stowing it inside her oven.
The pause before a *Krik*, a scream.

In Hebrew school later, Peter felt like he had the key but
no lock to turn. He knew it was just wrong to say Christ
(and all that stuff), just wrong for a boy like him, and he
just didn't care to say anybody at all. He just knew if he
had been living in Europe with all those other Jewish kids,
he'd be dead by now, and that was scary to him when he
closed his eyes to sleep. He saw Nazis and fires, and a
darkness spreading everywhere...and Izzy said, "Now you
know why we don't love Christ boychickle. In his name,
so many Jewish children died, in the name of God, or
Christ, or Hitler...."

"Or Stalin?"

"He too is no angel," Izzy admitted glumly. "But not
just Jews with Stalin...anybody...."

Fire, darkness, blood, Hitler, Stalin...Doesn't help him
to sleep any better.

Peter notices now from the wetness on his face that he's
been crying, his breath coming with little painful gasps.
The Lord of all Creation sits down when She pees, Izzy says.

He says they make Life kiddo, in their bellies, and men are just a waste of time, all of us, little boys, all of us, if we believe any different. Snot sniffling won't help neither....

He starts to back his way up the stairs in the darkness to find tissue...and now for the first time he feels the marks on his face and body from Mammileh's hands, an infinite soreness, achey logey feeling.

The way Umpapa looks so down-in-the-mouth and sore and lies to me all the time, and his crazy tantrums—bad enough, he thinks, though at least you can scream, kick out at those big crashing fists with your hands. From the mouth of God into my hands....With the Mammileh he feels paralyzed all over. When she carries on, he's locked inside his own personal block of ice. She has such powers. He can see it, even with Sam and Izzy....

And then the puny voice he used to shout back at her, "Please please"—was that his own voice? *Vymiru*....

It sounded like the voice of someone he hated inside himself. Voice of a *putz*. The last time that happened was when they took away our dog and Benjamin said to get even we should both make number 2 right outside their room at night on the rug, so we both did that together and they blamed only me. Did I get a licking then and soap in the mouth, and Benjamin just got a little soap. No hands. No slaps.

Recollecting the past, Peter has been truly put through the mill again in camp in Hagarstown, his buttocks and shoulder blades still stinging from the furious touch of Memsahib Lillian..."You filthy child...*filth*!"

I never promised you Bonamo's Turkish Delight....

After scampering past the sunbathing men along Tar

Beach and down the dark stairs beyond the massive steel
fire door Peter feels as though all he has left is as dark as
his worst thoughts.

It's twelve floors down to the Sanctuary on street level,
and he isn't wearing any clothing. A girl could see. Dog
bite. Who knows?

He reverses direction, takes quick steps up onto the
darkness of the next landing.

The pungent cinnamon of perspiration odor is so very
powerful here it must be the darkness itself perspiring with
such a stench.

He leans against a wall which abuts one of the four wall
courts. The thwack and sharp sting of little hard rubber
handballs rebounding makes thick concrete vibrate. Heavy
shuffling of feet, frantic ricochets, cries, alarms...as he
recalls Izzy's talk of mashed green banana and cow peas,
and dust settling on the windows of the blue Pontiac car,
when Izzy and Lillian and he went for that picnic in the
Hempstead State Park last summer; and Izzy told him so
much about Uganda and the fruit trees and the waterfalls
he was hungry and thirsty all at once, and when they
stopped at the Roadside Rest and he had a frank and orange
drink, he saw Izzy and Lillian close together, like a single
breath, and he thought to himself, Why should I care
anyhow? It's not my life...and Izzy paid for his second
soda and bought beers for Lillian and himself...and later
frozen custard....

"*Bobkas*," Mammileh said to Izzy, "I get nothing from
h i m ."

"You can't really believe that Lill," Izzy replied. "Give it a chance..." Izzy must love everybody, even Mammileh....

The walls are alive with rats and rubber balls. New sweat smells like carroway seeds. After handball Izzy smells dark and strong, like sulphur from a match. It's as dark now as his bunk at camp when they took away his flashlight and he sees little skunk eyes everywhere, he thinks.

"I feel like one of John L. Lewis' coal-miners down here," announces Dr. Piggy Baer, with unmistakable phlegm. "*Ergetz*!"

Piggy's creamy eyes are as large as campfire marshmallows. Friendly Henry Wallace eyes: "I bet you can't see any better...."

Peter sees through the dark where Piggy, like Mohatma Ghandi, stands with a big white bath towel tied around his waist in a skirt.

The dome of Piggy's large head, lighted by the stairwell from above, glistens like calve's foot jelly. Below the knees more darkness. Peter really can't see Piggy's feet at all.

He asks, "Are you all right Dr. Baer?"

"Actually coming down it felt like maybe another heart attack," he says, "so I stopped here awhile, passed gas, and now I'm perfect...better than ever...."

"I had a piece of stuffed cabbage last night for supper," he adds, "and it always makes fireworks with me...."

He breaks wind.

"I hope that don't scare you...."

Not an awful lot of stink to Piggy's smells, Peter observes, like ashes and almonds, and the water in the flower pot after the roses wilt. Mild compared to what they left that time on his parents' threshold.

"I'm sorry if you weren't feeling well," the boy says, as a ball thwacks hard against the wall where they're standing, one above the other.

"An old man like me," Piggy observes, oyster-eyed, "is a regular gas company. I could sell to customers...Right now I can't even make bail for a small cardiac arrest...."

"I'm sorry."

"What's to be sorry about sonny? Ain't your fault..."

He comes closer and stands on tip toes as close as hair to Peter, who smells Lava soap bubbles, and before he can say Stop! the old man kisses him on the lips.

He tastes brown of cigar and his lips are sticky wet, but it isn't terrible. A *haiseh gedempte* feeling, and then a clamminess.

Peter backs up two steps. "You didn't have to do that," Piggy says.

"You didn't have to do that neither,"

And Piggy replies, "I ain't giving you any bellywash. None whatsoever...I'd sure like to get to know you better."

"How do you know?"

"No offense Little Pintobasco...I'm a pretty lonely old man. A million kids I brought into the world...."

"....And not one to call your own, says Izzy...."

Piggy seems surprised by all the boy knows: "How old are you little Peter?"

"6½," he lies. "I'll be 8 April...."

"For sure?"

"Honestly," he says. "I skipped...."

He's very nervous. The trouble with lying is all the lies you have to tell to make the first lie do what it should.

"Even if you are only 8," Piggy says, "you sure are a big

little boy...."

His lips come close again, a smell like cauliflower, and a hand reaches across the darkness as though to pat Peter on the head, and then it gropes, even lower and then lower....

Static electric swa: He feels so warm he's trembling: "Dr. Baer please...I'm shocked...."

The hand so warm, and smooth now, just like his mother's hand when she would wash him in the tub. Against his will, he can feel himself hardening, and he doesn't really trust it. It could hurt.

His face like a fresh-baked hot cross bun. Piggy pulls a little, makes him tremble, and harden.

"Nu little boy?"

"Don't be nasty. Please," Peter says. "Please. You'll upset me so I'll tell Umpapa...."

"Be sure you tell him all about Izzy too," Piggy says, as Peter sidesteps around him and the old man's wrist bends, his hand unlocks.

He's heading further down into the darkness...

Piggy shouts, "Still only a baby...?"

He tastes the blind man's juices on his lips, his sweat.

"Come back up here. You liked it. I could tell, I'll pay you," Piggy says. "I got plenty money down in my locker. Lots...."

So far down on the stairwell, away from Piggy, he is certainly very glad to notice there are no lingering effects from that warm obstetric hand.

Light seeps through a fire door by Peter's foot. Piggy says, "I just wanted to touch...."

"I'm not ready for that yet," Peter shouts. "Can't you

tell?''

"*Moisheh Kipoyer*," says Piggy. "Upsidedown like always,
a fool and his money...."

Peter hasn't stayed to listen. Pushing his way through
another heavy metal fire door into this empty gallery above
the black spotted walls of the two busy handball courts,
he hears Piggy's far-off voice, ghostly, wheedling, on and
on again, though he can't even make out any more words.
A sound like surf against his ears, full of fog and fearful-
ness. A chortle in a cloaca.... He lied to Piggy. In April
he'll be 8½.

GALOOTS AT PLAY

"Grown-ups are the funniest people," he reflects some moments later, "animals, with furry hands like Jacob."

He knows all about Jacob, asweat, wrestling with an angel, passing himself off as his brother, Esau. Such a business, I tell you. Playing favorites, like Sam with Benjamin.

On Court #1, which is directly below where he now stands, alone as a stone—and if he comes up close to the edge of the balcony he can even overlook the front part of the court, though not rear court—Manny Keiserhof *Der Shiker* and Little Murray Teitel play doubles with Mike Tumulty, the cop with a Jewish wife, and Mr. Big Pockets himself, Sam Rostok.

Hands like catchers' mitts flail at the cool thin air of the handball pen. Peter thinks back to a time when Buster was riding Umpapa about the way he played. Calling him names. Klutz and so on. Suddenly Little Sam struck out with his gloved hand and hit Rostok right across the jaw. The big man was startled; he hadn't been expecting it. He swung right back and the blow sent Umpapa hard against the back wall. Then they both stared at each other like neither could believe what they'd just done. Izzy grabbed Sam who was staring down at his open hand. "Lemme go," Umpapa said, staring at his open hand like a murderer in the movies. "Calm yourselves down," Izzy said.

"Next time he tries that," Rostok said, "I'll throw him

off the roof.''

He rubbed his jaw, and picked up the handball and threw it back into play again and pretty soon they were all volleying, even Sam.

He's also thinking of the man with the runny nose said he was a policeman who offered to show him a banana that can spit in the bathroom at the Roger's Cinema two weeks ago. Peter ran back to his seat for the rest of ''The Return of Frank James'' with his fly still open.

''Where you been so long?'' Izzy asked, his host for the afternoon.

And when he told the Bwana about the policeman after the movie, Izzy said he probably wasn't any cop but he would talk to the manager anyway.

''Men like that don't usually mean too much harm,'' he said, ''but you never can tell. You did the right thing kiddo. That you don't need.''

And he promised someday to take Peter back to watch the parts of the movie he hadn't seen. The next day he asked Izzy what the manager said, and Izzy sang, ''Yes we have no bananas....''

''Hold your horses kiddo,'' he added. ''For all I know that was the manager, so just don't go to that movie theatre again unless you got somebody with you in the toilet....''

''Who is my partner?'' shouts big Sam Rostok now. Buster Crab. The only class-A player in his age group, he was beating Umpapa badly when their fight started that time. ''You can give it but you can't take it,'' he told Umpapa.

"So do you," Little Sam replied, "in spades."

Now Rostok throws the ball into play. A close match down below. Bodies wrestling with their shadows.... When they thrust out their arms to slap at the bounding black ball, they seem to be sparring with the front wall as well. Upper bodies knot and bunch, glistening like suet.

Safe to watch a while. They all hate each other. They all love each other. The comforts of home. Thick billowy sleeves of satiny flab pour from waistbands when they move, fat and sinew captured above or below their athletic trunks by rapid motion. To make each shot they step forward, or back, like burly street sweepers, and cut away again, in lindy hops.

Tumulty jangles a lot when he moves; around his neck on chains are St.Christopher, a Greek cross, big Jewish *chai* in gold from his wife's relatives. He calls himself "the non-sectarian goy," and is well-liked by all, except those who say he cheats at pinochle. "I'm in with a bunch of smart Jew boys," he explains in his own defense. "What else can I do?"

"Mine!" shouts Big Sam Rostok suddenly as he lunges, a Galoot, and Tumulty cries out, "What the fuck Sam!"

Below so much girth and gut, Rostok's long graceful stridings make the shadows move real fast. With excellent confidence of motion, he blocks out an area on the balls of his small feet, turns his knees in, squares his shoulders, lifts, lunges, swings, the powerful muscles on his back bunching up toward his neck like armor plate.

Teitel misses, the ball rolls free. "Who the fuck is my partner?" Big Sam exclaims.

"You made the choice," Kaiserhoff says who drinks because his wife ran away with the children to Larchmont. He won the silver star at Salerno, Izzy says, but he never was "a whole man" after that. Izzy says Kaiserhoff lost his wife at the Stage Door Canteen and he shouldn't look for her anymore. The War didn't make people any nicer kiddo....

Now Manny says, "Lets shmear them partner. Murder them. Easy does it. One point at a time...."

"I doubt if he can count that high," Rostok observes.

New serve.

You never know which way to go off which wall. The players wary, alert, looking every way, dancing, lunging. Teitel fussing with the straps on his jock. Sells mutual funds and not too many, according to Izzy, who calls him Keitel the Prussian. Our Little Field Marshall. All he's got to look forward to eventually is the Social Security.

Kiddo there are winners and losers in this world, Izzy says, and Teitel may act like a field marshall but he's definitely no Marshall Field. He never even had a chance, so his feelings are hurt. What does he do about it? Joins the fixers. The race was fixed from the word go. Always after the buck, and look what it gets you? I'm no fan of his and the feeling's mutual, Izzy says.

It just seems to Peter that Rostok would be doing better without any partner. Teitel muffs every shot that comes his way. Covering Tumulty's court Rostok seems plodding, slow but authoritative because his opponents are scrambling to hold themselves together while returning each shot. An armadillo matched against squirrels....

Peter observes Rostok's glistening distension of belly move as he moves, like a warrior's shield in place, little rivers running off him when he lurches, a deep nasal bellowing, "MY BALL...MINE!"

Another sudden shudder as Peter remembers Piggy: Has the old man gone and told on Peter? Can he still be waiting for me down there?

The ball rebounds again and again. Against my better judgement, Peter adds.

Moving sideways or back to take a shot, Rostok makes noises like engine knock, and nobody even notices. They are too engaged by the ball, movements, steps. Now Big Sam underhands a shot up close to the back wall and pivots with it, sends it flying forward, like he's panning for gold and casting off the leavings. *Changa*!

Once, sharp-faced Tumulty reaches out to swing and the knuckles of his gloved hand rap hard against the cheek of his partner.

Pained, surprised, Rostok pauses, with hands to face, and misses the return shot from Teitel.

"Mind what you do with your hands!" he shouts, in real pain. *Der Obote* cries real tears, then tries to shake them off, and after a moment does and the game starts up again: 10-8....

Rostok's got a wet face. Where's the ball? It's rolling freely about in some corner, or what....

Rostok glances up at where Peter sits, and frowns, as though the pain on his cheek has raced up to between his eyes, and was even now too much for him to bear.

Then Tumulty starts and bends and finds the ball, and

lobs it over at the server, Teitel. Feeling reproached for being witness to Big Sam Rostok's discomfort, though not entirely unhappy with the sight of it himself, the boy sidles over toward Court #2.

Empty, it seems, except for voices, Izzy's and Umpapa's, and then he sees them stepping into the light before the front wall, like cave men, when they begin to slap and punch. They move with such a stiffness at first, stolid above their shorter shadows. They speak echoes from wall to wall: "Attaboy Iz sidearm on the forearm...."

"Like this?" Izzy grunts.

"More like this. Block the ball a little with your body, and swing like you're throwing a baseball. Like this...."

Umpapa grunts.

"I see...I see...." Thwack!

The ball rolling free again....

Once their moves increase, as Umpapa shoves his friend to one side like a swinging door to come in very close to make the shot, practically next to the bruised white front wall, and Peter is aware of his father's sudden burst of speed and grace, and the long tip-toe reach of his overhead slam, and of Izzy's awkward physical befuddlement. It's upside down altogether of what he's come to expect and imagine from these two figures, and when the ball rebounds high over Izzy's head, he's excited by his father's sudden prowess....

The ball continues to sail up inside the balcony where he's standing and rolls about beneath some seats.

Both men turn at once, and stare at him, surprised

they've had an audience....

"Hi Petey child," says Izzy, black and shiny, and squat, from above.

"Hi!"

"We're playing a game now," Umpapa says, "and if you want to watch OK with us, but be quiet...and would you mind tossing down the ball?"

"Find the ball and you can have winners," Izzy adds. "Hoopla!"

He looks beneath the row of chairs on which he sits, stoops, snatches up the warm black sphere which is so heavy in his hand it's a real surprise to him, almost like soft lead.

Peter fancies he can even make the grenade toss such as he saw in "Sahara." From sailing too high the ball caroms off the ceiling, and drops like a cue, bounces off a cuff of wall in the rear by the floor, and up toward the meshed iron ceiling, dropping down sharply now among the seats again.

"Attaboy," Izzy says.

"Peter just throw the ball straight at me," Umpapa says.

And Izzy: "You know how boy...come on now...."

He tosses it underhanded in a big arc that lands and bounces up, right into Izzy's outstretched hand, and then both men turn and begin the rhythms of their play again.

The two men are edging toward and away from each other like zoo chimps. *Amhara*, Peter thinks, they are playing showdown and probably cannot be bothered with the likes of him now, being so absorbed by their game. Does it really matter who wins? Usually Izzy says he couldn't care less, but now he's struggling to look like he's still in the game while Sam has it all over him in spades.

"Chuck easy Izz," Peter calls out, and his father wheels about when the ball rolls free and gives him a look that would freeze a radiator.

Big deal! Peter has his own needs too, a hot empty feeling in the kishke and light-headedness from all the sun.

"*Mapapa*, I'm hungry and also broke. Give me dollar...."

"Dollar?"

Thwack-bam!

"For to eat something...Situate my stomach...Actually two dollar, for the milkshakes too...*naneke adu ao*...."

"Speak English," says Izzy.

"Can't he see I ain't got pockets?" asks Sam.

"*Teeta Teeta*..." says Peter.

"*Magafa avi*," Izzy says. "Hoopla kid hoopla!"

"Boogie talk again! Dinge!" Sam says. "That's your doing Iz...."

"*Fo Fo Umpapa. Fo Fo*...and I thought maybe down-stairs in the locker room...."

"Our money don't grow on trees kid. You'll just have to wait until Izzy and I finish and we all eat...."

"*Nuka Yassa!*"

"*Nuke nele ga!*" says Izzy. "*Aloko* and *a bi gezunt!*"

Next door they are really beating up the walls. He can hear. All he wants now is a trip downstairs to the drug store with the soda fountain. To the springs...Bomba with his big python....

Sam's turned his back on Peter to begin playing again.

"*DOME DUGPO*," Peter shouts at him. "*Foufou!*" His father has his own ideas about food from being born in Russia. Hotdogs and hamburgers are just *nosherie*.

"*DOME DUGPO*," Peter shouts again.

"Ants in the pants," says Sam to Izzy. "Imagine...."

"So give him Sam. What's he got to wait for?"

"He's just making a pain in the ass of himself," Sam says, "as usual...when I asked earlier...."

Peter replies, "Don't hurt my feelings...."

"He's got a point," Izzy says.

Peter feels so *nwene*, and peculiar, he just can't hang around anymore and wanders back toward court #1 where Micky Rivlin has replaced Rostok.

Behind a film of tears, they seem as far away from him down below as though they were on the round eye of a Philco TV. For just one minute sometimes Peter blinks clear and thinks what it would be like to be Mr. Rostok, even poor Micky Rivlin. to know their pleasure, even their sorrows, he thinks. It would make him feel so much stronger ...apart from his own miserable feelings....

"WATCH WHERE YOU'RE STEPPING IZ!" he hears Umpapa calling out.

Rivlin, who has not even begun to sweat, is truly astonishing, so fast. He's everywhere on the court at once, with eyes glazed over, a little windmill of motions. He don't say a word, but makes noises in his throat, like a dog straining against his leash; nothing holds him from the shot.

Open-handed, he leaps tall buildings in a single bound, fleet, fantastic, this former handball champ of Brighton Private, and when the point is won he shrinks into himself like a prick in the shower until the next big rally.

"We've got them on the run," Kaiserhoff says.

"You and what other army?"

Micky shrinks a little more and then springs up larger than life against the bounding shadow of the oncoming ball, a three corner killer that drops down dead and rolls aimlessly beyond the reach of ants.

"Beautiful," says Peter. He claps from the gallery.

Beautiful, he thinks, is the thought clearing his mind of the bad words he had with Umpapa on the other court, until the gallery door swings open, and Big Sam himself emerges, removing the dark stained gloves from his hands, to become another spectator.

"You still up here boy?" he asks. He's got eyes. He can see. Knows the answer.

"I can't believe what I see," Peter says, pointing down toward Micky who has just walked up a wall at a 45 degree angle to slap a shot toward the corner for another drop dead killer.

"Remarkable," says Rostok.

"And is it true he gets $500 a month from the Army for what happened to him?"

"Sure. Maybe more. But you gotta remember in every other respect Micky's practically out to lunch...."

"How can you say that?"

"The Government will take care of him the rest of his life," Rostok says. "Got a silver plate in his head from Okinawa. One good bop on the *keppileh* and he's a gonna ...The Government knows...."

"Maybe he shouldn't even be playing?"

"What's the difference? He's got no family," Rostok says. "From me he won't even hear the ball scores...They gave him so much electric shock at Walter Reed he glows in the dark poor Mickey...."

Pity is like wasted motion when Rostok *spritzes*. He calls himself a realist. Once Izzy was talking with Umpapa about the pension he lost from Eggy Brammstein's and Rostok said, "Why not just go to jail Berliner? That's the only place you'll feel secure, jail or the grave...." But Umpapa says the big man personally owns two Congressmen and a lot of judges, not to mention City Councilman Fox.

He tries to recall the look on Big Sam's face when he got hit down below. The same look of surprise and anger Gary Brisken had from my beebee, Peter thinks. When Rostok weeps the world must pay somehow, sooner or later....

"Why you looking at me that way?" he demands now. "Micky volunteered. He thought he'd really show Hitler something...I guess. So Micky's Micky and Hitler's in the Argentine with the Baron De Hirsch people maybe. Look who won the war...there are no more Jews in his part of Europe...."

"No more Hitler neither," Peter says.

"Maybe so," Big Sam says, "and maybe not...it cost me $20,000 to save my boy with an appointment to West Point and when they threw him out for moral cowardice Mr. Hitler must have had himself a good laugh...At my expense."

"Be that as it may," Peter repeats.

Umpapa says Rostok had his son yanked right from a fox hole in the battle field to go to West Point, and it musta cost him a lot more than he admits. Would Sam do that for me if he could? Peter wonders about a father's love. What should it cost in dollars and cents?

Peter knows all different theories about the origins of
Rostok's great fortune. Izzy told him different things at
different times, such as—right after landing in Baltimore
he developed appendicitis and they had to operate. A
month later he was still big up front like a pregnant woman.
They operated again and they found a hand towel stuck
in his *kishkehs* saying Walter Reed Hospital. A smart lawyer
got the Government to pay up $10,000 in damages, and
he bought real estate for his parents in the New World.

"You and I get sick like that" Izzy always says, "it costs.
Rostok he makes a buck off *shvegern* from a bath towel...."

"He sleeps in shit," Umpapa would sometimes add.

Peter likes to think if there was a towel there, Mr. Rostok
probably put it there. Always looking for suckers....

He thinks of telling Rostok Piggy Baer is looking for him
to make a touch....

"I'm real sorry about Hitler," says Peter. "I was practically
just a baby when all that happened...."

"Thank your lucky stars," Big Sam Rostok says.

The game has started up again, fitful and frantic, a burst,
a stall, another burst, and Peter and Big Sam are sitting with
the gloomy silence of recent Jewish History. Peter calls
Umpapa Mr. Hitler sometimes when he's real angry and he
gets called "Little Mr. Hitler," and that's the way bullies
are. A little coincidence like having the same half-birthday
in April becomes a big deal McNeil.

The bitter taste of ashes in his mouth is what he gets from
arguing with Rostok and Umpapa. They always know too
much and don't play fair. Rostok probably had his reasons
for being mean to Sam. It's not his problem anyway. Maybe

just Sam lost his temper and was sorry later the way he is
with me, but it was much too late for Big Sam Rostok.

"Too much water has gone under the dam," Big Sam is
saying. "They made soap out of all my little nephews."

What am I supposed to do about that? He's got nothing
more to say to Rostok, nothing more he wishes to hear said,
which only gives him nightmares and night sweats.

Peter gets up out of his chair to leave.

Already, Big Sam seems to be dozing again, but he starts
when Peter moves, and slumps forward a little more. Has
he just dropped dead on me for good?

Peter comes closer, inspects. Such calm regular breathing
you could play marbles on his belly.

He peers down at this detritus of so much energy and
thrust: Rostok's massive snowy chest, the sloping outward
of abdomen, nest of coiled vipers bunching beneath the
waistline of his trunks.

"*Hey mister Rostok*," he whispers. "*Are you still here?*"

"WHAD DO YOU WANT?" The great body rattles eyes
the size of China agates his way and Peter doesn't wait to
reply.

When he exits for the stairs again the huge door slams
behind him like a gunshot.

LIKE A LOVER

Groggy, only half awake, before sailing with Izzy in first class on the Ile De France, Lillian sits on a sling back chair to be served bullion by stewards in short white jackets with tricolor stitches on their starched fronts.

It's a real hot day for a bon voyage party. Lillian wishes she'd ordered iced coffee from the gimp in the drugstore on the corner, like her neighbor Etta, instead of watery tomato juice.

"Wait till you see Gay Paree, the City of Lights," Izzy tells her. He's as bronze as a statue in his stark white jock strap, a billion dollar bulge below the waistline like a muzzled dog; the late shadows wavering across his handsome face darken his lips.

"Just so long as we leave Tar Beach right now."

A horn blares. The great ship rumbles against its prow. Her bowels churn. An orchestra plays "J'attendrai." Izzy crouches alongside her chair on all fours scanning navigational charts.

Now they are on a beach somewhere in Europe, or Long Island, maybe even Florida. George Bernard Shaw has just walked past in a one-piece bathing suit. Izzy is rubbing Jergens lotion on her legs. He bends and kisses her at the place where they meet, now covered over by her hand: "In dreams I kiss your hand madame. Your gentle fingertips...."

Etta sits on the other side of Izzy and reads *Woman's Day.*

LIKE A LOVER   189

If she had a twin, they'd be bookends, a soft muzzy soap-
stone face. "A spectre is haunting Izzy," she tells Lill.
  "What do you mean?"
  "Who else but you?" she asks. "It so happens Izzy and
I have an arrangement, but as he's still attractive and I'm
not, and never really was, he looks at you and zing go the
strings in his heart. You can't blame me for hanging on,
though, can you? Now don't let her burn darling," she tells
Izzy. "Rub everywhere nice and soft...."

Next they are at Big Sam Rostok's Testimonial and Izzy
has been just asked to sing "Hatikvah." His voice soars up
toward the crusted gilt ceilings in the ballroom, as Sam
dozes, with one cheek slap against his open palm, the dead
grey ash of a cigar flaking into his dessert dish.
  Something's wrong. Izzy's singing Irish by mistake:
The Rising of the Moon, A Nation Once Again, *Gewalt*...
Kathleen Mavourneen.
  Sam going through her clothes, and even her letters, and
dresser draws, looking for clues about this man she's been
seeing, and she lets him snoop because she can't say no
to anything now. She's also just a little bit flattered. He
cares so much?

And here we are in bed now and Izzy has just asked her
to take him in the mouth, and when she says Sam wouldn't
like that she's really worried on account of her root canal
work; will he come in her mouth? As she also doesn't
really like the taste.
  Will he come? Will he come good? And will she swallow?
Gingivitis. Her doctor says salt water and peroxide. Feh....

She wakes up on her elbows and returns to composing a letter to her brother Abe, the manufacturer, in Hoosick Falls, N.Y.

"Dear Abe my brother...."

When he was little Abe got infantile paralysis. Lilly practically raised him at her father's house until he met his wife, Sharon, married, and moved upstate. Now he runs a filling station, repairs cars, and manufactures Masonic key rings with Sharon's brother.

Sam lent him $500 to get started in the key ring business, and if she's writing now to ask for the return of the money, it's for Izzy's sake, so she can lend again. No greed there. For the sake of love, she'd really like to help Izzy out, if she can. The last time she wrote Abe about the money he replied with curses.

"Dear Lilly

I am not going to write you how stupid it was of you to make me such a letter, as your conscience has probably told you so several times....

Now Lillian, try to think back several years, when you was a pretty sick pup with pneumonia, and my wife Sharon by herself nursed you back to health up here in Hoosick. Yes, and I believe you're right my wife is stupid just for doing that, and I know she would be just as dumb to do it ever again for such an ungrateful person.... Truthfully, I am a loss for good words...."

When she told Sam, he called Abe "chiseler." She won't tell Sam when she writes again. Sam was like a father to Abe once. He even fixed up his credit rating....

Her elbows ache, and her forearms sting when she falls

back against them. Inside her head Lill commences to write a reply.

"Dear Abe

Never mind about the money which Sam lent you and you have never returned a cent, even though you promised you would, and we never asked...."

But, if she wants the money for Izzy, she'll have to ask without equivocating.

"Dear Abe

It truly gives me such pain to write you again about the money.

Our youngest son Peter is not and never has been quite normal. He needs the care of a psychiatrist for which I do not have the funds, and there are reasons why I can't ask Sam.... Please Abe, to a sister have a heart...."

She glances up toward the hot fire ball sun. Aside from distant traffic sounds welling up from below, the only sound she hears comes from the clicking of mah jong tiles where the *Rebetzin* plays with her circle of lady friends.

If only she could talk to Izzy now. He would know what to say to Abe....

It really doesn't disturb Lillian to tell a lie about Peter. It's not entirely a lie, after all. Peter really isn't normal. Lillian thinks Sam is much too defensive about the boy, and maybe she knows why....

It doesn't do any good to think like that. Sam doesn't really know. Only she and Izzy know. Sam thinks they're all crazy in the head those doctors. He would never let Peter go see one....

She tries to start all over again:

"If you only knew how unhappy I was already Abe, you wouldn't try so hard to make me unhappier...."

Now there's a beginning, she thinks. Abe never liked Sam, nor she Sharon. Lill preferred the first wife, Dora, a saint to early breast cancer whom Abe divorced practically right after the diagnosis.

He always was such a louse. No conscience. What's the use?

Lillian asks herself: Am I that unhappy? Was I ever really happy? *Where?*

She's got to admit she loved Abe once, almost as much as Izzy. He could be such a sweet little brother when she was nursing him well again....

The memory throws her into panic. She feels herself thinking, and her thoughts are without content. A hot dazed look on her face....

Lillian can't quite shake the memory of an afternoon in early Spring when Izzy took her up here on a slab before anybody was even out sun bathing. They'd met in the pool; Izzy wore nose plugs for his drip and a rubber thingy on his beautiful big head looked like a condom....

Nobody saw them together when he took her hand and led her up through the dark stairway.

He took her to the womens' side where the benches were so much wider. Afterwards they showered together, cold, clinging, close, for a long long time, and it was the best ever, until the sun started going down rapidly, and they were all pebbles....

"The world will little know, or long remember," Izzy said, some minutes later.

"What are you saying? What's to know?"

He said, "It's a Civil War we're waging you and me...
Don't you know? The animal the human," he told her, "the
human the animal Lill...Manassas Bull Run Gettysburg...."

"Does that scare you?"

"It makes me very happy and then very sad. I really like
Sam and the boy...."

She asked, "Do you want to stop?"

"Do you want us to stop right now forever?" she asked,
a second time.

A shadow crossed his face.

His eyelids blinked.

Izzy was shivering.

Izzy was crying.

"I'm being so silly because I love you," he said. "I love
you, like I've never really loved anyone before in my whole
life, even Etta... How can I stop? I can never stop now...
or ever...."

It was the first time he'd actually used that word. Said
Love....Lill was so frightened she started dressing right
away. She had dinners to fix, children to feed. And ever
since it was hit and miss, a couple of hours here and there,
meetings on trolleys and busses, in the private rooms at
Michel's, the bar opposite the Navy Yard, the Christian
Science Reading Room, his friend Eggy's flat in London
Terrace (Did he tell Eggy who he was with?) There was
never enough time to say love again, no more words between
them, as though he were running away from her all the time
with his goddamn love....

Once, over the phone, Izzy told her, "If I had it to do
all over again...."

"Not if! Please Izzy no!" She didn't let him finish. "Never

in my life! No!"

"Izzy," she cried out. "Izzy!" Well she'd promised Etta she'd never take Izzy away but did she say they'd stop seeing each other?...Impossible! Izzy on the phone to Etta: "Something just came up, a meeting, It just came up Etta," while smirking at his lap: "Couldn't be helped. See you later darling...."

Lill slaps a hand across her mouth as she feels Etta's weight falling against the slab, and her sigh, which is the introduction for everything inappropriate Etta Berliner ever asks, or says. "I could fry an egg on my tits...." Etta says.

"Two," Lill reminds her. "Two eggs," trying to keep alert.

"Thank God I still have two."

Abruptly, Etta asks, "Anything I can do for you Lill? Any little thing honey?"

A dull white skin like lard. Such a doughy unattractive woman this wife, my friend, she thinks, with strap marks all across her naked shoulders. She wants to say, "Jump off the roof!"

"Go away please!"

Lill says, "Pins and needles in my legs. I was dreaming again. My legs are fast asleep...."

She shimmies a little to bring back the sensation.

Etta says, "Izzy always calls that Seventh Avenue legs. Did he ever tell you that?"

"We don't talk that much Etta."

"You probably don't have to...do you?" She offers Lill a sip from her lilly cup of iced coffee.

"It clears the mind."

"I'm clear enough," Lill says. "I suppose you overheard?"

"I heard enough thank you." Etta sighs deeply. "Some

things just keep coming up with him. My magnetic husband
...Just don't ever lend him money...."

"If I could help I would," Lill says. "Why not?"

"When it comes to money," Etta says, "Izzy's still a
Communist. He don't mean to but he forgets...."

"That's too bad...."

"It's Izzy. It's his way. Money for him is *drech.* We're
all comrades under the skin, pocket books and all...."

"You make him sound dishonest...."

"I love Izzy," Etta says. "But honest is a different world.
Izzy may talk about integrity and all sorts of stuff like that,
but he really thinks different than you and me. He gave
away all my mother's money to the Russians when he was
supposed to buy her war bonds, and when I complained
he said he was saving Russian lives, Jewish lives, which was
better than keeping it under a mattress...."

"I've heard of worse" Lill says.

"I love Izzy," says Etta. "You won't hear bad things about
him from me...I just love him to death...."

"I'm real sorry for you right now," Lill says. "I feel awful
about us, for you especially...and I never meant it to be,
but if Izzy asked to see me, even now, in front of you, I'd
come running to him...."

"I know...." She's got the tears in her eyes. Dirty with
mascara. She reaches out to touch Lill, as though she were
petting her, and Lillian backs off, afraid for herself.

"Why does a woman like you need two husbands? What's
it like? You *shtup* one and think of the other? What are
you going to do with Sam? *and me?*" she demands.

"I don't know about you. I hardly even think of Sam
anymore...."

"Whatsa matter he don't get you hot? *What*?"

"I don't think of him at all," Lill says. "He's just there all the time...."

"What a pity. And Izzy? Tell me? You love him?"

She peers at Lill closely as though studying a result in agar, though surely not the cause. "Do you love him to death?"

Shyly Lill nods.

"Does the boy know?"

Lillian doesn't know for sure; she doesn't even want to guess.

"What does it matter?"

"The boys don't count. I don't count...." Etta shakes her head sadly. "A hot box is all that matters...."

"It isn't only like that," Lill adds, softly. She has no anger herself. She's been expecting conversations like this for some time. Sam too. He'll find out. If he has to... She was blue for three months when Izzy went to Spain and no explaining it in a pregnant woman. The same now... She knows she has responsibilities. She's not just being flighty. But to feel something finally for another person, and to be loved, adored... She can't just let it be like that entirely.

"Etta, if your Izzy was down below on the ground," not so shy anymore, "and he just like that asked me to jump, I'd jump right off the roof into his arms...."

"I know all about it," Etta says, "but you really shouldn't...."

"How can you say that? You of all people?" Lill asks.

Etta is smiling at her dimly through grey tears. "Darling," she says, "you must be reasonable. Izzy can't catch. He never could...."

"Butterfingers," she adds, big horse teeth showing.
"Always so, and always will be...Plain and simple butter-
fingers."
Laughing like it's funny when it's not....

A CONFESSION OF SORTS

It's 45 minutes later. Izzy and Sam, having finished their game, and showered cold, are splayed back out along the baking deck. The future is steam, and heat, hot showers, mustard, mint and honey massage, a shave, perhaps a final game of rummy, and a *shmoose* with the guys. For now they are baking again, loose, and limbered, like the other men, after handball, a cold gushing down across their shoulders on the roof. No time for goose-pimples, a sly half hard-on maybe, and a doze before the evening begins.

Peter has also returned, after a brief visit to the Women again where, once again, he was quickly expelled by Lillian and Etta.

Off to one side of the grown-ups he spits into the shower drain and watches for results. Thinks about angels. Are they former people with wings? Just regular people? Folks like you and me who have departed? Children with wings? The idea first or first the angel? He's surely love to know, just to see one just once, as Izzy promised....

Birds are twittering. The afterglow of twilight isn't awfully far off. Arty Katz, the bookie, arrives shirtless in Smiling Jack sunglasses to announce another Dodger victory; Reese hit three singles, drove in 5 runs for the Preacher, and Stankey, stinky little Stankey, hit an inside the park homer.

Rostok has bet the Dodgers for the pennant and seems real pleased with his prospects. He orders cokes from the gimp downstairs for all the players, and Arty, and a buttermilk for himself.

"Arty," he says, through creamy yellow buttermilk lips and mustache, "it's a good thing you don't have any family to support...."

The bookie's face inflamed, with acne, like a pineapple. "I'm covered all the way," he announces.

"Go take a shower," mother hen Rostok tells him. "A little soap for that greedy face...."

"Can I help it?"

"I'd recommend a short arm examination," Halpern says. All the grown men cheer "yea hooray for Arty...."

Peter thinks an angel could look Rostok straight in the eye and be even more beautiful than the Memsahib, lovely, lovely beyond compare, and winged, like the creatures on the Sanctuary ceiling. They would shine down upon him and be gracious unto him with love and understanding. Not like Umpapa. Sam The Man. Sam What Am, Sam too busy to give me the right time of day, as Mammileh used to say. What does he really know from angels?

Umpapa and Izzy are all alone again, acting exclusive; in a far corner of Tar Beach, they sit on towels. They've not yet showered and shaved, or shampooed themselves; now they are resting, slouching, with their faces cast up at the sun, spillways, run-offs.

Izzy has just borrowed another $500 from Sam, which means two or three months later maybe he'll pay back, or indefinitely, or just until his next commission check, Peter can't be sure which, and Umpapa still wants to know, in a nice way, how Iz'll ever pay him back all he owes because there was the money for Etta's milk farm last year too....

"I may just have to do some concertizing in the mountains again," Izzy points out, by which he means a weekend or two at a hotel singing "*Belz*," "Black Magic," and "June in January", and fucking his brains out with *mieskeits*.

Needless to say this should all remain confidential. Sam is not to breathe a word to Etta. They have an 'arrangement', sure, but she gets jealous whenever he goes off to the Mountains "with those tramps."

Etta in the dark means Izzy is truly grateful for "the monetary help" and "keeping it on the QT", an essential for "domestic harmony Sam...."

From the back, hiding behind Izzy's reflector, Bwana Solly Cohen looks like the devil with wings coming out of his ears. Still trying to get his money's worth from the sun.

With a towel scarfed across his shoulders, Mushy approaches their bench. "Come to think of it," he says, "I have the impression you guys are in utter ignorance about all the landfills East of Flatlands Avenue...."

"Mush if you don't mind this is a private conversation," Sam explains.

"Please forgive me," says the little man, with a bow, as he backs away again, like the waiter at Joe's after he gives you your table. "Matter of fact, I was just about to leave...."

"Not to be disparaging," Izzy says.

"What's the difference? Sometimes I think his brain is mostly landfill." Sam frowns.

"Would you believe," says Izzy to Sam, changing the

subject by picking up from where he left off before asking
for the loan, in the middle of nothing, "a grape the size of a
plum flown here from Lisbon, Portugal, to New York in eight
or ten hours? Also Belgian endives. Melons. *Pajaritos*?"

"Chickens?"

"Little swallows skewered," Izzy says. "A delicacy...."

"Must be an awful lot of spoilage,"

"Not with refrigeration...."

"Expensive?"

"A penny or two more...but you make it up at the point
of sale...."

"What's in it for you?"

"For one thing I could stay out of trouble, and out of
Etta's hair. Chaperone sort of," he points out, "I know my
Iberia...My Uncle Phil also had vegetables and I used to
help out...."

"Must be awful hard on the seat of the pants," Sam
replies.

"They call it commission broker but Eggy says...."

"Eggy this Eggy that," Sam says. "No more Eggies please
...What about Etta? What about the High Holidays Iz?"

"Just making small talk conversation," he replies. "It
was an idea Eggy gave me I was just playing with...The
swallows won't catch on just like that any way...."

"Eggy shmeggegy," Sam says. "Some friend. He never
paid you what you were worth...and when he had that
bucket shop on Nassau Street everybody took a beating.
His best friends...."

"He's in business to make money Sam...."

"Well, no skin off my ass," Umpapa says. "You don't
seem like no commission broker to me Iz. Anyway, what

can you charge for sparrows?''

"I guess not...."

"Who's guessing? I know...."

"Anyway," Izzy says, "I'm no businessman. I'll survive ...without Portugal or Spain...and thanks to you Sam...."

Silence, the twitters from starlings aroused in the park by waning daylight. Arty does sit-ups, his face as red as raspberry jam. Rostok dozes again. Micky Rivlin mouths a muted "O Suzannah" on his harmonica. "The West's awake," sings Izzy through the side of his mouth.

Sam says, "You'll drop by the office Monday or Tuesday I'll give you my personal check. No strings, only try not to make a habit... You ought to be thinking about putting some money away for the future...."

"How am I gonna do that on what I make?"

"Maybe I can cut you in one of our deals someday," Sam says. "You could use Etta's funds. Meantime no more borrowing after this...."

"The last time I swear," Izzy swears. The sun blazing forth one final spell before it starts to swing downwards to blaze off other buildings makes him squint. "I promise...."

"I'm not asking for promises. Just don't give me from sparrows, or rabbits. You've got a God-given gift...."

"It don't pay."

"So I'm your patron *nu*?"

"You're a true friend," Izzy says. "I shouldn't be telling you this, but I will. It's to get a lady fixed, *kalyeh machen*, a scrape job...."

"So if Etta knows," he adds.

"It ain't for me to say," Sam replies.

"Etta is a real trusting person," Izzy says. "I'd hate to

lose her trust over an *abortnik*, a story...."

"What story? About the money? What trust?"

"What price glory?" Izzy says. "The scrape. I mean the woman I told you about...she needs my help...."

There is, of course, no woman this time and no 'spoiling', nor scrape job needed. Without such money Izzy will lose his car and TV to the Amalgamated Bank which is why Etta especially shouldn't know. He's been thinking about it off and on all day. One bad season....

He adds, "Everything's kosher. The doctor has a degree from Vienna...."

"No license?"

"Not at the moment." Izzy clears his throat and thinks of using what's left over to buy Etta something personal, maybe freshwater pearls.

With saliva Peter draws Spitfires and Messerschmidts in aerial combat. One plane dives low dropping bombs like turds. He wishes he could hear better. Izzy looks so worried, like he's sitting on the can pushing.

"So many women you've told me about," Umpapa says, "For that alone you ought to be ashamed of yourself. What falls into your lap at the showroom is one thing. But this woman with a husband is a genuine slap in Etta's face...."

"Something happened over lunch," he replies. "I couldn't help myself...."

"Something always happens to Izzy...."

"For better or worse," his friend adds, glumly. "We both couldn't help ourselves...."

"It seems to me you've helped yourself to plenty," Sam says. "If it was my wife we'd have it out in an alleyway somewhere...."

"She isn't anything like your wife," Izzy points out. "A one-night stand. No more...."

"So hit your head against the wall," Sam says. "It can't hurt you any worse...? He's broke and he's buying scrape jobs for someone he hardly knows? Sir Walter Raleigh," Sam adds, broadly.

"I'll never understand what gets into me," Izzy nods. "Do you?"

"Me?" Sam is exaggerating with his shoulders, his eye sockets suddenly deep-bitten behind glasses. "I don't see what I got to do with your bad habits?"

"Don't you ever look elsewhere?" Izzy peers hard at Sam's back, and sees his Peteyboy drawing what looks like something between a woman's legs...with a Spitfire coming out of it....

Sam Pintobasco, attorney at law, is not given to confessing much of anything in the presence of his sons, if ever. "*Der yinger*," he says. "*Zog nisht*...."

"I don't care if you look, you two," says Peter.

"You shut up," Sam says. "This is not your business."

"He means no harm Sam," Izzy says. "Neither do I...." He winks at Peter: "We're strictly tribal stuff here, boychick, millet and maize...*dibi, maffe, yassa*...."

"*Yassa yassa* let's all shut up," Sam says. "Let's all do ourselves a big favor and all shut up until the ladies are ready to leave...."

"Starting when?" asks Peter.

"NOW!"

Umpapa's shoulders droop and he falls flat against the deck once more.

Izzy whispers, "Thanks again for the help Sam. You're a true friend...no questions asked...I don't underestimate...."

"NOW! I SAID NOW!"

Sam slaps his hand against the deck.

Izzy whispers at Peter. "Your father is a friend and a half," he adds. "I don't underestimate...."

"IZZY WILL YOU STOP EXAGGERATING?"

"He's also modest," Izzy whispers.

Then Peter starts to sing:

"She had 29 Cadillacs

29 sables from Saks

29 fellas who never had their arms...."

"Boychick," Izzy says, "why not go sing in the shower?"

He's coloring a lady's face with spit. It's the lady, Izzy's friend, with the husband in the alleyway. Suddenly Peter gives her a scrape job with the blade of his palm and she disappears in a wet blur.

Umpapa says, "Life is not like the Exchange Buffet. Some people don't like being cheated Izz...."

"I promise you'll get all your money someday," Izzy says.

"I wasn't worrying about my money. I just don't want you evicted...."

"No chance."

"Well don't try singing for your landlord," Sam says.

"Where's 29 Palms?" Peter asks.

"In Miami I suppose," Izzy confesses.

"Do you need more? I'll make it a bigger check," Sam says.

"It will suffice for now," says Izzy. "Three hundred for the doctor, and two hundred for overnight in his clinic ...My conscience will be clear...."

"CUT THAT SHIT OUT! TIME IMMEMORIAL IZ SHUT UP!" Sam says. "CAN'T YOU BOTH SHUT UP?"

Peter spits on where the lady's face was once to make more color. "There," he spits. "I told you so lady. It's all your fault...."

He starts to get up.

"I'm sorry kid of mine," Umpapa is talking softly, gently. "I've been trying to grab twenty winks and I just lost my temper. You and your Uncle Izzy...The scrapes he gets into...."

"Sam!" Izzy's blushing. Flustered. Peter has never seen him this way before. "It's not for the boy's ears. It's not his business Sam...."

"I should say so," Peter replies.

"So at least," Sam says, "tell me the lady's name...."

"Out of the question. Come on...."

Sam shrugs. Micky switches to Clementine and Izzy starts to sing:

"In a cavern
in a cavern
excavating for a mine...."

"The last time he hit me was for root canal work," Sam says.

He winks at his son, and closes his eyes again, looking very pleased with himself for giving such a good lesson to his son in what his "Uncle" Izzy is really all about.

SEVEN

DOWNRIVER

On the high plateaus the distant Moon Mountains wear a fringe of snow. Mist clings to cliffs, trees, and waterfalls.

Um Peter descends to Kampala which must be a lot like Memphis, Tennessee, where all Memsahib's relatives still live, only a lot blacker, probably, and dustier. As Solly Cohen might put it, "*Shvartz*!"

Peter sees his big fat cousin Katey holding baby Ralph on a porch before a latticework arbor. Heat wilts the puffed sleeves of her frock. She's grinning right at Peter's face, as though he were a camera. Won't he join her with Ralphy for a nice cold glass of lemonade? A Doctor Pepper. Stop your crying child....

"Mississippi water ain't for drinking," Katey says. "A Pepper or a Cola make you feel a whole lot better...."

When he asked his cousin Katey why she sounded so *shvartz*, she told him that was just Southern talk. She could put it on or take it off, like her shawl, she said, but all Peter saw was an abundance of bosomy arms, the big wooden ceiling fan turning slowly, churning dust motes. Coils of fly paper dangling....

He settled for a Nehi orange and the promise of a trip to his Uncle Ben Frankenstein's sausage factory in Yazoo City.

Once, when Katey was nursing Ralph and the smells were milk-sweet in the heat of the porch behind the hollyhocks and sweet tea roses, he asked Cousin Katey if she knew what Egypt was like.

Katey shrugged with her eyes closed.

"Have you gone up?" he demanded. "Been to the Holy Land?"

She shrugged again.

And Peter asked, "When Cousin Jep went into you he knew you, did he not?"

Which stirred Katey a little, though she did not respond directly.

"Boy," she simply said, "Land of Moses was Egypt. Memphis is named for such a place in Egypt because of the River, the Mississippi. It musta looked just like the Nile ... Green and muddy, hip deep muddy from Cairo Illinois on down...and as for the rest of your questions I don't know what they tell little boys in New York City but hereabouts we call that *shmutzik*, and a boy can even get his mouth washed with Ivory soap, if he ain't careful...."

She was switching Ralph from bosom to bosom, softly and gently, so he would not be stirred to cry out, and wake Jep who was sleeping off a night of 'bowling' with his friends.

Memsahib was visiting with an old beau and his wife. It was very hot that day.

Peter said, "It's so hot I can't help myself...."

"Don't even move," said Katey. "That's the only way...."

"Cement mixer putty putty," he replied, still as mud, thinking again of the big river, and Mud Island which he'd been shown only yesterday, with Arkansas on the other shore.

"Moses was a little lost boy in the bullrushes," Peter said.

"The Egyptians made our people lay bricks without mortar...."

"It's hard being a Jew anyplace under the sun," Katey said.

"Was Egypt almost like Hitler?"

"It ain't that simple. It's never really easy," said big fat Katey with her milk smell. "Egypt was like Bilbo for the *shvartz* but Hitler, everybody he hated, his own people, and worst of all Jews. I could live with Bilbo, but not Hitler. The same for Egypt, I suppose."

He has dreamed a lot of Egypt ever since he went up to Memphis, on the headwaters of the Nile.

He dreams a lot of a heat so sappy and thick, like syrup on his pancakes, a brown and glowing heat, like the sun in old photos.

Dreaming of running water always means Peter pissed in bed. He pulls the needle of his piss back inside his bladder. He can hold it a long long time if he has to, like in cars or on the train, but at night sometimes the river runs freely against his will.

Downriver to Memphis, Peter is supposed to be going again, for the Jewish High Holidays, to the Land of Cotton. Days of awe in the City of Memsahib's relatives, eland and waterbuck, his ancestors, Mem-Phis, away, away, away down South....

They will be taking the Dixie Flyer on the Southern Railway in a Pullman by night, with a dining car by day, and the men in the Smoker all flirting with Mammileh, and buying him and Benjy treats. Grits and bacon and all those smiley black faces *Goydedooda day*....

Inshallah. They'll arrive at the old Union Station, Uncle
and Aunty will be there, Katey and Ralph, and Cousin, or
is it Uncle Ben, from Yazoo City, and he will be pulled away
after hugs and kisses by fat Viola, Katey's maid and former
mammy, to a sandbox in a backyard to play with all his
littlest cousins while Memsahib calls her old beaux, readies
herself for a round of parties, late night darky jazz shows
on Beal Street, and Umpapa must stay back in New York
City with his closings....

Um Peter really likes old Memphis by the big river.
Though it is as hot as Tar Beach, maybe even hotter, when
you sit under a big cottonwood tree on the banks of the
Mississippi the whole colored world struts by, like marching
bands, and Viola sings in her big loud voice:
     "Big fat momma
     big and round
     Big fat momma
     coming to town...."
Fafafoom. Big muddy river and the taste of Aunty's fresh
eggs, which have a bite, Viola's peaches in violets, and when
she sings to him at night with Mammileh gone stepping she
sings peach songs specially for him:
     "Don't sit unda da
     peach tree
     wit anybody else
     but me
     anybody else but me
     anybody else but me
     no no no"
Viola's big voice, like hardballs rolling in a barrel:

BIG FAT MOMMA
BIG AND ROUND
BIG FAT MOMMA
COMING TO TOWN

She sings blues, Izzy songs. Makes him think of Izzy when he's far away..."Don't the moon look lonesome shining through them trees...."

Once, in the middle of the night, he woke with a nightmare piss iron and it had him scared stiff it was so hot and stiff, and when he got it soft again he went into Aunty and Uncle's room, and they too were lying stiff and silent, just like mummies while, down by the river, a boat horn rocked the levees: NA THA BO NIM BO NIM....

He thinks Memphis is a place where a boy like him can behave because people just aren't so respectable down South. *Na Nanana*! Aunt Katey and her Jep do it every afternoon at Siesta and Uncle Ben in Yazoo calls his daughters "sweet stuff" and "Bonny Roo." He calls his wife "Okra" because her name is "Cora," and the pretty colored girl who cooks he calls his "Sharon Eileen."

In the cool dark stairwell Peter sits on cold stone as though he's stuck in the middle of a rapids. The walls are slammed again and again by caroming bodies adrift at handball, and he smells the sweat of bygone games mixing with honeysuckle and magnolia, and Viola's Cashmere Bouquet when she bends to tuck him into bed at night. Constant reverberations through the walls of feet and bodies crashing together, where Umpapa's handball buddies cavort in twos and foursomes, pull him back from the White Nile again, and the long slow dark river down south bends and twists ahead of him....

"GOD DAMNIT!"

Somebody crashes against the wall, and shouts, and bounds back on to the court again.

Katey would call such language uncouth, maybe *shmutz*, and Viola would say "rude talk."

Umpapa and his buddies play and talk that way all the time. They don't know shit from shinola about being rude.

Just thirty steps down from Peter is another floor where in the old days when he was six he was taught to swim and play water polo by Tobias, the Hungarian, as soft and sleek as a dolphin, but Peter has been staying away all summer long from the pool because he knows that's where the Memsahib and Izzy sometimes meet, as Sam is afraid of the water, and it's better all around if they aren't putting on a show for him all the time.

Besides, the chlorine makes his eyes all red and sore, and he feels like a garbage can, so wrinkly, as though in danger somehow of rattling, falling, or even drowning.

He edges sideways, a step or two further down, and then around a bend in the stairwell, where light streams suddenly down from a window onto all the dusky darkness, as in a church, or a movie theatre, and he is thinking of floating as a baby boy on the belly of Tobias in the chemic green waters, as lovely golden-haired Miss Eleanor Holme, assistant to Tobias, urges him to "kick kick kick Peter kick," — and she's so pretty with her bubbies floating half above her straps sometimes he calls her bubbies names, sweet names, like toffee and cookie, says "I love you love you Eleanor," and when she laughs he's so ashamed he's sitting on the toilet, and...and wait a minute fella. What's this? What's he seeing now? Can it be? All the way down below? *Mecheieh*?

It's as though a match has flared and then almost gone out
again before burning slow and bright. Hot. Ten feet away,
no more, Peter thinks he can almost touch this angel.
It's an angel for sure, this little naked person like himself with
long blonde curls and angel eyes.

The wings are folded back, of course, out of sight, to make
room for passage on the stairway, but she is slim and angelic,
with gold dust in her hair, a radiance of aura about her. The
most beautiful soft and golden shoulders, and a behind
too....

What she doesn't have Peter takes no notice of, at first,
and when he does it's more like a dimple he never even
thought of before, much less seen, and he can feel all his
bullrushes exploding with orphans: "*Vos machstu shaney*?"

Izzy's words but he likes to say them nonetheless.
"*Shaney*," he says, "*shaney*, you must be sent straight from
Heaven above."

"Don't be so primitive."

Like flickering candles, her image fades with her words
and grows vivid once again; she climbs a step or two up
toward him and the light pouring some sort of heat down
against his face. "You're a key where there are no locks."

She comes even closer into the light like water held in
place behind glass. "With us it's very simple. We don't
believe in disappointing kids, or spoiling them. You asked
so you got."

"And I like...I like," Peter says. "But how did you ever
get here?"

"I don't travel by the IRT," she tells him. An Iriam smile

like Miriam makes his ears burn. He wants to praise. Wants
to adore.

Little bit of honey. He wants to touch, too, but holds
back.

"My name is Peter."

"Surprise me."

"What's your name?"

"Jezebel."

"I never heard a name like that on a girl."

"As I live and die. You can just call me Jezzy. My parents
named me Abby...It was either that or Adrienne after
Grandpa Abe. Or Jinja because of my hair...."

"Blondie's nice too," Peter says.

"Too *goyische*...your mother's name is Lillith...?"

"Lillian."

"Big difference. She wishes you were born a girl...."

"Cheese it! Nothing we can do about that now."

"Not the way you're built."

And when she shrugs her naked shoulders the light is
almost blinding like the little ring inside the bulb that glows,
or maybe flash bulbs going off. He says, "Can I love you
Jezzy?"

"Don't be silly...."

"So maybe I love you already."

"Love?" She seems truly dubious. "Love is not natural
Peter, like they say in all the songs. It's something you have
to learn...Let's just say you're interested...."

"Very! Very interested."

"So maybe I'll call you Moon Mullins cause you got such
a pretty round face kiddo...."

"Please don't call me that."

"Moon Mullins? Your mother thinks you got a pretty round face, and should have been a girl...and she don't like being on the bottom anymore...."

"Leave my mom outta this. It's kiddo I mind," he says. "That's what Izzy calls me."

"So? Who gave him exclusive?"

She's laughing and he finds himself laughing too, and then he wishes he could sing for her, as Izzy sometimes does: "Love can make you drink and gamble/stay out all night...."

"Personally I'm not impressed one way or the other by Jewish men. How about we do something together?"

"Like what?"

"Something absolutely blasphemous," she says. "What else?"

She waggles a finger, turns, and starts to walk on down, and, sure enough, he is following her.

Seen from behind she is really half his size, a candle flame, thin, bowing out below the waist, with her small round buttocks, that seeming silence tucked below, and no wings. No wings anywhere that he can see, just long blonde curls adangle above a wiggle. Shelagh from the river Shannon. Or *shaney*. A sheeny wouldn't do....

"Where are your wings?"

She stops, and turns again.

"You do have wings somewhere?"

"Everybody always thinks they want wings," Jezzy says. "Wings are like white wall tires. They never got anybody anywhere. Good angels or bad...."

She says: "Hot makes me perspire...." With a little bump and a grind, she adds: "*Visen is Glusten*! Knowledge is desire.''

"What?'' For lack of understanding he offers her a look like he's swallowed too much water in the pool. "What are you talking Shaney?''

"You and me,'' softly, "and Izzy.''

He's blushing. Benjamin told him once how Izzy's Sigmund died when he was so little he never even went past kindergarten. He was overweight, Benjamin said, and a cry baby "with a strawberry birthmark on his ass just like Harry Halpern.'' Peter can't remember knowing about Harry Halpern's strawberry and he can't remember if he ever met Sigmund. He remembers a baby crying once in the car when they were all driving to Washington together. It could even have been Peter.

"Kindergarten's dismissed,'' Jezzy taps him on the shoulder. "This isn't school Peter so please don't daydream.''

"As you've plainly noted,'' she adds, "curiosity is our chief asset. Mine and yours.'' She wiggles again. "Show business means no *shtiklech*. Being pre-pube, we could do it all we liked and never even have babies....''

"Ain't it a shame,'' she adds, and, turning, starts on down again.

He thinks she is probably being very naughty but he loves her as he has never loved other girls he's seen. She moves beyond cobwebs with undulating grace, so pretty, clean, and small he must have made her up. To be standing about like him, without a shred was certainly something he'd made up a few times before, but what about that honor roll smile? Those perfect white chicklet teeth? That mouth

...Such a personality, he thinks. She could be in the Movies or on "Quizz Kids," or "Let's Pretend." When he asked her where were her clothes, she said, "Don't ever expect to get a boner from me. I'm a lefty, too, only I don't happen to have a *haccent* like your uncle Izzy and his friends...."

"You know Izzy?"

"I knew his son Sigmund a whole lot better. Siggy and I were made of the same dust and therefore equals. Ever hear of Medranov?"

Such a mouth! "Where?"

"G.N. Medranov," Jezzy says. "Like Olgen, a deep thinker, and certainly not Party Line. He was the salt of the Earth to Izzy, once upon a time. But Siggy that's another story. Izzy felt nothing for the boy compared to how he feels about you...You want to swim?"

"Na...."

"How come?"

"I'm good just the way I am...."

"Your whole face is a mess with tar," she says. "You need a wash...."

"Later," he tells her, "please."

"Well don't do it for my sake. I won't be impressed...."

"I promise later."

They've stopped in half-light again and Peter feels his eyes upon her belly, and in between her legs, and maybe even the spaces in between her toes, and so does she, it seems, because she says, "The Medranov faction resigned from the Party in 1939 over Hitler. They would have been expelled anyway for adventurism...."

Then she notices his adventurism is getting out of hand. "Peter when I said no boners I meant no...Equals, got it? Knowledge? Desire? Just forget about gender. This is not show business...."

"*Shuldik*," he says.

"Sticks and stones," she replies. "You can do better than that. Think of your aunt Etta, or someone else. Or count up to ten. Or make a *shimilecha* on the old man's back...a simulacrum...."

"Where?" he asks. "Why?"

"Sacrifice," she urges him.

"That's my whole life this summer...."

"I'm not just talking about a little ass." She turns away to show him just what she means and he should bear it in mind.

He follows her then.

They have passed through the vacant gymnasium with its flying rings and pulls adangle, mats bedecked with clumsy weights, and sleek wooden indian clubs strewn about like duck decoys, tiny dumbbells, dynamic tension coils, so now they are standing in the practice golf room among autographed photos of Byron Nelson, Bobby Jones, Gene Sarazan, regular restaurant window.

There are group portraits of the wrestling and basketball teams in repose, and a photo of Izzy and Sam together as college boys skulling in Sheepshead Bay in Anshe Israel sweatshirts. When Peter swings a club face against the tiny red balls the soiled old cushion mats on the wall go Wack Bam!

WACK BAM! Caps exploding....

In the alcove Jezzy spins on the horse.

"*Maron*!" she says. "Madonna! Nothing for kids to do in this whole goddamn place except jerk off to High Heaven...."

When she dismounts he thinks he sees something cut on a bias. "Hey."

"Mind you don't look!"

WACK BAM! he answers her with his club.

She's standing by a closed glass case full of trophies: Micky Rivlin's handball cups from Oriental Beach, and squash trophies from the time of Abraham Abraham's young manhood, a big tarnished loving cup with ears of gold and silver inscribed to Tobias Kovack for Graeco-Roman wrestling, and another smaller soft-boiled egg-sized cup for the "Coney Island Olympiads, 1907."

"What about big Sam Rostok's truss?" she asks. "They could have it bronzed like baby shoes...."

"Be careful what you say!"

Peter is thinking about Izzy's army joke: A man tries to get out of the Army by borrowing a friend's truss. Next thing you know he's in the camel corps in Africa. When he demands an explanation they tell him anybody who can wear a truss backwards should serve in the camel corps in Africa....

Peter goes WACK BAM again.

She stands in the doorway framed by vestal gloom, her face smiling, radiant for him like Ebbets Field just before a night game.

"Izzy's funny, I know. But should that suffice?"

WACK BAM says Peter with his mouth, and almost drops his club.

"First they learn how to swing a club," she says, "and

then they move out to Long Island... It's happening everywhere you look...."

Peter drops the club upon the thunky mat below his
feet. "Izzy says that's not for him...never!"

"Izzy prefers up down up down on the bed," Jezzy says.
"If you ask me Izzy's got you and your mom over a barrel
emotionally...."

"You shut up!" His ears are red hot coals.

"Objectively speaking," she adds, "he's a flop, a failure...."

They're down below, near the synagogue offices: Rabbi,
Cantor, sexton, trustees all closed for the day. They've left
behind only their fading photos under glass, a brown shot
of the original Temple site, a framed blueprint from Rostok
Construction for a Memorial Hall to the six millions in the
parking lot. All the rest are gone gone and gone again. The
slow season upon us, right before the Days of Awe, when
God seems to have abandoned all of Park Slope and Crown
Heights to heat and dust, and then twilight and dusk and
his parents' dressing up for the evening's activities, cards,
movies, whatever.

Last summer Izzy and Aunt Etta and his parents went to
Zionist camp for two weeks with the kids and harvested
tomatoes, musk melon, onions. In Heightson, New Jersey
there was no lake and late into the night he saw fireflies
and heard the adult voices arguing with the crickets about
"the new State that would be" on the rec room porch
beyond his bunk.

He heard the man from Palestine with his funny British
accent denouncing "terrorism," and pleading for support
in "British Yiddish," as Izzy joked later; and when Izzy

asked about the "condition of the natives," he was lectured over *tsimmes* at the dinner table about the wicked Mufti in Jerusalem and his Nazi friends, and the man said Socialism doesn't mean we should all slit our throats for our Arab brethren.

Then Izzy said his feelings were hurt for being so misunderstood and he went off for a walk with Etta and Lillian while Sam played cards with a man from Milwaukee, but, even later, Izzy sang "*alenu*" and "Bandera Rosa" and "Red River Valley" for the people at the campfire, and Memsahib danced with Etta and the older women. O beautiful in the firelight....

"Are we being nostalgic again?" Jezzy asks him, suddenly. "*Gib noch a simon!*"

She would have a sign from Peter. If blushes could blister, his face would be all puss.

Izzy a failure....

She has moved beyond his sight toward the Robing Room, and Peter will follow her once more. The stairway brightens when they pass the Hebrew School walls plastered over with children's drawings of Joseph and his brothers, the coat of many colors, Jonah, Noah, the story of Esau and Jacob, FDR and Eleanor.

The air so chilly as they descend past the Annex for the High Holidays dark as his momma's walk-in closet; and he thinks again of his naked self hidden in furs, a second skin of some sort. Jacob and the sweaty angel.

In Memphis momma went with Cousin Katey and Aunty Pin to the Luxor Baths. I was not allowed. Of course....

"Because you got a teeny weeny," Aunt Pin said.

"It's so small who'll even notice?" Aunt Katey teased.

"Never you mind," his mother said, only last summer in June. "He's at an age...." She didn't have to finish. His feelings were definitely hurt. He stayed home with Viola and Little Ralph in the sand box.

They have gone down as far as the stairs will go, and are standing on marble floors before a huge brass door. Bitten brass letters spell out SANCTUARY. "Your momma got to have a life of her own," Viola saying, "Pretty woman like that she need to...."

A push away is the chilly marble steps, a vast darkened hall with plush seats, the painted ceiling beams recessed with graven images dropped from the Bible—or beyond— of the building of the Temple, of Lot's wife, Aaron and the Golden Calf, the Tower of Babel.

There are slim white angels with flaring fiery wings above him everywhere, slaves with inky shoulders, Nubians and Samarians, camels and lions, a wilderness of dunes, palms, oases, ponds where Israelites drink prostrate in the desert, then the great arc on the stark marble bima with the Ten Commandments cut out of mahogany, a ruby drop lamp glowing with Eternity, directly ahead, resting inside a clos- ed coffin of cedar woods, the little stiff puffy body of Abraham Abraham beneath a couple of overhead spots.

Hatishpa! This is the hallowed place, hot in the summer, cold in winter, stuffy with furs, Chanel no. 5, and warm floating farts on the High Holidays when the congregation attends. Air biscuits, Izzy calls them, though now it's cool and dark, mostly reeky of disinfectant, and an afterburn of incense.

The ceiling is a place of dreams. During services he has kept from dozing by keeping his neck cricked up until it ached, and during responsive reading he would mouth words of his own making: "I will adore thee ever loving fool! God of Abraham, Isaac, and Izzy...."

Jezzy's smile is frozen water. She enters naked on tip toes and he follows her on chilly marble feet to where the light is brightest from overhead spots set above them.

The large covered coffin of dark wood with silver handles sinks among heaps of flowers, like a giant pressure cooker on wooden horses, before the bima, arc and pulpit, and Peter thinks of his mother, over her stove, when she turns the brisket, her face lost in steam, and immediately hears Jezzy again.

"Wouldn't you like to take a peek?"

"It's not allowed."

"Who sez?"

"God sez so...."

"So what? The facts of life."

"But this is death."

"So? That's part of life too...."

She walks among the glistening banks of white flowers beckoning him on, and before he can say another word she's released the hinges and is raising the pot cover, her face lost in blossoms....

In the strong overhead light of the bima a face as white as a Yartzeit candle. Abraham Abraham is a little pocked beneath the eyes like tripes, and his set lips seem to reproach the floral fuss surrounding him.

"These old fashioned German Jews from Brooklyn Heights always look like great big dolls," she says, placing the coffin lid down against the marble floor with a clang.

"He never was very big," explains Peter. "When I was 7 I almost was his size. Must a worn Adler Elevators...."

Side by side they peer down into the casket.

Dressed for Eternity in a morning suit of striped trousers and a cutaway coat, Abraham Abraham seems to peer down at his pince-nez which dangles on a black ribbon across his vest so that it glitters coldly back up at the viewer.

Adorned on both lapels with sextant and T-square, he's been slipped inside a handsome doe skin vest with side vents about his middle, and sports a wing collar and a lavish large grey silk four in hand tie with a pearly Lodge stick pin. On his feet are black shoes with smoothly polished tips, wraparound spats. He holds between his hands the Jewish Bible.

There is the same grumpy look on his face he used to wear when seated on the bima during services. A little puffy face with a white brush mustache, as though he can't find where they put his glasses, or is dissatisfied with the state of his health, all these arrangements for his public viewing.

Standing so close to this waxy little man in his great boat of a casket, abandoned to wreaths and floral tributes, Peter feels himself in a cold shrivel, peers up at the ceiling where Moses just clopped a rock with his staff and made Vichy water gush forth.

The smell of flowers rotting overwhelms their perfumes when they come closer to the casket.

"Death is really crass," says Jezzy. "...Am I being too blunt?"

"Just a little, and I like it. How is it with you?"

"I sure as hell wouldn't trade places."

They laugh together, but Abraham Abraham remains mute. He was never much of a regular fella, Izzy says.

Peter thinks death doesn't make us all that sociable. It's as awful as they say, if it looks like this.

"It's not supposed to be any fun," she says, as though reading his thoughts.

Peter was reluctant but he said, despite himself:

"I love you Jezzy."

"You only think you do."

"Suppose I think I adore you?" he asks, "like Van Johnson. What then?"

"It's fine with me. Just don't confuse that for honesty. You adore your mother and she's chippying with every guy on the roof...."

"Shut your trap!"

"Honest Injun."

"Don't say that!"

"If you don't want to know the truth," Jezzy says, "turn off the radio. My mother was no angel either. None of us really are, you know. It's a woman's way, Love...."

The dark humid reek of lilies almost overwhelming. Above them, the choir loft, a vented cage where two carved lions face each other with their paws raised. They wear crowns, as in the story books, above a pair of sliding doors which Peter recalls the rabbi opening with a pull cord, and golden light invading the Torahs and all their silver ornaments.

In those days Abraham Abraham always slept more soundly in a high-backed velvet chair upon the bima than in his mansion on Jerolomun Street. One year he cut himself shaving and there was a little stickum plaster on his face throughout Kol Nidre. It was Indian summer. A black fly kept buzzing his face in search of blood, but he seemed to doze between attacks.

When the chords of the great organ woke him with "Rock of Ages," the old man stood up and slapped his hands together like a cymbalist and the fly vanished. Umpapa told Memsahib, "Next year there should be air conditioning."

"What's the matter," she asked, "the flies can't stand the heat?"

Jezzy circles the casket like Izzy and Sam window shopping for new cars. "Does it come with white walls?" "A heater? radio? What about service?"

"Personally I like the 4 door job with the V 8 engine...."

"What? No trade-ins?"

She stops at the feet of Abraham Abraham. "This is the LaSalle of corpses, the Zenith," she declares. "If you're thinking of high performance...."

"Not funny McGee. It just isn't right making fun," Peter tells her. "He's dead and really can't answer back...."

"So?"

"He'll be in the ground by tomorrow. Let's show a little respect...."

"You're such a good boy...."

"I try...."

"If only they knew upstairs."

"Don't you dare tell them."

"Who? Me? I'll never say...."

Her grin is her farewell. She mounts the bima, is standing to one side of the big mahogany pulpit: "It's the end of an era I tell you...."

"He really was very old," Peter says. The air smells of lemon wax.

"Down with capitalism," she declares. "Down with the bosses with the big bellies...."

"He never ran the stores. He jut clipped coupons," Peter says.

"Sustained by the sweat of his workers...."

She starts to sing:

"None shall push aside another"
none shall let another fall
Stand beside me o my brother
all for one and one for all...."

She has turned her slim marvelous back to Peter, finds the velvet pull chord, gives a yank. "You can tell by the doors," she says. "Most of the new cars sound so tinny...."

Light swells against the silks and silver of the unevenly-sized family of three Torah with their large crown finials of silver, bodies of gold embroidery. Peter blurts, "Don't touch...."

"Give me one good reason why...."

"Because you're naked. God will see...."

"God sees right through my step-ins," Jezzy says, "God has x-ray vision...."

"You're a girl...."

"Boy girl, is that all you can think about?"

She reaches inside the arc and removes the smallest of the Torahs, cradling it like a babe in arms so that silver decorations tinkle. Approaching the pulpit she starts to

nasalize: "Shield of Abraham, thou art holy and thy name
is Holy and they who are Holy Praise thee daily. One bull,
one ram, seven sheep and a *katchka* in a pear tree...."

"That's all mixed up together," Peter observes.

"Duck soup just like Sarah Rachel Rebecca and Leah
...Wanta buy a duck?"

"Rostok says all women are *kurveh*."

"To him they are," she says. "A girl's gotta make a living
when she's on her own. But did you ever hear of Ruth?"

"Wither thou goest?"

"And it should also happen to the Capitalist State," she says.
"At which point we have a dictatorship of proletarians...."

"What did you say?"

"Wither," she repeats.

"I'll keep on trying," she adds. "That's a yuck. You get
it? *Fort Tryon Park*? *Town House*? *Tannhauser*? *Withering
Heights*? Pass me a pointer and we'll read...."

Suddenly the hall blazes with light. "Jesus Mary and
Joseph," Peter shouts.

"GET DOWN OFF THERE YOU...."

"HOOLIGAN WHAT ARE YOU DOING?"

This outburst comes from all the way down the aisle
of pews at the entranceway to the Sanctuary. Standing
beneath the balcony Leo Treitner, executive secretary and
sexton, has his hands on his hips, and his sleeves rolled up
to the elbows of his white shirt, a bird of paradise on his
tie knotted into a windsor between his open collars, and
perched on his brow a little white skull cap with the candel-
abra logo of Fruchtman Caterers in gold.

"HOLY HOLY HOLY," Trietner shouts. "SACRED!"

"Crap," Jezzy says, "I thought this was a reformed *shul*...."

"I'll fix everything," he yells back. "Don't touch another thing."

Treitner comes charging down the center aisle toward Peter who finds himself with two hands around the Torah facing an irate shamus. Trietner's shirt is soaked through, his heavy eyebrows dripping sweat.

"So what's the big deal?" says Peter. "Jesus Mary and Joseph, she don't even menstruate...."

"*Vos hot er gezoght?*"

"Bleed," says Peter. "She's just a little kid like me...."

The shamus examines his state of nakedness and dirt and shakes his head, sadly. He takes the Torah in his arms and places it back in the arc, pulls the velvet chord, and the lights go out when the doors close.

"You're coming with me, Mr. Rostok and the other trustees they got a right to know about this...your family got a right to know...."

"Please don't do that, please Mr. Treitner...."

The shamus is irate: "This is a place of worship, not an amusement park...."

"She just wanted to show me something."

"Stop that *she she* business," Trietner says, as he grabs the boy's forearm so tightly Peter feels his knees begin to tremble. There's no place else to run or hide. He reaches out with his other hand for Jezzy's hand, and she can't be reached. A vanishing radiance, and he's pulled by Treitner down the bima in the posture of a supplicant. In the blood-red glow of the Eternal Light he freezes, and feels a string inside him loosening like someone just yanked on his pajamas real hard. Before he can say "Excuse me" Peter is dribbling all over the marble steps.

"The most High bestows gracious favors, BWANA PISCHER," says Jezzy. "Hasten Jason Get the Basin! UMGAZU!"

"Somebody get a mop," shouts Treitner, as he leads Peter across a rivulet of pee down the aisle toward the great brass doors again.

Where are we going?

What is my sin? He sees his father's fist, his mother's look of rage. Izzy always appeasing Sam: *What did I do to be so black and blue*?

Treitner leads Peter to the elevator where the janitor stands with his hand on the lever. "There's a puddle you need to clean up right now in the Sanctuary," he instructs the fellow as he pushes Peter inside and grabs the lever. The chain link door is squeezed closed. They are rising up up and away....

Trietner tells the janitor. "The undertaker's men should be coming to take Mr. Abraham until tomorrow...They should have been here hours ago. Be sure you let them in and give them a hand...and close that coffin!"

"Yas boss...."

"O LORD I HEARTILY THANK THEE...THOU ART ALL POWERFUL TO SAVE," Peter's thinking: "GRACIOUS LORD O PLEASE...MOTHER MARY FULL OF GRACE," while they continue to ascend, past the white-jacketed caterer's men setting up for the *harabee*, until, stopping at last on the sixth floor, the gate is pressed back, racks of bleak steel lockers are revealed, endless processions of drab olive boxes on boxes just like at school, only larger, and a zooey smell everywhere, dim yellow lights hung from the ceiling inside little bird cages, the clatter of dropping shoes and gushing showers, cries, alarms, the snap of a towel against flesh.

"You have to be spoken to," Treitner says, "a boy like you, while there's time...."

"To tell you the truth," Jezzy says, "That's not a bad idea. I been in a lot of funny places in my life but this is the first time I was ever inside a men's locker room...."

"Will you shut up?" Peter says. "He can't hear you. Nobody can...."

A man in flip flops rushes past, wearing nothing but a towel, belly abulge.

Without further resistance he (and she?) are led by the hand down a cavernous room between aisles of lockers until they come to an open area where a number of the grown men lounge, covered only by towel skirts, or peering at themselves in mirrors, or shaving. Peter thinks of the big apes grooming themselves in Tarzan land.

"What have we got here?" Big Sam Rostok asks, supine against a wicker chaise lounge.

"I caught him red-handed desecrating the Sanctuary," Treitner says.

"Me too," Jezzy puts in. "And don't forget it."

"Hey come on girl," says Peter. "Quiet down!"

"Boychick is this true?" Izzy appearing suddenly from nowhere like rain in the 4th inning. Umpapa nowhere to be seen. God be thanked.

Peter says, "I don't even know what the word means...."

"It means making number one on the bima," Treitner says. "That's what...."

"Nerves," says Jezzy. "Just nerves."

"Leo, calm down all ready," Rostok says. "It ain't the end of the world. Somebody call his father from the steam room...."

Peter stands alone, abandoned for a moment, with no place left to hide. It's gonna be pillar to post this time. He's sure of it. It really feels just like the end of the world.

A radio clicks on.

"What will I do Little Nick?
Here's what you do Mr. Quick.
Just drop in at the nearest Nedick's store...
For vigor and vim and zip
it's a pleasure to take a sip
of a cool Nedick's orange drink...
Be one. Nedicks...."

Rostok says, "My old friend Marty Glickman tells me they found a guy pissing into the orange drink at Madison Square Garden...."

"Is that really true?" Peter asks.

He can't believe stuff like that. Tastes so cold and fresh.

Mr. Rostok ought to know, but he really just can't believe it?

"Why would somebody do such a mean thing?"

"Y is a crooked letter," Rostok says.

A door slams; a naked man appears.

And Peter prepares to greet his naked father and the fully dressed Treitner with a declaration: "It was an accident...."

"*Vos?*" asks Sam.

"I didn't mean to do nothing. Mr. Rostok knows a guy

who deliberately pissed into the orange juice at Nedicks...."

"In a manner of speaking," says Rostok.

"*Vos?*" goes Sam again.

"I'm innocent," Peter says. "An accident...."

"More or less," Rostok adds. "As it were. *Comme ci comme ca!*"

A COURT FULL OF KANGAROOS

It's now Bulova watch time five PM. The balance on the big white porcelain doctor's scale, recently vacated by Rostok, trembles toward lopside in the torpid locker room air like Justice unbalanced. A rich crematory smell of roasting beef rises from the caterer's ovens on the ballroom floor and mingles with piercing wintergreen and soapy shower odors inside the commodious locker room.

Izzy starts to sing:

"When we Jews awaken
to the smell of frying bacon.
Grits and syrup on the table,
and a greasy slab of sable...."

"Shut up Berliner," shouts Rostok. "I want to hear the news."

On Harry's yellow Emerson news mostly is of ball scores, twisters in the Plains states. Harry Truman has been visiting his aging mother in Independence Missouri. British authorities in Palestine will be hanging two Jewish terrorists and deporting three others. The Reverend Adam Clayton Powell Junior is organizing a protest.

Lillian and Etta and the other women are even now upstairs, in the locker room with dusty mauve walls, powdering their bodies, their breasts and large soft padded fannies flailing when they move to inspect themselves before one of the fogbound full-length mirrors. Yetta-Thelma takes a Schick injector to her prickly underarms. Downstairs, the air chokes on talc, the viscous smoke of Garcia Vega naturals. Izzy will not be deterred:

"Mr. Frog went a-courting and he did well
yo ho yo ho
Mr. Frog went a-courting and he did well...."

Summoned from his wooden perch, prone, midway up the far wall of the vacuum-proofed steam room, Sam Pintobasco appears without a yoho, rolled up inside a towel like a Roman senator. First Halpern whispered: "*Der Shammes iz dort gekumen*," and he was on his feet before he could even ask why. Now, in the cool minty air of the locker room, he's the color of a small parboiled russet potato, his gnarly knees and fine slim calves the stems on cocktail glasses. "Sword and *petzel* by his side," Izzy thinks, but he keeps quiet.

"*Gai gezunter hait* Leo," Sam says, "I haven't got all day. What's cooking?"

The crust of drowse about Sam's eyes breaks open when he sees his naked son being thrust forward for his inspection by the fully dressed shamus, all in a sweat. He stretches out one sweaty hand against a locker, to stay himself from dizzyness.

"With such a millstone around my neck should I be studying Torah?" Treitner asks. "Is this your kid Pintobasco?"

"The only kid," Rostok says, wearily. "All goddamn summer long."

"Piece of cheese and a lemonade squeeze," sings Izzy. "Kiddle eat ivy...."

"Cut it out!" Trietner says. "I ain't kidding...."

"A *mentsch* and a half," Izzy says, "What does it matter this sexton can't keep track of the petty cash... and drives a new blue sedan. Nicer than Sam's or mine."

"Hold off," Sam says.

He's misplaced his glasses. "*Vi zinen meineh brilen?*" He's asking of the heavy air near the steam room, salted and balmy with sweat, herbal Aqua Velva, Wildwood Cream Oil, delicate Lilac Pineau, as Izzy mumbles, "*Menschigaboola* ... The saints preserve us...."

The best he can, Sam examines the scrawny figure of a quaking boy pushed toward him by the shamus, as though he is not really sure this really is his own son Peter. Such a filthy *ponim*. What's he been up to now? Waterbags from the roof? The coal shute in the sub-basement?

A midrash group of naked men, creamy with self-importance, has formed behind Treitner: Halpern, Solly, Anuskiewicz, eternal commentators, cluckers of the communal tongue. "What now? What's this? *Vair vaist?*"

Such a summons from his place of steam at such a moment can only mean trouble for Sam, thinking of his election tonight and possible advancement. He feels this dim anger at Treitner for interrupting him in his mental preparations (he was making notes for a speech), but is not sure how exactly to behave now that he's been brought forth.

"What's going on here?" he demands in the responsible voice of a trustee.

"Behold this *goniff*, this hooligan," Treitner says, still sweating heavily.

"Mr. Treitner is really not a physical culture person," Rostok laughs: "The sexton is here on Temple business Mr. Presidenke...."

"It's your boy," Leo explains. "You've got to discipline him . once and forever...."

Being sure to seem always subservient to this trustee, and potential President-elect, Treitner nonetheless tries to sound suitably indignant: "If a child has an evil impulse," he points out, "our sages say he should go to a place where he is unknown, wrap himself in black, and do just what his heart desires...."

"Leo I'm sweating and I'm cold all over with goose bumps and I can't find *di brillen*. Come to the point...."

"Piece of cheese and a lemonade squeeze," Izzy repeats.

"Your son has committed sacrilege, and that isn't very funny Mr. Berliner." He talks at Izzy but obviously means his words to be heard by Sam: "I found him fooling with them Torahs downstairs. I had to evict him, naked in the sight of God...."

"I wanted to see for myself what God wrote," Peter says.

"Liar," Jezzy says. "You were just being nosey like me...."

She's hiding behind Izzy's naked leg which has been wrapped up mummy-tight inside an Ace bandage coated with Ben Gay, her knees locked tightly together, too, with her small legs and hands hiding the wens and fens of her privates.

Once, some years back, Izzy recalls, he spent an afternoon with Ada Treitner, Leo's war bride from Norway: big hands and feet, and when she came she sounded like Ma Rainey. As Rostok put it to the guys once, "Mister Izzy is like the *Parents' Magazine*. Always trying out the toys for all the fellas in advance, but he never tells afterwards who should be a bride and who shouldn't...."

Izzy warns his friend: "Don't listen to this crank...."

"Any fool mocks understanding," Leo snaps back.

Izzy starts to speak but Sam says, "*Haltzichein.*" He holds him back.

Treitner has lotsa fog in his spectacles and his face looks like somebody has just taken a styptic pencil to his lips. All white and scrunched up, a prize fighter's eye. He is innocent and simple, but pompous, disapproves of nearly everybody who doesn't wear *tfillen*, but he wishes to remain employed so he'll compromise up to a point: "Please Mr. Pintobasco, you must keep this boy under lock and key. I have a body on my hands down there could be desecrated and the undertaker's men are late in coming...."

"Did you do all these things Peter?" asks Sam.

"It's only kid stuff," Izzy says. "Nickels on the railroad track...."

"A synagogue is not a locomotive Mr. Berliner," Treitner points out.

"He's no goddamn shamus neither," Izzy replies.

His Ace bandage comes undone. He wouldn't mind one of Rostok's panatellas but would never ask. Pride...Peter hears his father's voice like metal being banged and twisted.

"Shut up Izzy. I'm talking to my son." Sam wraps a patrician inside a bathtowel banded with the blue and white stripes of the Hotel St. George pool: "This sounds like serious business...."

"What Treitner don't know about kids he'll never learn in this locker room," Izzy comments.

Immediately, Harry Halpern tunes down his Zenith, and Solly puts the jar of Vaseline he uses to oil his eyebrows after a day at Tar Beach to one side. They are both expecting hellzapoppin fireworks about the corpse. Like race horses at the starting gate, caught between a snort and a whinny.

Izzy is thinking about Ada Treitner. She put eye make up on her nipples, and rouged her cheeks the color of persimmon flesh. He should have tried again some other time. He will try again now: "Must everything sacred be kept under lock and keys in this *shul?*"

"Viva la quince Brigada," shouts Jezzy. "Long live the sailors of the Potemkin!"

Cute kid I got my boy, Izzy thinks: a *shaney* all right....

"Answer me Peter," Sam says.

"So I had an accident. I peed on the bima...Only Number one...."

"You what?"

"It happens," Jezzy says. "Nerves. He couldn't keep it in...Through the form of a beautiful female many are destroyed...."

She faces Izzy: "And you Little Father, turn your eyes from your neighbor's wife."

"Gotta hand it to that shaney," Izzy says, bending over to refasten his bandage, and Peter, momentarily grateful that someone else is aware of his companion, thinks he hears Izzy humming.

"The Jacob's Ladder," he says. "Sing Jacob's Ladder Izzy please...."

"If you ask me that's like Esau and Eyore," says Jezzy. "*Kimoshe anu.* Different Indians mean different things. Friend or shithead. Take your pick...Stolen waters are sweet and bread eaten in secret is sure enough pleasant...."

"Would you please mind your own business?" he demands.

"Don't talk to me that way," Sam says. "I'm your father...."

"A likely story," she blurts. "As Izzy says, God is dead and everywhere men are in chains...and his mother ain't the Virgin Mary."

"Don't talk to him that way," Peter says.

"I see it doesn't take too much to make you feel guilty," Jezzy replies.

"Come here son. Right now, come over here...." Sam points like a recruiting poster.

"*Heynani!*"

Sam has stepped closer. "Give him to me," he says to Treitner. "Come here sonny...."

"In my *shul* I don't want this happening again," the shamus says.

"Bad enough bodies left above ground...."

"You can depend on it," Sam says.

"I got caterers to see to, 300 couples expected, and the beef is running tough...."

"Tough beef. Tough shit." Izzy says. "That's the ticket...."

"I have to be this way," Treitner adds. "I'm responsible...."

"Property is theft," mutters Berliner. "What's the difference? To keep his wife from chippying he bought her a new washer-dryer."

"Just forget it," Sam says. He stares at his son.

Peter knows what to expect next, an upraised hand, a shout, sudden blow, and cannot back away. He must comply. "Come here," his father says, as he steps closer.

"Sam," Izzy pleads then, "the boy meant no harm...."

"My boy Izzy?"

"If you like," says Izzy, cricking his back up straight with a grunt. "You know what I meant. We both love the child...."

"You're making a fool of yourself...." Sam's teeth are clenched inside his jaw as though he's just come from a session of root canal work in the Henry Street clinic. "Shut up Izzy just shut up!"

"But after all," Jezzy says, "Izzy is almost like a father to him...."

"Don't you talk fresh to me!" Sam grabs the boy, but does not strike him. He pulls him trembling to his side. "Never you mind Leo," he says, "I'll take care of this. I'm sorry if he caused you any problems. The boy has his problems and he's sometimes a big problem to others...."

"I'll say," Rostok shouts, echoed by a tuba fart from the chaise on which he now sits up.

"As I live and die," Jezzy says, behind Izzy's leg once more.

She starts to sing again:

"None shall push aside another
None shall make another fall...."

"Beethoven," Izzy exclaims. "*Dein nomen grois gemacht!*"

"Cut it out," shouts Peter from the clutch of his father's hands.

"Cut it out Uncle Izzy. Can't you see my father's angry at me?"

"If you know I'm angry why do you do such things?"

"Why?" Sam shakes the boy. "Why?"

"How should I know?"

"That's a *meisseh* if I ever heard," Jezzy says.

"It's true. When I see things they upset me so I talk to

myself and tell him I could learn to be good if we only tried a little more," Peter explains. "Do you think I wanted Uganda? It felt so bad to me, the whole thing, but I wanted to know a lot of things...."

"Know what?" asks Sam. "What do you think you want to know?"

"That's really the problem once again in a peanut shell Umpapa. I don't even know what I wanted to know. It wasn't dirty. I told myself Izzy and mom...."

"That's what you wanted to know?"

"So I told myself," Peter said. "I shouldn't know, it wasn't right to know, I should try anyway, we all should try a little harder, and then I knew anyway because I have eyes, and Izzy sings so beautiful in the Annex where momma goes...But it really isn't right me knowing all these things...."

"It is *not* right, you're right," Sam says. "Much obliged. Tell yourself that and it will all go away. Pretty much. I know, I'm your father, and I promise...."

"I tell myself that too," Peter adds, though he is still not convinced. "Do you think it makes a lot of difference?"

"Listen to me," his father says. His eyes are very bloodshot, and he has a famished look on his face, popweed capillaries in the temples. Sam wets his dry lips with his tongue. The moment of danger is at hand. The other men, who have been staring at the way the floors are kept, now check out the ceiling for plumbing leaks.

"Listen to me once and forever. Listen, and don't ever talk about that stuff with your mother!"

"Don't worry. I have a mind of my own."

"Whoever said you didn't?"

"She must know I know anyway," he says. "I've seen them both...together...."

Then he's shaking and feels himself being shook very hard by Sam. Shaken and shaken but not yet walloped even now. Shaken until his teeth knock together, the blood rushes with pins and needles in his head.

"Are you listening? Do you want to get hurt? Drive me crazy?"

Another hard shake, the world starts spinning. A twister picks the dust up from the veldt, blows it down across the high ridge country of Uganda, and he's got blood in his eyes with polka dots, can't quite catch his breath. All the loose parts a jangle.

Peter shakes his head as though he's been hit, he nods, as after a blow. He could even be nauseous, but he won't be, if he knows what's good for him. The world is slowing on its axis once again. He reaches out and holds himself against the cold flesh of his father's chest. "Much obliged," he says. "If this keeps up, I won't be responsible...."

"A boy only has one father and never mind what Izzy says. Izzy don't pay your bills. Izzy is all talk but no action...."

"Don't be mean to Izzy."

"Izzy should know better. He was our friend. Is this what we deserve? We take you to this nice place? Teach you to swim? Send you to camp? Answer me Peter?"

"I'm sloppy and shiftless, a shirker."

"Always. Exactly," Sam says, "against my better judgement." And then he stops himself from saying more. They are no longer talking, even touching.

Apart from him again, Sam looks like a big cotton rag blown against a wall somewhere in a windstorm.

"Shirkers of the world unite," says Jezzy. "Jepthah was a mighty man, and he was the son of a harlot...."

"She should talk," Izzy thinks. "Jean Harlow."

Standing with the others, trying to be only as conspicuous as a caper in a plate of salad, Izzy laughs softly to hide the pain around his heart.

He wishes he could bleach into the walls, feels dismissed, put down, the dunce in school again, though no longer in jeopardy as he was feeling just a few moments ago. Izzy can't explain why in words, but it's a relief all this father and son stuff. Sam isn't saying to his son Lill's a whore; he's just saying put it out of your mind.

A shmear job, a cover-up. It makes Izzy indignant to think of Lillian as whore. Why her? *Why not me?* he asks himself. Women are always called names for doing just the most normal things, he thinks.

A normal woman, he believes, who needs loving, and cuts herself when she shaves beneath her arms, and often has cystitis. That Ada Treitner she was a whore, probably even back in Norway, but he tried to be good to her until she started worrying about Treitner finding out.

"I've always loved and respected your mother," he wants to tell the boy (and Sam) also, but holds back in front of their friends and Sam. Now let me die for I have seen Lill's face of love, he thinks.

"What I don't understand," Sam is saying to his son, "what did we do to make you so unhappy? So naughty...."

"Boring! I felt bored...."

"At camp you were almost homicidal."

"These kids nowadays got it so soft," comments Haplern.

"See you all later," Jezzy says.

The feeling of loss is dark, sodden hunger pains. Peter would definitely like to punch somebody back in the face, Halpern, Treitner, anybody, he thinks, or say something, like what Izzy says about his mom and other women all the time. That she's the best, a true *shaney*. Power over wild beasts." How do you like that *boychicks*?"

Peter is shaking just to think such thoughts by himself. He searches the room for Jezzy's sweet angelic face and it is not anywhere anymore. Nowhere. Nothing. No more. Now. A big hole in the afternoon... the air like plate glass windows.

He knew then he would never see her again anymore. Lost forever. Dreadful sorry, but he's not really ready for what Izzy and his *shaneys* do together.

"Go into the shower," His father says. "Wash. Your mother and I will have something to say to you later...."

"And Izzy?"

"Forget Izzy now," his father says. "Wash. I'll have a talk with Little Mr. Izzy. You'll see...."

He's standing all by himself again as his father leads Treitner and the other men into a small corner room to talk confidential. Buzz Buzz, they are talking so he can't overhear. He can't see Izzy and he's lost Jezzy forever. Like being told prove you exist. A wicked child hardens his face....

Peter says, "I didn't mean no harm. I still love Izzy and Uganda... my whole life long... not just you Umpapa. Sorry about that...."

"He breaks my heart," Sam overhears, "and then he says he's sorry?"

"I really am sorry, but I still love Izzy. You'll see...."

"I'll see?"

"Because Izzy may be a big failure, but he treats me like a son and I don't have to be good all the time just to get his love...."

His father is in the room next door so maybe he can't hear, thank God. But Peter has certain things to say to the whole world. For all he cares. It's a free country after all. "Izzy likes me. I really like Izzy...."

"Have a heart," says Rostok, who has never left his chaise. "*Shah*! Your own father boychickle is not like a trade-in on a new Eldorado Caddy...Go wash your tears and your *shmutz*, and relax. Your dad has other things on his mind. You're lucky boychickle I'm your only audience."

"You and your beefcock and your bathtowel. You and what other army?"

Kindness from Big Pockets he'll never get used to. The garbage can is more accepting. Rostok never owned me, he thinks, but he's also got shares in the Syndicate.

Seeing him makes Peter want to say the worst things of all, piss and shit, *even*, and true things too, like *shtup* and scumbag. "It's all your fault anyway," the boy says. "They were getting along just fine. You gave my father dirt. Gave him the air...."

"I got a new lawyer," Rostok says. "It's my privilege...."

"You really made him feel bad you know...."

"I did what was right for me and my investors," Rostok says. "You'd do the same if you were in my shoes...."

"Charity begins at home," he replies.

"*Nu?* Why not?" Rostok shrugs. "You got a big mouth boychickle....and good instincts. Don't argue so much.

Anything else on your mind?''

"Izzy's really Mr. Fuckherfaster," Peter says. "And Mammileh likes it a lot. I've seen her...And you should have heard the look on their faces...."

"Seen?" Rostok asks. "I probably did. That's been going on such a long time it's got *payis*. It really ain't nobody's business anyway boychickle...what two grown-ups do is what they do. Believe me. I know. I was young once...So long as you pay your bills...."

He gets up with his *shlong* pendent like hernia, and takes Peter by the hand and leads him into the shower and mixes hot and cold water taps until they are lukewarm like spit, and then pushes Peter gently under. Says, "Nothing like a warm shower to wash away your cares and worries and all boychickle...Men and women are always doing things like that. They always are. The laws of attraction. You'll see. They can do worse. As you say, it's a free country, in the bed and out...."

And only when the water falls across his head and shoulders, and he knows no further physical harm will come to him, does the dirty thinking stop. Rostok says, "Someday you'll do it too...."

He musses Peter's wet hair.

Alone, and safe here, like Bomba in the Cave of Falling Waters, Peter thinks if Sam did not hit then, he won't hit now. Maybe he really didn't hear? He probably knows anyway. Rostok knew. Everybody knows. The talk of the *shul*...The shame of it. No wonder he got a shaking... No pillar to post this time, just hurt looks, anger, the world shaking beneath his feet, and a face like he don't really understand even now. He that keepeth his mouth keepeth his life. Things that get all stirred up eventually have to settle.

Peter lets the water turning chilly beat into his flesh, and feels the sting of the sun numbing, easing. Closes his eyes and makes whipped cream in his hair, just like Izzy, with the Creco soap; and he's thinking back to that time at the Roadside Rest when they were all so close, he and Izzy and the Memsahib.

It was after his second frankfurter when Mammileh and Izzy stood together smiling at him and then they were all inside the same cabana putting on their bathing suits, and Mammileh was behind the shower curtain, and when she came out he thought she was prettier even then Rose O'Day, and she said to Izzy if only she could lose five pounds and get rid of her stretchmarks, and Izzy said, "They make your skin look just like satin;" and she blushed and he blushed, Izzy suddenly smiling so sweetly so full of joy and asking him, in Yiddish, "Do you know you have a beautiful momma?"

"*Seist du mein kind was far a shaineh mamileh du hast?*"

Izzy shouldn't have said that to him, even in Yiddish. He was saying too much. It made Peter feel so *nweny* again as far as Umpapa was concerned. So sad for Sam. Sadder than he'd ever felt in his own life. And he told his Mammileh, "Don't you even feel embarrassed?"

"What have I done? Why should I feel that way?"

"Izzy and you," he said, "and me...."

"Izzy is like a brother to me." "I'm almost like a father to your," Izzy said, "an uncle....I'll watch you grow up and I'll be proud...."

"Izzy loves you," said the Mammileh.

"I'm almost like a father," Izzy said. "Believe me. You can call me Uncle or Little Father."

He was sweating, his face very red. He really only had eyes for Mammkleh. Because they're doing it together. Everybody knew. Rostok, maybe even Treitner....

Beyond the crashing of the shower, his father appears in the doorway again. Steam clings to his hair. He looks the way their dog looked that time when they left him out in the rain. Maybe Izzy's Sigmund was dead and his parents were comforting the Berliners. A condolence call. Pretty soon they forgot all about the dog steaming in the rain.

So now Sam stands just beyond the splashing, like he's collecting rain checks, and he seems so wet and wrinkly, like rags. Is he still angry with me? He seems to be inspecting, flesh and bone. I'm almost like a son to him....

"Wash good," Sam demands. "Your momma wants you clean and neat when we go out on the street. A little *mensch*!"

Maybe clean and neat means the cafeteria tonight, so that Peter has escaped the worst again. He'll be alright now until tomorrow. Piroges and sour cream, ice tea with lemon in big cold yellow glasses slide right out of your hand, maybe coconut custard pie, or Boston cream, with strawberries on top. The big blue seltzer bottles, and the little jugs of red and white horseradish.

Summer's ending soon and the hot days and then Dixieland and Memphis, maybe Uganda back again. She'll be so good to me if Izzy the Flop is not around to flatter her all the time, and so will he, Umpapa, when we get back home to *shul* for Yom Kippur....

Peter starts to sing:
"Don't despair
use your head
save your hair
use Fitch shampoo...."
"And be sure you wash your *hinten* too," Umpapa adds.
"*Ma poppa*," he assents. "*Dugpo. Umgazu....*"
"And no more silly talk...."
"I didn't mean what I said about Uncle Izzy...."
"That's really not your business Peter. Mind what you say," Sam says. "Sing all you like but mind what you say...."
"*Mpapa....*"
"Mind," Umpapa says.
"But Izzy," he says. "*Uncle Izzy....*"
"Don't ever call him that! Never ever call him that to me again."
And long after the little man has disappeared behind one of the rows of lockers, Peter continues to sing:
"Don't despair
use your head
save your hair
use Fitch shampoo...."

FUGITIVE THOUGHTS

Izzy also hears Sam's words. And Peter's. He's right next door in the toilet, crouching like a catcher, a woman giving birth in a field. He's been taking a shit and there's no paper to put around the seat. The other stall is empty. No more than a *petit bleu* of paper there either.

Izzy feels a little let down, a little sad, heartachey, "*noch Siber in Kalten nord*," but is still trying to be careful about some things. What's the point of talking with Sam now? Having it out? He's lost everything, Lill, Peter, his hopes, everything. "Never call him that again!"

He pushes at his bowels. Goddamn Treitner goddamn ignoramus bringing things to a head like this. Not only Sigmund is *not*, Peter is *not*....

Basically Izzy's in hiding, on the crapper, as though expecting a posse to come arrest him any minute. The charge: adultery with the wife of a trustee...Worse, betrayal of a friend, of love itself perhaps...or maybe just being a perfectly sincere phoney, of a sort. Regular playboy, as Etta says: The morals of a Socialist "where love and money are concerned."

Behind a copy of *Jewish Affairs*, the world is dying, though not entirely without new *chochmes*, fantasies of hope and safety, whether false or not. Izzy can dispense with personal depression eschatologically.

His pamphlet-sized magazine may be about the same

scale against his hands as *Reader's Digest*; socially it's so much more responsible.

Editor Morris Shnink is presently discoursing on the possibility of a revival of Naziism in the two defeated Germanies.

The coated page of his little pamphlet is splotched with drops of Izzy's perspiration. He's also running at the eyes, he notices. Doesn't want to be seen this way, but can't finish, stop, wipe himself even.

Shnink believes the German national territory under the control of Britain, France, and the U.S. is highly likely to become a hotbed again, especially the Ruhr valley, and Bavaria. He favors the Morgenthau Plan and Peoples' Democracy, and other such whooha.

Writes: "Let us turn to freedom of the worker in Washington's puppet states...."

"It's business as usual," Izzy tells himself. "The same old gang...with the same old lies...."

The magazine is really Izzy's cover story anyway for a broken heart, and just in case he gets interrupted, he wants to seem preoccupied. Underneath he's thinking real thoughts, *goodbye thoughts*.

He doesn't have to stay and have it out once and forever with Sam and Lill and Etta. Why should he? The boy don't care. Lill don't care. They've rejected him. The true *goldeneh Medina* calls him forth....

He could go to L.A., to Silver Lake or Echo Park, a small efficiency, maybe a terrace, a patio sheltered by gum trees, his old friend Maurice and his wife, the film editor. Barbecues. Hootenannies. There a man on the left can still have *yichus* and voice his mind, and his worth is not to be bought and sold as it is with Sam and his friends....

A lot of good people went out there after the hearings. The newness of that place. Light touching everything. Balmy air. Summer in winter, and never snow. They wanted to live a good life. Couldn't even be touched if they were union members. Free love, squeezed orange juice daily, abalone shell walks, palm trees. Lift up your voice and sing!

In Silver Lake or Echo Park there's a regular community. Good people. Left people. People with convictions. Support for civil rights, the rights of man, Izzy thinks, the underdog. Maurice once sent him a postcard a while back: "*Ich shikdir a greis fun de trenches*' (Greetings from the trenches). Maishe."

He could go there even now, and be happy even now, with or without Lillian. O *mayn amor*! Even open up a little *krom* temporarily, a store, sportswear, bathing suits, with his connections back East people like Eggy would help out sure. Maybe open up a *schenk*, a *kretchmeh* along the beach in Malibu or Pismo, fresh seafood, good wines, artichokes steamed in butter. Everything nice, fresh linens smelling of the sea, of brine, the furze of Catalina....

Would Etta want to come? Could he bring himself to do it without her? Just abandon her like an old suit? Dreyfus in the Devil's Island? A car smashed on the Pulaski Skyway? Because in thirty years she couldn't give him what he got with Lill in ten minutes?

He turns back to his magazine and an article on paid informants. When he took Sam to the party that weekend at Camp Beacon he could tell his friend was making mental notes to himself and maybe he told his old college friend, the FBI man, about Meltzner and Biberman, the Fortgang Brothers, Ruby and Elaine Kagan....

The words of a tale bearer are as wounds, he recalls, but Sam is the type his feelings always come first. A good heart but selfish, no politics, a selfish person in bed, too, Lill says...never remembers to wash his mouth before bed and love, according to her, a 60 second man. His pleasure matters, not the other's, Lill's, her pleasure. Shameful....

Izzy thinks Sam might have informed on him and his friends just because he wanted to make a good impression with his old friend, the G-man.

A man like Sam, he thinks, doesn't betray you for money, but out of vanity, so he will be better liked and appreciated. It's the same thing as running for President of the Temple... the need to be liked, to be someone, with information to impart...ego! *Where ego is there Yid shall be*...an ignoramus basically, with cunning, *amharetz*...doesn't know to turn away when he farts in the bed...*Undercherets!*

His bowels suddenly release a loud shunting of stool and noise, and he sees himself on the Twentieth Century Limited heading West to his friends in the City of Angels and palm trees. He could go to Echo Park, Silver Lake, an efficiency near the beach in Santa Monica. He's right now in the club car with a highball. A good looking woman in black sits next to him. He asks if he can buy her a drink. She asks if she can leaf through the copy of PM on his lap. He has an erection. "Berliner, aren't you forgetting something?"

"Forgetting? What?"

"Forgetting Lill? Your girl friend."

"I don't forget I'm running away," he tells the redhead.
"Don't be such a child!"

("A red headed woman asked me out to dine....")

Songs again! What has he ever gotten from that type of activity? A canary? A laughingstock...No *kests* for Izzy with the sweetest voice this side of Brownsville, and no *yichus* either. He never could remember lyrics. Lots of hard selling and *shtupping* the *maidlech*, and now Rostok and Sam could buy him ten times over. His old party friends never understood: He couldn't remember. It was for the boy and Lillian he did all these things, stayed around, for Peter, my only son, my *ben yachud*, sang until his heart broke. Hung out...Wasted his life, his little talent, until his throat hurt. Till the end of Time, Izzy thinks: "*A liebslied zing ich far dir....*"

In L.A. it would be different. He could probably be his old self again: a *tummler*, friend to Man. Maybe he'd have to work at a job in the beginning, or with a little store, odd job lot outlet, bathing suits or sportswear, but he could eventually put together another sort of living: concerts and benefits, The Peoples' World, Fairfax Group, his old friend Farfel with his Kibbutz By-the-Sea nightclub in Santa Monica—he could use an act like Izzy for MC. He even said so....

"Your Social Baritone, Iz Berliner."

Except that he's really more comfortable in the tenor range...The Kagans are making industrials in Sherman Oaks. He always wanted to do voice-overs...and in San Luis Obispo Stan Lax (ne Laxinoff) is organizing cannery workers...and smoking lots of maryjane. *Gai gezunterhait!*

A different world out there. Antelope Valley, the Town-

send Plan. Even capitalists are more progressive. Henry
Kaiser. Kaiser Plan...Berkeley and Oakland, Jack London,
Henry Miller....

Venice, The Valley, Laurel Canyon. It's really a totally
different world out there, so much warmer, more tolerant
of lefties. Easier. The good life as I live and die.

She said to him once he never talks to me, never looks
at me the way you look at me. He comes home eats dinner
reads the paper. Like that. You make me feel your love.
It's different. But in L.A. it really would be different...no
Etta to check him out, and they really would be free, but
Lill just won't go. The kids. He would take Peter, sure, but
not both. That would destroy Sam, and she won't leave
the other behind. She thinks the other one is normal. Her
normal child....

He told her once, "In L.A. I know people with connections, from the old days."

"I'd be miserable," she said. "I'm a mother. I sometimes
think I'm not but I am. They depend on me...."

"If Sam found somebody else," she said, "it might be
different...."

"Not likely," he told her.

They never spoke about it anymore. They probably
never would again. What's the use?

He'd make out...first an efficiency around Echo Park,
the Silver Lake, and maybe later, with some luck, a place
in Malibu, Redondo, on the beach in Venice. Nothing like
New York prices. You could live on oranges and fish from
San Pedro when the fleet's in and, in two hours, you're in
Mexico south of the border down Mexico way ayi ayi
Mexicale Rose don't cry....

Izzy knows he will grieve his whole life for leaving Lill
and Peter behind, but it might as well be out there in L.A.,
with palm trees...and the sun after all....

He'll need to wipe himself in a minute and he doesn't
know how. Treitner's fault. There should be a big full roll
in every stall, a chicken in every garage, Izzy thinks. But
maybe somebody will come? The Gimp? or Harry? *Kiddo*?

He'll try to be gentle and understanding, as if everything
smelled like roses where he's sitting.

"If you ask me," he'll say, "your friend Jezzy is quite a
young woman kiddo...see what I mean? Ask and you'll
get from Jacob I. Berliner," and boy will be so pleased he'll
purr *Izzy*....

Never again!

Or he'll talk eating, food. "Kiddo are you hungry?"

"I could have clams."

"On Tar Beach my prayer?" Always make a joke if you
can is Izzy's motto. "*Trife* is *trife* even, in a reform synagogue. Hows 'bout some collards and black eyed peas?
Hog Maws? Barbecue poke sanwich?"

Anything to get a rise from the kid? He loves being
teased. Means someone is paying attention.

The way Lill ignores him and then lashes out...Phadoo
...Etta knows. She's told him more than once...He expels
a windy emptiness against the clutter of waters under his
bum. It's like she's sitting on a volcano lately, Izzy thinks.
It would be better if he could get away. Go for good.
Forever and forever. Maybe change his name? Izzy Bell
...Ira Bell...Ed Bell...That's plain American...Ike Bell,
that has the proletarian click....

From L.A. he would write letters to both Lill and Etta,

and send Sam checks, and eventually save more money and
have a trust fund for Peter when he goes to college. A
special fund for travel maybe, Mexico and Europe, Paris,
Dublin, maybe even the Soviet Union in good time. Fly
around the world. Fly like a *feigele*, a bird, free, or in the
great ships, his *tierer yingel* Peter.

And even without Lill he, Izzy, could make it on his own
again. Women like and trust him. So do men. He never
had any trouble meeting people. Sure I loved you Lill I'm
crazy about you but I really can't wait any longer because
it's getting everybody crazy: Peter, Etta, Sam, even yourself.
You just will never leave Sam and you know it. Because
he gives you so much. Maybe not everything, but certain
things. All the comforts, he decides, aside from breakfast
on the beach at Venice with the *Morgen Freiheidt* and some
good old friends.

He just won't ever get involved with a married woman
again. "*Fun Poylan kimt kein gits*," he says aloud. "From
Poland nothing good comes," he thinks, meaning Lillian
again.

Then what about Etta?

Izzy loves Etta as his sister, his friend, little Terry Fagin
from around the corner on Blake Avenue when they were
both six years old. Pretty Tillie Berger out of Omaha. A
good heart. Not much sex appeal... Would she ever be able
to make ends meet without him? Would she find another
man? An *agoonah*? Awful... She deserves so much better
from me....

Nobody's coming. He don't even hear anybody talking
anymore. He could be locked in here for the night.

He thinks of Lillian again. Should he try to see her before

leaving? What to say? *I love I'll always love you*...I knew this would happen to us from the day you talked about your stretch marks in front of Peter. They always got me hot you knew that. I never minded. Like clear water running over sand.

He will not try to talk to Peter unless the boy comes looking for him. Then what will he say? I hope he brings a roll of paper....

"Dear Lillian," he writes, "this had to happen someday. I'm like a rolling stone...You and me: Oil and pumice, even worse...Hopeless...."

Izzy's head has slumped almost down to the level of the bowl against his knees. He'll have a ring around his ass like a Valentine if he don't get off right away. What to do? *Shrecklech*....

Maybe he could make a quick flush and a run for the showers. A good thorough washing there. What difference? There's plenty of soap and hot water. A land of milk and honey collapsing into the weight of his own contradictions....

He stands up, flushes, pulls his buttocks tight together with a deep breath, sits down again.

He'd probably need a couple of thousand just to set himself up in L.A. Where to get the money? Etta? Sam? Lill?

He couldn't.

"Dear Etta, You are better off without me. I'll always love and respect you. I won't fight the divorce...."

"Dear Peter, Some day you'll be a great scholar or a poet, an actor, *a lamdan*, a scientist, but not a doctor I hope, and you'll understand everything and, I hope, forgive...."

"Dear Sam...
"Dear Sam...
"Dear Sam...."

Izzy gets up again. He's got no choices. He flushes, and
runs. The floor is slippery but he's gotta make it to the
shower room....
"Dear Sam
Please forgive us as Lillian and I have long since forgiven
you...all the years wasted and loveless. But you should
try to be kind and loving to your wife as she's a very good
woman. A regular marriage counselor might also be of
some help...Brush your teeth before you make love...Take
your time...She likes it slow...Long and slow and full, and
she's doing all the moving on the top. You'll see. You'll
get to like it after a while...."
Cancel that. Lill and I had something special. He would
never want to see it replaced...surpassed....
"Dear Lill
I love you. I will always love you. Try to teach Sam some
of the things you know that I taught you and you taught
me. He can learn...."
He hasn't moved, is standing a few feet from the bowl,
redacting his own thoughts, when the boy enters, dressed
in shorts and a new striped polo, moccasins with little
beads, and seeing Izzy there starts backing off again.
"Don't go," he says.
He holds up his hand to stay the boy by magic, as it were.
And he's feeling so damn jealous of Sam for having them
both now, Lill and Peter, that he wishes he had the shame
to hide his face, banish himself.

Absently, Izzy declares, "She'll never love you."

"What did you say? Uncle Izzy are you okay?"

"Right as rain," he says. He whispers: "If you can get ahold of some willy roll."

"Willy?"

"Toilet paper. Hurry kiddo. Ask the gimp. I can't stand here forever...."

"OK. I will...But Izzy," Peter adds, "don't blame me for what I said...."

"What you said?"

"Fuck," Peter says. "You and Memsahib...."

"Not to worry," Berliner says. "It's just another word for love...."

"But I'm sorry anyway...."

"I need to wipe," Izzy says. "Quick Henry the flit!"

And the boy leaves him there again, and standing as he is, with his shorts down around his ankles, Izzy Berliner the Flop commences to weep. He is crying for the love he never took, for the courage he always lacked, for the sneaking around, the son who died, and the son who was born to another man, and the child of his young fair love, Lillian, his daughter and lover, who he will never lie with again.

And when the boy comes back brandishing the roll of paper, it is Izzy's conviction that his child's face has been transformed. It is Sam's face he sees before him, Sam's child, Peter boy...If nothing else, he thinks, I've taught him charity....

"Have a nice evening," he tells his son, "a good movie...a million bucks kiddo...whatever you want...."

"I already got."

"This I know," Izzy says. "Certainly."

And he hides his face from view inside his hands and feels the heat of desire and sudden terrible loss moisten his palms.

"A good life," Izzy says, "it's as simple as that."

Childless again, alone, he's already stepping aboard the sleeper bound for the City of Angels.

IZZY DARLING MY DEAREST

Izzy Darling My Dearest,

When you come to the showroom Monday this you'll find there.

Please don't be upset.

I'm saying goodbye now. Forever.

It's really so much better this way.

Don't call me unless you're a free man. Don't even call me personally anyway.

The same for me and Sam. As a wife and mother, I know it can't happen that way anymore without doing terrible harm to everybody we love.

I know now I don't hate Sam. I don't love him neither. I love you Izzy Berliner but I can't have you except in the bushes, behind peoples' backs, one or two days a month at most. It gives me diarrhea just thinking of you sometimes, anticipating.... The last time we had four hours together I was so upset I couldn't even enjoy myself.

I'll always miss you. I still desire you Izzy Berliner. I'll never stop. It ain't good for me, but I can't help myself. It's better we stop right now. I need a dependable life. Dependable is not what you and I give each other. We're disposable.

I'll try to live with Sam. I'll even try to make him happy if I can. Thank God he don't know anything yet... you always told me that.

You, too, try to be happy, with Etta, or without. You are so wonderful and precious. You could have such a good life. Don't swindle yourself. You gave me the best years of my life in dribs and drabs....

With a woman, Izzy, it's so different. I can't go on like this forever. My body will betray me sooner or later. You'll always be young, but I'll grow old, a stranger to you, to myself. It's terrible. I need a full-time person in my life right now.

Goodbye my sweetest love. I'll never know anybody like you again. I never will. Honest....Even before certain things happened between us you gave me so much happiness just being with you, the four of us. So now we'll have to be like that again. I'll try real hard not to lead you on, and you, too, Izzy, you'll have to try, just like me. Promise me, or we shouldn't see each other in any way at all....

I'll miss your touch, your voice, your skin, your funny words, all the sweet reasons you gave me for being happy with you like that—the smell of your breath, and your sweat when we were making love....

Yes I'll miss even that *mayn amor.*

You told me once Peter was our love knot. Peter is our souvenir. I see your face every time I look at him, and it makes me think of you, makes me sad and angry, and only sometimes loving, but I'll try harder, I promise. I'll be good to the boy for your sake even if it kills me....

Goodbye again.

I love you.

I'll miss you. And when we see each other now we'll be just like friends, strangers....

Farewell forever *mayn amor.*

   Lillian

KHIDESH (AWE)

He will never forget the sun that late August 1947 afternoon on Eastern Parkway. Standing outside the Temple
with his father, who was clad in his loud red Hawaiian shirt,
canary yellow pants, and pink cubavera jacket, the light
took the colors of his father's outfit and then flashed them
back so gaudy with bright hues he never saw light and color
like that until he went to Mexico once; and so then he
squinted to look at Umpapa, and, as Peter glanced away,
his face was seared by heat from the sun reflected off the
windows in the facade of the old Temple building, and the
car windows moving along the Parkway blazed with garish
amazing light.

His mother would be coming downstairs presently to join
them. "She's still fixing her face, her hair," Umpapa said.
"Sure you know women."

It didn't really matter that what he knew he rather liked
and approved of, unlike Sam, who was mostly too busy
even to look. Sam was telling him the facts of life: Men
always had to wait. Mammilehs were usually tardy.

His father took his hand and held it warmly, asked,
"About that movie? I'm game if she's game tomorrow
night, your momma I mean. She wasn't feeling so well this
morning...."

"So am I," Peter said, and then he realized how quickly
he'd been bought, if not forgiven. His father said. "We got

to hurry home and dress formal for the big dinner tonight, and you'll be staying home all alone because you're getting to be a big boy. You'll manage without a sitter tonight...."

Alone pleased Peter a lot. He said, "Hotsy totsy dad...." He wondered if he would have gone to Etta and Izzy's, if not for what just happened up by Tar Beach.

His father said, "I'll get you Chinks for dinner take out, and you can listen to the radio until 10 o'clock. Then if we're not home you should go to bed, and mom will come in and kiss you good night and tuck you in when we get back...."

"Is everything alright Umpapa?"

"Perfect," Sam said. "Ipsy pipsy. Why do you ask?"

"Because...." He shrugged. The light flashed off the new streamlining of cars and dazzled his eyes so that they started to tear.

"I hope I didn't cause any trouble," Peter said.

"You're just a little kid," Sam said. "How could you? It ain't your fault."

They stood there some time until the sun dimmed a little and a cooling breeze from Canarsie laved his forehead. His father seemed righteous about himself as though something he'd long predicted was now fact. First he talked about school next week and Peter's need to study and learn if he wanted to go to college, and then he talked about the Botanical Gardens across the street.

He said people came from all over the world to see the rose gardens over there. Didn't that make Peter feel good? He would take him there someday when the roses were in bloom. There were greenhouses, designed by a famous architect. His father said, "I never dreamed when I was a boy I would have such nice surroundings to raise my family...."

"No kidding," Peter replied, flatly. He was missing Izzy already, but trying hard to give Umpapa the benefit of the doubt.

"Brooklyn," his father said, "is a city almost as large as Chicago...they call it the Borough of Churches...."

"I'd really like to go to Africa someday when I'm grown up," the boy said, dreamily. His father frowned, as though he knew what to expect next, but said nothing, wishing neither to encourage nor discourage. He said, "You've just got wanderlust. You'll grow out of it someday. *Kainenhurah*!"

Nothing was said about all the *parshe* Izzy shocking things he said in front of Sam and Rostok in the locker room. Nothing about Tar Beach. The day was ending with a sort of truce.

Peter said, "Do you still love mommy?"

"I love you. I love your brother Benjamin. And I'll always love your mother," Umpapa said, slowly, between loud slow breaths. His glasses glittered, and his face was as closed as his eyes. The sun from behind a building corner made his cheeks ruddy, aglow He spoke quietly: "I want us to be close boy, close as can be. You'll see from now...."

"Yes dad," he said, glancing away.

"Because I'm your father son," Sam added. "*Yichus* you understand...."

"Yes dad I understand."

Lill found them standing there outside holding hands,

though apart somehow. "My two men," she said, as she came outside, and when she turned their way, father and son were astonished by her humid beauty, the hothouse smells of talc and cosmetics. To Peter it seemed as though she'd actually changed on them in some way, passed through whatever had kept her locked in gloom and self for so long. She seemed alert again, pert, somehow fresher to his eyes, as though after-showering, and also after something else, he could not know what.

She smiled at him, and picked some lint from his collar. Her step was light and airy.

Dressed for the street, she seemed so slim and youthful, her waist cinched tight, her cotton skirt full and pleated, her cheeks afire, hair smartly combed above the blaze of her soft cheeks and bright green eyes. "Say will you look at your mother boy," Sam said. "A movie star...."

"Sure," he said. "Momma's beautiful. I always knew that...."

"O come on you two," she said, but Peter could tell how pleased she was.

Lillian seemed to smell of autumn flowers and honey. She was breathless. "Where's the car?"

"Just around the corner," Sam said.

She took both their hands and they started to walk together around the corner.

That evening he was alone, but neither scared nor unhappy. He listened to "Your Hit Parade" and "Can You Top This?" on the radio; around 10 Umpapa called to ask if he was tucked in. "I'm definitely the new President," he told Peter.

"Congratulations," the boy said.

"Are you happy for me?"

"I don't know," the boy said. "Maybe...."

He pretended he had a stuffed nose and put vicks in the percolating humidifier to keep him company until they came home.

The next night was the happiest Peter ever could recall. His father was now Presidenke-elect by unanimous vote, and they ate at Dubrow's and saw two movies, one in color, with Betty Grable about South America.

His mother and father seemed so happy together that when the divorce began to take place, just a few months later, and all of a sudden Sam moved out to the Towers Hotel downtown, Peter always thought back to that one evening in late August, after he'd lost Uganda and Izzy and Jezzy, when he wanted to remember what the good old days were really like. Dubrows and two movies, Sam urging him to try cream pie for dessert....and Benjamin not coming home for three more days....

The next time he saw Izzy he saw an old man, brown and toothless, like a prune, at the Memorial Service for the late Etta Berliner.

Peter was just home from his first year at college, real snappy, in a cocoa linen jacket and tan slacks, cordovans, with perforations. Izzy kissed the boy on the cheek wetly, and when they were alone together, for just an instant, with Sam and Lillian (who'd arrived separately) talking to some of the other guests, Peter said: "*Shuldik* Little Father. I'm so glad to see you again," and Izzy's voice was hoarse and rasping with the throat cancer that shortly after murdered him as he said, "Thanks Kiddo thanks a lot. You looking good, looking like a million bucks. How are the girls treating you?"

"I've got myself a *shaney.*"

"Dot's good," Izzy exclaimed. "Dot's what I like to hear. *Heynayni!*"

And they both laughed and hugged, and were blushing with the contact of their bodies' flesh.

"Peter are you coming with me?" Lillian called out. Her hair was colored blonde; it was done up thickly, piled above her brow. She stood beside her new husband, Morganbesser, a clothier, and a nice guy, everyone said.

She looked at Izzy as though he were a speck of dirt on the fabric of her life and didn't show she'd seen anybody. An ice sculpture on the wedding buffet she was. Then she seemed to soften, said, "Ah Izzy, you should have taken better care of yourself," and the tears came to her eyes as she turned away to her new mate, Morganbesser. "Coming Peter?" she called out, hoarsely.

But Izzy was still blushing from even so much attention, and Peter said, "Yes momma, I'm coming. Goodbye Iz ...Goodbye...."

"Uncle Izz?" the old man corrected him.

"Of course Uncle Iz," he agreed, with tears smarting in his eyes.

"Do you know you still have a beautiful mommy?" Izzy asked, and he heard his Uncle Izzy add in a soft raw voice: "*And who knows better than you how hard it is to bring up children?*"

He went to join his father and his new wife, also named Lillian, and she kissed him on both cheeks and gave him a watch his father wanted him to have, and when he looked back through the crowd of mourners for Izzy he simply wasn't there anymore. Like a light just went out again.

His father came up beside him. "I know who you're looking for," he said. "We talked...."

"I'm glad," Peter said, "but I'm so sorry...."

"I never thought I'd outlive Izzy Berliner," his father said.

"Never in my heart," Peter whispered. He was a head taller than his father by now and he spoke above him, almost as though to the room at large. Then he thanked Sam for the new watch and they gathered up his stepmother and Benjamin and his wife Sherry and started out the door of the funeral parlor into the viscous hot air of New York summer.

"Another scorcher," Sam remarked.

"*Hamduillah*," said Peter. "*Gewalt*."